GAMER ARMY

ALSO BY TRENT REEDY

------------------o------------------

MIDDLE GRADE

Words in the Dust

Stealing Air

YOUNG ADULT

Divided We Fall (Divided We Fall #1)

Burning Nation (Divided We Fall #2)

The Last Full Measure (Divided We Fall #3)

If You're Reading This

GAMER ARMY

TRENT REEDY○----------

ARTHUR A. LEVINE BOOKS

SCHOLASTIC INC. / NEW YORK

J

Library of Congress Cataloging-in-Publication Data

Names: Reedy, Trent, author.

Title: Gamer army / Trent Reedy.

Description: First edition. | New York, NY : Arthur A. Levine Books, an imprint of
Scholastic Inc., 2018. | Summary: Even though he is only twelve, Rogan Weber is
an obsessed gamer, whose motto, ego sum maximus, declares his confidence in
his own abilities, and whose parents are also deeply involved in ultra high tech (a little
too deeply sometimes); naturally he is thrilled to receive an invitation to join a tech
giant's virtual reality TV gaming contest—but as the games become more and more
intense and dangerous, he and his fellow gamers realize that something sinister is
behind this particular game.

Identifiers: LCCN 2018016854| ISBN 9781338045291 (hardcover : alk. paper) | ISBN
1338045296 (hardcover : alk. paper) | ISBN 9781338045307 (pbk. : alk. paper) | ISBN
133804530X (pbk. : alk. paper)

Subjects: LCSH: Virtual reality—Juvenile fiction. | Video games—Juvenile fiction. | Video
gamers—Juvenile fiction. | Video games industry—Juvenile fiction. | Secrecy—Juvenile
fiction. | Conspiracies—Juvenile fiction. | Parent and child—Juvenile fiction. | CYAC:
Virtual reality—Fiction. | Video games—Fiction. | Video games industry—Fiction. |
Secrets—Fiction. | Conspiracies—Fiction. | Parent and child—Fiction.

Classification: LCC PZ7.R25423 Gam 2018 | DDC [Fic]—dc23 LC record available at
https://lccn.loc.gov/2018016854

DEDICATION

----------------o----------------

This book is dedicated to Cheryl Klein, with gratitude
for seven wonderful years of work on seven books;
for limitless patience, compassion, and understanding;
and for opening the door to my Dream. I will always
salute you, Colonel Kidlit.

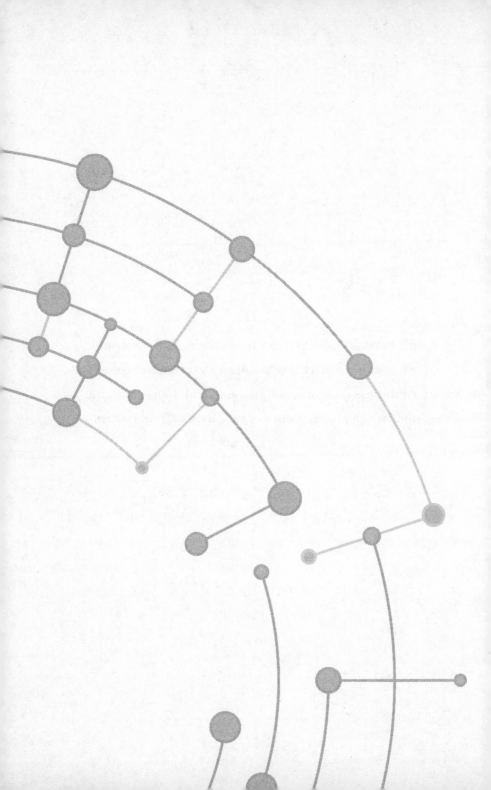

CHAPTER 1

Rogan Webber laughed, folding his arms over his armored chest, leading the other laser viper advanced combat robots out through the sliding steel doors into the empty corridor.

"It's not that funny," said TankerForce. He'd been the sorriest excuse for a Tank that Rogan had ever had on his fireteam. IRL he was a thirty-nine-year-old father and teacher who was just getting back into gaming.

"I said play on easy or practice with a solo campaign," Rogan said. "I don't get why any of you are surprised I was the one who captured the enemy terrorist and destroyed Scorpion's super robot."

Shaylyn Spero, the flyer mod, and the only other nearly max experience laser viper on the fireteam, shoved Rogan in the shoulder, stepping past him as if he didn't matter. "You act like you did it all yourself. I helped take out that robot, and I kept those little gunner drones off your back." Flyer turned around, walking backward, the sleek green aerodynamic robot holding its arms wide. "Next time, I'll be so far ahead of you that I'll already complete the mission objective and bring down the entire Scorpion terrorist organization before you get, like, even close to the target. That's all I'm saying."

The engineer and healer mod vipers followed her, saying nothing, probably mad or embarrassed about being almost totally left out of the last battle.

TankerForce hung back with Rogan, his giant feet clanking on the floor as they walked. Tanks were large, with a ton of armor and weapons, and Rogan's stacked Ranger was no noob, so the two of them hardly fit side by side. "You're good, kid. One of the best gamers I've ever seen."

Rogan sighed. Here was another old guy, calling him "kid," acting like he was so much better just because he was old. Like it should be a shock that a twelve-year-old would be a good gamer. Apart from some strict age rules for the adults-only nightclubs and the teen hangouts around Virtual City, what did age matter in digi-space? Rogan had chumpified tons of old guys in lots of games, but especially in *Laser Viper*, his favorite.

They emerged into the massive *Laser Viper* war room, the expansive domed chamber packed with advanced combat robots, the hangout for out-of-game players. Gamers could meet and joke with one another, form fireteams for group campaigns, and trade tips about the missions.

"Of course you think he is," Shay said. "Rogan always gets his Ranger up front, never mind the rest of his team. He only cares about stealing all the achievements and XP even though it was totally a team effort."

"I was right in the center of the danger," Rogan said. If he hadn't rushed into the middle of it all, the others probably would have been destroyed. Why shouldn't he earn the best rewards when it had been up to him to risk the most? "You all helped a little, but I'm the one who got the job done."

"Who flew in to save you from that rockslide?" Shaylyn shot back.

"I *said* you helped. It was fun. But I now have a level one hundred viper and three upgrade points. So I'm heading to the upgrade bay to buff my Ranger. Don't worry. You'll get better someday. You know? *Ego sum maximus.*"

Shaylyn's metal hands clanged on her metal head. "Stop saying that! It's so dumb!"

Once in an MMORPG, an ogre had dropped a Latin phrase before a devastating battle-ax attack. Wikipedia later told him the words meant "Fortune favors the bold." The ogre had sounded so cool that Rogan had been slow to defend himself. After that, a quick Google Translate gave Rogan his own motto: *Ego sum maximus,* Latin for *I am the greatest.* Cocky, maybe, but that was part of being a great gamer, and if it threw Shay off balance, well, he'd take every advantage he could get.

Rogan ditched the others and went to the upgrade bays. Leveling up to 100 made available new abilities that would make his Ranger even tougher. He installed titanium alloy close-combat claws— basically three six-inch razor-sharp claws on each hand that popped out like Wolverine's.

As if those weren't cool enough, he finally hooked up the tech he'd been waiting for: fifteen-meter grappling cables that could be fired from each arm. The ends of both cables looked like frayed steel ropes, but they were really programmed steel microfibers.

If he fired a cable at a brick wall or other solid substance, the tiny filaments would weave into the microscopic gaps in the surface. He could then reel the cable back in, pulling the object to him or pulling himself to the object. Rogan had watched videos of other leveled-up Rangers just killing it with these cables, swinging through battles like Spider-Man. He smiled. Shaylyn's flyer wouldn't be the only one in the air anymore.

When he finished the upgrade, Rogan left the *Laser Viper* building on Gamer Avenue, transforming in an instant from a tough fighting machine to his regular, barely customized avatar. His fairly generic kid body, for whom he'd bought a black leather jacket and a *Gamer 4 Life* T-shirt, picked up the pace—he had to get home soon.

The saying, "It's always sunny in Virtual City," was only partially true. The city was set to East Coast time, but daylight perception hours were different for everyone. It might be midnight in New York, but someone from Hong Kong, for whom it was noon, would see Virtual City in full daylight. And for Rogan, the two-hundred-foot-tall statue of William J. Culum was casting a long shadow in Culum Square as daylight faded in Seattle.

On the street in front of him, a Lamborghini, Ferrari, and an old 1960s Batmobile raced past. A man chased them on a hover-cycle, laughing the whole way. Rogan watched them tear away down the canyon between the hundred-story buildings.

A clown lunged and roared at him, his face stretching and long sharp fangs showing. Rogan kept walking. The blue-green holoscript bio-bubble above the clown showed the guy was nineteen. Who could be that old and still think pop-scares worked or were funny? From the beginning, William Culum and his team at Atomic Frontiers had hard-coded Virtual City to be violence free. Nobody could hurt anyone else here, so why be scared?

Not for the first time, Rogan wished he had enough credits or real-world money to enable site-to-site transport. Every few years, initiatives sprang up, demanding the feature be freely enabled for everyone in digi-space, but they never succeeded. Too many businesses wanted to sell virtual vehicles and needed people walking by their stores and ads. So Rogan continued down the street, past the movie theater, karaoke club, and coffee shop. Farther down, bright light spilled out of a crowded store where people shopped for digital clothes for their avatars. The place sold everything from tuxedos and formal ball gowns to jeans and T-shirts to space suits, saris, and sombreros.

Three fourteen-year-olds jumped from the top of the two-hundred-story Sky Mall, laughing and somersaulting all the way down. One of them chickened out and tapped back to the real world about fifty feet up. The other two vanished in flashes of white light upon impact, their avatars sent back to their Virtual City starting points with safety violation warnings.

Two blocks away, a group of about a hundred people from all over the world held up signs and chanted loudly, demanding official United Nations recognition of Virtual City as an independent nation with the same standing as established IRL countries.

High above the skyscrapers, a giant green-and-yellow zeppelin glided through the sky. Airships cost millions of credits—tens of thousands of real-world dollars. In the large gondola under this particular ship hung the Virtual City home of Mario Alverez, the fifth-ranked gamer in the entire world. Rogan had watched a video about his airship. It had three decks, with a dance floor, a boxing ring, and a sweet retro arcade with built-in video games.

Millions of people played and worked in Virtual City. Some worked there full-time. Some spent nearly all their time there. Mario Alverez held the world record: nine and a half months' uninterrupted time in digi-space.

Mario Alverez was the best. Someday Rogan would take the title and be even more famous.

Always and everywhere, on the sides of buildings, buses, and airships, even on *people*, advertisements competed for game credits and real-world dollars, promising satisfaction, instant access in digi-space, and same-day, even same-hour, delivery by drone IRL.

Just another day in Virtual City.

-----o-----

Rogan smiled as he reached his fiftieth floor apartment. His happiness shattered against the door, though, which had been affixed with an ugly blaze-orange sheet of digital paper.

NOTICE OF E-VICTION! OVERDUE RENT! SECOND WARNING!

Rogan Webber, being the current occupant of #509 Mega Modern Building 5, Virtual City, is hereby reminded that rent must be paid in full, with a 450-credit late penalty no later than . . .

Rogan skipped all the legal jargon he had already read in the first notice, his eyes drawn to the last few lines again.

. . . by the aforementioned date and time shall be **_immediately e-victed from the aforementioned premises_**, with all access thereto restricted. All digital property within the premises shall immediately become the property of Mega Modern Digital Property Management Corporation.

Rogan sighed and entered his cozy little rent-overdue apartment. He loved the tiny place, and was lucky to have it. Virtual City real estate was expensive, and some digi-homes and offices cost more IRL dollars than some IRL properties. His apartment was more valuable than plenty of properties left out in the middle of the so-called brick-and-mortar blight, once business had migrated to digi-space. He'd saved gaming credits for three years to score this place, but he hadn't really thought about how he would continue paying rent. He'd assumed he would become an even better gamer by the time rent was due, and that he'd have more credits by then.

Only it hadn't worked out that way.

He couldn't lose his apartment. It was his sanctuary. When he was by himself in his virtual apartment, it was because he chose to be alone, safe in his own space, and somehow that wasn't as boring or lonely as his IRL house where his parents were often too busy to spend time with him.

Rogan had painted his apartment walls black with sparkling stars. He'd spent some credits on some cool Zelda, Mario, and Metroid posters in which the images moved, Harry Potter style, with Link slashing his sword at an Octorok, Mario leaping for a 1-Up Mushroom, and Samus Aran blasting Mother Brain. He loved those games. Even after decades and dozens of sequels, in gaming, the classics never died. There was no kitchen in his place, because what would have been the point of one? You couldn't eat anything you hadn't scanned in from the real world anyway. Best of all, the bed, beanbag chair, and his desk and computer were all scanned in from real-world anchors. So the steel hover chair was actually a plain plastic-and-fabric office swivel chair IRL, but usable here in Virtual City. Rogan could sit down and do his homework in his own virtual apartment.

Now his stomach rumbled. He checked the antique grandfather clock in the corner of his living room. It was 6:18 already, but when Rogan crossed his fingers to activate the floating blue-green holo-script screen in front of him, he wasn't surprised to see both Mom and Dad online in his family contact list. He didn't bother logging out and shutting down, but simply slipped off his headset and then his gamer gloves, surprised as he often was by the darkness outside the game. He had switched on the laser torch lights in his apartment, but his IRL bedroom was nearly pitch black.

He felt a light, pointed nudge against his hand and smiled. "Hey, Wiggles." He reached out and scratched his fuzzy black-and-white spaniel mix behind the ears. "Sorry, pooch, but I was in the middle of a *Laser Viper* battle." Rogan turned on a lamp, placed his hands on either side of the dog's face, and raised Wiggles's little pink nose to his own face. "You hungry too, buddy?" Wiggles jumped around, panting, happy and hungry.

Rogan switched on the hall light on the way to his father's game room, petting his impatient dog again to apologize for being late with his nightly dinner of dry pellets. "Dad?" he said, poking his head inside.

His father stood in the middle of the room, wearing his VR headset and gamer gloves. Only one small desk lamp by the computer provided any light. Dad carried the Eagle Sword of Azeroth as he walked in place, moving his character in game. He'd ordered the sword in a Virtual City shop for over fifty thousand credits, and a delivery drone had dropped it off in its special carrying case a few hours later. The sword was equipped with computer chips, which worked much better with the VR sensors in the room, and it was properly weighted to improve its owner's fighting skills.

"Dad?" Rogan tried again.

"Yeah," Dad said.

"Are we going to eat soon?" Rogan asked.

"No," said Dad.

"Well, I mean, it's getting late. I'm kind of hungry and—"

"Trust me, he's right down there around those rocks. It's a mega ogre." Dad laughed. "You're going to want my sword for this, Zarganon."

Rogan sighed. Dad had one of the best VR headsets on the market, complete with the most high-quality noise-canceling headphones available. He couldn't hear anything but his game.

Of course, Rogan could log into *Warcraft Universe* and search for his father's avatar across the seven worlds, but that would take forever.

He timidly reached out to touch Dad's shoulder.

"Look out! Lightning bolt!" Dad shouted, ducked, and swung his sword.

The foam-plastic blade smacked Rogan in the face. He stepped back, holding his hand to his hot, stinging cheek and watery eye.

"What?!" Dad lifted the headset a little to see. "Rogan?! What are you doing! You OK? Hey!" He crammed the headset back down and frantically swung his sword back up. "I'm hit! I'm hit bad! I'm almost — Where's our healer?!" He pushed half the headset up. "Seriously, you OK? I told you not to bother me when I'm in a campaign!"

Rogan nodded. What else could he say?

Dad slipped the VR headset back down. "No, all good. My son got in the way, that's all. Wait!" He spun around and tried to bring his sword up again, but cursed before throwing it to the floor and pulling his headset off. "Great, an enemy goblin just took my head off with a sword! A weak little *goblin*!"

Dad turned to Rogan, his face a little red, looking like he was trying to control himself. "Really great. My Paladin is dead and has to respawn. My whole guild is about to raid a dangerous dungeon for some major gold, and now I can't help them! What is so important that it couldn't wait, Rogan? What?"

"Nothing." Rogan kept his hand on his stinging face. "Sorry. I didn't know you were in the middle of such an important part."

"Nothing." Dad threw his hands up. "Great. I died for nothing." He rubbed his hand over his eyes and forehead where the VR headset pressed hardest on his face. "Come on, Ro. You're getting too old for this kind of thing. You always told me you wanted to be a good gamer, maybe join my guild someday. I want you to join too, but you can't pull stuff like this."

Rogan couldn't meet his father's eyes. "Sorry."

"Hold on a sec. . . ." Dad's voice brightened. "If I use my last summon Pegasus whistle, I might be able to fly back there in time to help them with some of the battle. . . ."

Rogan looked up with a grin, but it was too late. Dad was already back in his headset, back in his game. He stood for a long moment in the shadows at the edge of the room, watching his dad pick up his sword and, after a while, return to his guild, calling out to them enthusiastically. Rogan turned away and headed back into the hallway.

Mom's office door was locked, as usual, so Rogan fed Wiggles and went back online to his apartment. Checking his family contact list, he found that Mom was in her Forum, hosting another meeting. He went down to the end of the block and spent a few credits to use the portal to warp to the Forum.

Rogan's parents had met in the computer science program in college, and they'd both started their careers working to design and program video games. Dad had stayed there. Mom had started a video blog about technology, politics, and society. She'd built up a big audience with segments about online privacy, the government's role in the internet, cybersecurity and cyber warfare, and other topics. That was way back before everything went virtual reality.

Rogan's mother was one of the first to move into Virtual City when it launched, and the audience she brought with her quickly scored her enough game credits to buy some of the best digital real estate. She established the Global Forum, a four-thousand-seat modern auditorium that hosted speeches from technology leaders, politicians, and the organizers of political movements from all over the world. They might discuss the importance or danger of a proposed new law about digi-space, hold rallies in support of or in opposition to political candidates, or talk about the best ways of creating political change in a certain country or around the world. Because people from many countries were interested, the Global Forum hosted events at odd hours, sometimes in the middle of the night. Because it was his mother's forum, she often gave speeches, just as she was doing that night. She was kind of famous. And usually very busy. Rogan moved his real-life chair into position to stand in for an empty seat near the back of the packed house and watched his mother's passionate performance.

". . . and since apathy on the part of our elected representatives is our problem, apathy among us can be no part of the solution. The meeting of two apathetic forces only bolsters and validates the status quo!"

She paused for applause and paced the stage, nodding to Rogan, not because she could see him very well all the way back where he was sitting, but because her VR system was programmed to alert her when he entered the Forum.

"Some people in the media have tried to dismiss our digi-space concerns as petty partisan bickering, but the reality is that neither American political party, and very few parties around the world, are taking this seriously enough. They're too committed to so-called real world initiatives, trying to get people out of digi-space, but failing to understand that the digital world is now a very real part of life. The government has an obligation to maintain a stable internet and hypernet and to protect its citizens here!"

Louder clapping and a few shouts resounded through the room.

"These so-called temporary hypernet disruptions, which so many leaders around the world have tried to downplay as simple inconveniences, are in fact devastating. With websites and digi-space offices out for hours or days, important communications disrupted, even family members kept apart, we deserve an explanation of the cause of these disasters and of governments' efforts to prevent this from happening in the future.

"Now I want to delineate several action items, some practical ways we can all influence our political . . ."

Rogan slipped off his headset. *Looks like it's gonna be another Hot Pocket night.* He'd become the master chef of frozen foods and hoped there was another Philly Steak flavor left in the freezer. If there were only plain old pepperoni Hot Pockets left, he'd have to microwave some fish sticks. He couldn't take any more pepperoni.

Ten minutes later, he'd scanned his Hot Pocket and PowerSlam energy drink so that he could see his meal with his VR headset on, and returned to his apartment. Wiggles pushed up against him, and he petted him before slipping a VR headset on the dog. Rogan had adapted the extra headset himself so his fuzzy buddy could go with him to his apartment. The dog had resisted it at first, pushing it off every time Rogan had tried to put it on him, until Rogan had supplied enough bacon treats to convince the pup that VR wasn't such a bad thing.

Rogan had to be a careful, though. After several bumps into real-world walls, Wiggles had finally figured out what the blue-green Limit of Advance grid meant, but sometimes when he got really excited he forgot, or failed to react fast enough when the grid appeared.

Calling to his apartment's computer to play music from the video game soundtrack channel, Rogan sat down to eat and look over his homework. Not for the first time, he was glad to be enrolled in Steve Jobs Middle School in Virtual City, where the entire system was designed like a game, where students didn't have to wait for the end-of-semester test but could work hard through individualized instruction to see how far, and how fast, they could take their education, with cool bonuses for education achievements unlocked. He'd worked himself light-years beyond minimal proficiency, so now he could also just enjoy his Hot Pocket and watch some gamer vlogs. Either way, he'd probably sleep in his apartment tonight.

Rogan had stayed all night plenty of times. He loved it, dreaming of the day when he could finally log in and never leave, provided he could figure out how to pay the rent. Other crybaby kids whined for mommy and daddy, but he always prided himself on being just fine on his own.

Really. He was fine.

Rogan took a bite as he went over to his window. The Mario Alverez airship glided across the sky, eclipsing most of the very large full moon. Rogan wondered once again how great it would be to have not this little apartment, cool as it was, but an awesome zeppelin, a giant symbol letting everyone know that Rogan wasn't kidding when he said *ego sum maximus*. Dad would come up to play video games. Mom would mention the airship in one of her speeches and maybe hold a political rally on board. And as an added bonus, Shaylyn Spero would have no doubt that he was the better gamer.

The main theme from *Super Mario Bros.* brought Rogan back from his thoughts. He laughed a little at the primitive old music that he'd set up instead of a doorbell. He'd almost forgotten about it. Nobody ever came to his virtual apartment.

He turned from the window and smiled. Mom or Dad, maybe?

A warm hope glowed inside Rogan as he reached for the doorknob. He flung the door open. Then he froze.

Was this a trick?

Standing in the hallway were a man and woman he'd never seen before, and between them, William J. Culum.

The William J. Culum, computer genius, global technology innovator, Virtual City creator, and world-famous founder and CEO of Atomic Frontiers Corporation.

CHAPTER 2

Weirdly, William Culum did not speak first. Before anything else could happen, Wiggles started barking like mad at the newcomers until Rogan quieted him with a treat. Next, the woman took a step closer. She had long, straight black hair and wore a bright red business dress with gold buttons and crisp shoulders. She and the other two must have been wearing expression monitors, expensive little scanners that fit on each side of the VR headgear to transfer the user's facial movements to her avatar. She smiled brightly. "Rogan Webber?"

Rogan nodded.

"I'm Sophia Hahn."

Rogan had noticed that older people lots of times said things in VR that were already obvious from their bio-bubbles. [Sophia Hahn. Female. Age 33. President of marketing and public affairs at Atomic Frontiers Game Division. Arlington, Virginia. United States of America.]

Sophia continued. "I'm the president of marketing and public affairs for the game division of Atomic Frontiers." She stepped aside and motioned at William Culum like a woman on a game show presenting a prize. "And this is Mr. William J. Culum."

Mr. Culum's smile deepened the wrinkles in his forehead and the corners of his eyes. He ran his hand down to smooth his trademark large cardigan, which was as gray as his hair. "It's great to meet you, Rogan!" He went on to introduce himself by reciting information that already hovered in holoscript right above him. [William J. Culum. Age 56. Founder, president, and CEO of Atomic Frontiers Corporation. Arlington, Virginia. United States of America.] Information that every respectable gamer already knew. Information that even nongamers knew.

William Culum was one of the most well-known figures in the world. Besides being worth over eighty billion dollars, the guy had won the Nobel Prize in physics for his work in creating the incredibly more efficient hyperstream data cable. The invention had enabled much faster transmission of the massive amount of data that made digi-space, and Virtual City within it, possible. He had also been awarded the Nobel Peace Prize for personally·funding the expansion of the hypernet all over the world, including in isolated countries and regions, allowing digi-space access to more people than ever before. Rogan knew all about William Culum.

But this couldn't be the *real* Mr. Culum, could it? Celebrity impersonation was a complex issue in Virtual City. Impersonating real living people, or people who had died within the last sixty years, was illegal. But any half-decent avatar artist could change the height, hair color, or other features of a famous person just slightly, so the user could claim it was a tribute, not an impersonation. Then there was the whole other problem of people who wanted to be Luke Skywalker, not necessarily Mark Hamill, the actor who played him. The issue of digi-space identity appropriation was an unending argument on many forums and in the courts, but no one was more aggressive about suing to prevent the use of his digital likeness than William Culum. Rogan had read that many of the shadiest programmers didn't dare create any avatars or NPCs that looked remotely like him. Maybe this avatar *did* belong to the real man.

"This is my associate Xavier Johnson." Mr. Culum motioned toward the large, tough-looking man standing behind him. The light glinted off the man's brown, glass-smooth shaved head. He offered only a nod.

Rogan wondered if Mr. Johnson was here as a bodyguard. He almost looked like a soldier or a Marine from some of the war games Rogan played. But who would need a bodyguard in Virtual City? His mother had even done talks about how virtual reality could bring the world together, allowing people from all cultures and backgrounds to interact without the threat of physical violence.

"Come on in," Rogan said.

"I think somebody forgot his apartment's parental security measures." Mr. Culum laughed as he reached, or tried to reach, through the doorway. His arm vanished at the point where it crossed the threshold, ending in a laser-straight sparkling stump at the elbow. It reappeared when he stepped back. "Adults can't enter. In fact, we have a limited time to talk to you here before we are respawned to our origin points."

Sophia Hahn refreshed her smile. "That's why we'd like you to warp with us to Atomic Frontiers virtual headquarters!" Every time she talked, it was with the gushing enthusiasm of a kid on Christmas morning. "We have a *very* exciting offer for you. We know you're going to be thrilled."

"I should probably ask my parents first," Rogan said.

"Of course!" said Mr. Culum. "And they're certainly welcome to join us."

"They're real busy," Rogan said. He figured he had nothing to worry about. His real body was safe in his real bedroom. And if they somehow managed to get around Virtual City's protections for minors to say or show him weird stuff? His gamer gloves came basic programmed so that three hard taps to the top of his left hand would instantly call the Virtual City Police and remove the caller from the situation. Plus, this was William Culum!

Rogan made up his mind.

"Let me take my dog's headset off. He gets pretty lonely if I move to a different virtual environment. If he's IRL and can see me, he'll be fine." He set Wiggles up, then stood. "OK, let's go."

Mr. Culum didn't need to bother with portals, but instantly transported all of them, so that they stood in a large octagonal rotunda with a high domed ceiling and hallways on the second floor from which people could look down into the room. Huge windows offered a view across the river of the Lincoln and Washington memorials and the US Capitol building in the distance. The floor was made of black tile, and in the middle of the large center circle was the Atomic Frontiers logo, three electrons orbiting in a sort of star pattern around a globe nucleus.

Suspended from four steel cables about a dozen feet above the floor was an enormous brass sculpture. Four big hexagonal panels were supported at the ends of several brass bars. Each bar protruded from a large central column that had several tiny glowing windows in it. At the base of the central core, a large dish with a rod emerging from its center pointed downward at an angle toward the floor. Three space capsules hung from the hexagon support struts on thin, shiny gold wires. Rogan recognized it at once.

He'd seen over a dozen Star Wars movies in 3-D and VR. He'd flown plenty of starfighter ships in different games, and he'd always been disappointed that IRL all the cool space stuff had been done long before he was born. The old International Space Station was garbage compared to the Death Star, a bunch of tin cans that floated in space, doing nothing. But a few years ago, they'd begun construction of this beauty.

He looked up at the scale model of the sleek space station and smiled. "Sun Station One."

"Glad you recognize it!" said Mr. Culum, his voice echoing in the open chamber. "We keep this model here in the atrium as a reminder of our latest effort to ride technology into the future, and as a celebration of one of Atomic Frontiers' crowning achievements. It will become operational very soon. When it does, it will reflect massive amounts of solar energy into the station's collector/converter, then transmit that energy back to a large ground receiver on Earth. Enough energy to continuously power a large modern city. All with absolutely no pollution."

Sophia put her hand on Mr. Culum's arm and beamed at Rogan. "Atomic Frontiers has always pushed back the frontiers of science and technology, Rogan. You're here today because it's done so again—this time in the realm of video games."

"Is this like an ad for a game?" This was the company that made *Laser Viper*. Maybe they had noticed that Rogan played the game a lot, and wanted to sell him other games.

"Not at all," Sophia said. "Full details are on the way to your inbox. In the meantime, I'd like to be the first to congratulate you. That was some very impressive gaming in *Laser Viper* today! We've been watching your progress and advanced style of gameplay for a while. Amazing. You are one of the five best American *Laser Viper* gamers in your age division, from a pool of hundreds of thousands of others. One of the best in the world! Your dedication and your skill in combat have earned you a chance to compete in the most exclusive and prestigious video game contest ever held. Atomic Frontiers is proud to invite you to the *Laser Viper* Final Challenge!"

"Really?"

Mr. Culum leaned down into Rogan's field of view with a super cheerful grin on his face. "We hope to see you in person, two weeks from now, right here in our nation's capital, where you and four other gamers will be the stars of Atomic Frontiers' first promotional reality show. You'll all compete to become the first *Laser Viper* Grand Champion."

"Washington, DC?" Rogan said. "I don't know if my family can afford such a big trip."

"Don't worry." Sophia patted his shoulder. "Like I said, all the details are in your inbox, but this trip is just for you. Airfare and room and board are all included. Wait until you see where you'll be staying. We've converted a large section of one of the floors of Atomic Frontiers headquarters into luxury dorms, and the gameplay for the contest will be far beyond anything you've experienced with your basic VR headset and gamer gloves. We have a state-of-the-art, full-immersion gaming experience that you are going to love." She waved her hands wildly in the air. "Oh. I can't describe it. You will simply have to experience it to believe it."

Rogan tried to play it cool in front of the adults, but he wanted to scream and dance. Wait until Shaylyn heard about this! She was always giving him a hard time, trying to one-up him in every game, especially in *Laser Viper*. When he won the title of *Laser Viper* Grand Champion, he would have absolute proof that he was the best.

Sophia laughed. "By the way, did we forget to mention that the *Laser Viper* champion will receive a $250,000 cash prize along with one million game credits?"

"Wow," Rogan said quietly. He laughed when he remembered that orange e-viction notice on his Virtual City apartment. Were there any twelve-year-old Virtual City millionaires? There couldn't be many.

Mega Modern could keep the apartment. With a million game credits, he could get a whole house. He'd be a lot closer to owning his own airship.

"I expect even your busy parents won't be able to ignore this opportunity," Mr. Culum said.

"They'll be so excited, so proud," Sophia agreed.

"And you'll need their permission, of course." Mr. Culum smiled. "Sophia has taken care of all the relevant permission forms. All of it is—"

"In my inbox," Rogan said.

Mr. Culum burst into kind laughter. "He catches on fast! We may have to hire him, Sophia!" Sophia laughed with him. Xavier did not. "But seriously, Rogan, assuming your parents agree to let you participate, we still haven't heard what *you* think."

"I think . . ." How could Rogan explain how he felt about something as unbelievably awesome as this video game contest? "All I've ever wanted was to be a great gamer."

"You *are* a great gamer," Sophia said. "But the *Laser Viper* Final Challenge will be a wonderful way to recognize and showcase you and other great gamers your age. To really let you and the game shine."

"No, but I mean—" Rogan motioned to the world-changing computer genius standing in front of him. "Mr. Culum, I made a video report on you for technology class last year. My dad has a William J. Culum action figure. You press a button and it says—"

"Ride technology into the future!" Mr. Culum proudly proclaimed.

"Yes!" Rogan agreed. "I mean, yes, the figure says that, and *yes*, more than anything I want to play and win this video game tournament!" He laughed now too. This was really happening.

After they'd all exchanged goodbyes, Rogan warped back to his apartment. He wasted no time shutting the system down, but tossed his VR device onto his bed. His Hot Pocket and PowerSlam forgotten, he rushed out of his room to find his parents. He didn't care how busy they were. He had to tell them all about this.

"MomDad!" Blinking to clear the afterimage left behind by digi-space—a temporary side effect for any hardcore VR gamer— his socks slipped on the wood floor, and he crashed down hard. His

Ranger might have been super athletic, but he was not. He sprang to his feet and scrambled down the hall faster than Sonic the Hedgehog. "You'll never believe—"

His mom came out of her room, smiling and blinking, a red rectangle print around her eyes from her VR headset. She held up her all-powerful "just a sec" finger for a moment before she tapped away on her tablet. "Hang on . . ." She stopped tapping and stared intently at her screen. "I just need to finish this one thing. . . ."

Dad emerged from down the hall. "Hey, Ro. Sorry again about getting so frustrated earlier." He smiled sheepishly at Rogan. "You just need to learn to be patient sometimes."

"Oh yeah . . ." Mom was talking in that drawn-out, almost zombie-like voice she used when she was actually concentrating on text messages. "You have to be patient, Rogan. Or, you know, send a message to our inboxes and get our attention that way. You have to learn that you can't get everything you want in this world right away."

Rogan thought about pointing out that it had hurt, at least a little, when Dad hit him with the sword, and that Mom was usually no better at checking her inbox than she was at actually coming to the door of her office. But he didn't want to lose this opportunity to talk to his parents, so he put all that aside and told them his big news.

"Kid, are you serious?!" Dad patted Rogan on the back. "That's awesome!"

Mom wrapped Rogan in a big hug. She had finished what she was working on and heard most of what Rogan said about the contest. "RoRo! This is wonderful! We have to celebrate!"

Later that night, Rogan's family enjoyed pizza and soda as they chatted excitedly about the contest, and his parents went over the fine print of the contracts and liability waivers that had been sent to Rogan's inbox.

Rogan's mom put down the tablet. "It all looks legitimate. Of course, I'll be making some calls tomorrow with more questions. But I guess my biggest concern is this vague language in paragraph seventeen, subsection C, which talks about how parents will have relatively little contact with their children during the contest."

Rogan was about to point out that they rarely hung out a ton anyway when his father spoke up.

"That's just because they need to maintain secrecy so there aren't too many spoilers for the reality show. Subsection D lists emergency contact numbers and makes it pretty clear we can get in touch with Rogan if there is any serious problem." He chuckled. "Wow. *The* William J. Culum. Atomic Frontiers: Ride Technology into the Future."

Mom frowned. "You'd be so far away, RoRo. The first time away on your own. Are you sure you're ready?"

Rogan rolled his eyes. Was he ready? He was twelve, not two! And he'd been on his own plenty of times when his parents were busy in digi-space. He had his own apartment. Practically.

"Yes!" Rogan said, a little too loudly. "Yes, I'm ready for this. Please. This is a gamer's dream. I was born for this."

Dad laughed. "Rogan, you are absolutely my son. I would have given anything for a chance like this when I was your age. Heck,

I wish I could be in this tournament *now*. Don't worry, buddy. We just need to check on a few things, but I think this will work out."

"Really?" Rogan's insides leapt like Mario on a springboard.

"Really!" Dad said.

"Probably," said Mom.

"Most likely," Dad said.

"Thank you!" said Rogan. "Thank you so much!"

Mom checked her tablet. "It's getting late. I need to meet with some Korean activists in Virtual City, and you should get to bed. More about this in the morning. Brush your teeth, and don't forget to run your updates."

Rogan went off to get ready for bed, though he doubted he'd be able to sleep. He washed his face. Then he reached behind his right ear and pulled back the synthflesh cap to reveal the data port into which he plugged the cable from the maintenance module. Software updates for his neural electrical stimulation implant ran automatically while he brushed his teeth. Fortunately, the maintenance module connected to the hypernet so he could still run his updates while away at the contest. Since the implant had been installed, he hadn't had a single seizure like the ones he used to get. The device worked far better than the old primitive drugs, but his doctor always said keeping the software up to date was essential.

After about thirty seconds, the red light on the module switched to green, letting him know he could disconnect and close up. He pulled the data cable out of the port in his head with a slight scrape-click, spit, rinsed, put his toothbrush away, and was ready for bed.

Rogan returned to his room, his IRL room, and lay against a pile of pillows on his bed under his *Call of Duty: Alien Wars* poster. He tried playing a quick round of *Castle Crushers* on his tablet, but couldn't concentrate. He gave up after too many of his catapult shots sailed too far.

He set the tablet down on his chest and closed his eyes. All he could do was replay the events of the day in his mind over and over. Had all of that *really* happened? Had William Culum really showed up at his apartment door? Was he really invited to the best video game contest in history?

It was all so incredible. If he won this, nobody could ever ignore him again.

Rogan had just begun to drift toward sleep when his tablet pinged with an incoming message. He picked it up and tapped in.

Shaylyn: Guess what I just did!!!

Ugh. The last thing he wanted was his worst video game enemy cutting in on his perfect night, to brag about some cool thing her new level had unlocked. Well, this time, Rogan would be the one bragging. He laughed. She'd freak when she heard his awesome news.

I have something to tell YOU, he started typing, just before her next message popped up.

Shaylyn: I'm heading to the Laser Viper Final Challenge! Quarter of a million bucks and one million game credits! All mine!

Rogan's sophisticated tablet was worth a lot of money — money that his parents probably wouldn't be willing to spend again all too soon. That fact was the only thing that prevented him from smashing it into his wall at that moment. He had tried so hard to be rid of this girl, to beat her in game after game, to leave her in his digital dust. Shaylyn was the Bowser to his Mario, the Ganon to his Link, the Covenant to his Master Chief.

Shaylyn: So what did you have to tell me?

His head thudded back against the wall. He looked at his VR headset and gamer gloves on the stand by his bed. "Fine, then," he said quietly to the universe. "Shaylyn and everybody else better bring it. *Laser Viper* is my game, and I *will* win this tournament. *Ego sum maximus.*"

CHAPTER 3

Two weeks later, Rogan and his family stood outside the house with a yellow self-driving robotaxi waiting in the driveway. Rogan had thought Mom and Dad might come with him to the airport. After all, it was the first time he'd ever been on a plane IRL.

But Mom said Atomic Frontiers had arranged for an airline rep to greet him at the airport to help him get to his plane. "We want this to be an opportunity to practice independence, RoRo."

"I would have liked to get you to the plane myself," Dad said. "But coming out of SeaTac, your flight will definitely be delayed," he'd said. "Sorry, buddy, but I can't miss this game licensing meeting."

Rogan took a half step back from the cab. "I really need—"

Mom put her hands on Rogan's shoulders and looked him deep in the eyes. "Anytime you want, use our family hypernet account and slip on your headset. You can be right at home in your apartment." She smiled.

And so with some goodbyes, good-lucks, and quick hugs, Rogan and his suitcase were loaded into the robocab.

Please verify your prepaid destination is: Eagle Terminal, Seattle-Tacoma International Airport.

"Yes," Rogan answered the computer.

Please fasten your seat belt for safety, and thank you for choosing Robotaxi of Seattle.

The flight was late departing SeaTac, but after that, it all went smoothly, and after five plus hours wedged into a crowded aircraft with hundreds of other people who were also off in their own digi-space worlds, the plane bumped down on the runway at Dulles International.

Rogan had been playing the newest Zelda game. Gaming on a plane wasn't so great. To keep passengers from accidentally hitting one another, gamer gloves were prohibited on all flights, so Rogan was stuck using old-fashioned push-button controls. But the game was a reminder of the gift his mom had given him early that morning before he'd left home, and he reached into his pocket to squeeze the pendant that was "for courage and good luck." It was a little shield from *The Legend of Zelda*, a red bird shape on a field of blue, and at the top, the three gold triangles of the Triforce. "Your father gave me that pendant when we first started dating. Once a gamer, always a gamer," Mom had said. "Bring that shield back when you return with the championship."

Since he was a minor, a woman from the airline met him at the gate and escorted him to baggage claim, where Sophia Hahn waited for him, wearing a bright yellow dress with a pleated skirt that came to just below her knees and four oversized black buttons off center to her left side. She showed some papers to the airline rep. Her smile was almost as blindingly bright as her dress. "Rogan!" she squealed, bouncing a little with giddy happiness. She looked a little older than her avatar, a not uncommon occurrence among adults in digi-space "It's so good to *see* you in real life."

Xavier stepped up to join them and reached out to offer a handshake. "Good to see you again. My job is helping all the gamers in the tournament with whatever they need while they're here," he explained in a deep, even voice. "So don't hesitate to come to me for anything."

"Thanks, Mr. . . . ." Rogan struggled to remember the man's last name.

"Call me Xavier." He almost smiled. "Or just X, my nickname since high school."

Rogan spotted his dad's enormous battered blue suitcase making its way around the luggage return carousel.

X followed his gaze. "This your bag? The blue one?" He was already reaching for the suitcase when Rogan nodded. "No problem," X said. "I got it."

The suitcase was heavy, but X hoisted it like it was empty. He put it down next to a bright red roller bag with the double W wing logo for Wonder Woman. Whose was that?

"There she is!" Sophia chirped.

"Rogan?" At the familiar voice, he turned around to face Shaylyn Spero, in person at last. Her light brown hair sported a freshly dyed blue streak and was pulled back in a ponytail. She wore tan short pants and a T-shirt with a picture of the simple old Nintendo Entertainment System controller. Holding a Starbucks cup, she offered her free hand, smiling as if handshakes were normal, like any of this was normal, like they weren't blood enemies in every game they'd ever played together. "You're shorter than I expected," Shaylyn said. "Not quite as big as your *Laser Viper* Ranger."

Rogan scrambled for a witty comeback. Why was it so hard to communicate face-to-face IRL? He knew that if they had been in digi-space right then, he would have returned fire with the perfect reply.

Grudgingly, he shook Shaylyn's hand, wishing his palms weren't so clammy, wishing she wasn't almost three inches taller than him.

"You two know each other?" Sophia bubbled.

Shaylyn smiled. "Rogan always tries to beat me when we play online."

"Tries?" Rogan forced a laugh. "Your little Flyer hasn't taken down my Ranger since—"

"Since the last two times we've battled! Boom! You were down. Then I dropped you off the cliff. Boom! Ranger busted into a hundred pieces on the rocks below."

"So you know each other very well!" Sophia said. "I love that spirit of competition. It's going to make for great gaming and even better reality TV!"

"Yeah," Shay said. "We're pretty much gamer BFFs."

What? They'd known each other for only two years, so they'd have to drop the last *F*. And despite her cool gamer shirt and the way she could be useful on his way to total game domination, the girl was annoying! They weren't even Fs, certainly not BFs. They were more like Bitter Gaming Rivals. BGRs. Boogers.

Sophia bounced on her toes and stretched her neck, looking around for something. In a moment her movie star smile reactivated, and she motioned to a boy with giant, expensive-looking headphones, sitting on a bench a little farther away behind his own suitcase. "You were the last one getting in," she said to Rogan. "Our car should be waiting."

Headphones guy rolled his suitcase up to join them. He seemed to be trying really hard to look bored. He was way taller than Rogan, at least six inches taller than Shaylyn.

"Beckett," Sophia said. He didn't change his expression or look at anyone. She laughed and tapped his shoulder. "Beckett?" He took off his headphones and locked his eyes on Rogan, sizing him up a little like the way Rogan's dad sometimes looked over steaks in the grocery store. "Beckett Ewell is joining us from Atlanta. Beckett, this is Rogan Webber from Seattle."

"Hey." Beckett cocked his head back in a reverse nod and slipped his cans back over his ears, already done with everyone.

Shay shot Rogan a look like *Who does this guy think he is?*

"This way." Sophia led the group toward the exit.

X carried Rogan's and Shay's suitcases, but Beckett clutched his tightly to his chest.

A few minutes later, a driver pulled up in a huge black SUV. X sat up front, while Sophia and Shaylyn took seats in the middle. Rogan and Beckett had to climb all the way to the back row. Beckett sat down first, and instead of scooting across the bench to let Rogan flop down beside him, he placed himself right in the way on the passenger side, forcing Rogan to scramble over him.

Rogan took his seat and buckled his seat belt, shaking his head. This was just the kind of crap that never happened in digi-space, the kind of petty awkwardness that made him wish he could log in forever and leave the so-called real world behind.

Well, Beckett could be a jerk all he wanted. As soon as the game was on, Rogan would blaze right past him.

-----o-----

The digital brochure for the *Laser Viper* Final Challenge said contestants would be living in dorms. It should have said "luxury hotel suite." When they arrived at the Atomic Frontiers headquarters, Sophia and X led Rogan, Shaylyn, and Beckett through heavy double doors at the back of the big curved wall of a huge, horseshoe-shaped room. Three doors lined each arcing side of the horseshoe, and straight ahead, a movie-theater-sized screen dominated the one flat wall.

The center of the room offered a big, round wood table surrounded by a poofy-looking circular sofa. Two other kids, a girl and boy, who looked their age too, lounged far apart from each other.

Immediately, a cambot rolled up before the newcomers, a white elongated teardrop shape about a meter high, fat on the bottom just above its wheels and narrow at the top where the iris in its big black lens adjusted to zoom in on them like a giant alien eye. Rogan remembered what he'd read in the guidebook about the importance of all the contestants ignoring the cameras. He tried to look away, but it was tough because cameras were mounted on the walls and hanging from the ceilings, and kept spinning to face them.

The place had been pretty quiet as they walked in, but now Sophia Hahn marched to the middle of the room, holding her hands up high and spinning grandly. "Home sweet home!" She motioned toward the new boy. "This is Takashi Endo from San Francisco. He's one of the best healer viper mods in the world."

Takashi smiled and offered a little wave. "Great to meet you."

Sophia introduced the last girl. Her white *Star Wars* T-shirt was bright against her deep brown skin. "Here's Jacqueline Sharpe from Cincinnati, Ohio."

"Hey, guys." Jacqueline smoothed her shirt.

Next Sophia introduced Rogan, Shaylyn, and Beckett. "We at Atomic Frontiers Gaming Division are thrilled to have you all here. Now Xavier's going to show you to your rooms and let you know how everything will work while you're with us. Then we'll have a quick orientation in the game room." She leaned forward, folding her hands over her knees. "Just wait until you see the fabulous game system—basically game *arena*— we have set up for you. But we want to get you back to your rooms tonight with plenty of time for you to prepare and rest, because tomorrow is the first round of the tournament."

An electric thrill coursed through Rogan. Video games were in his blood, and judging by the expressions and postures of the other contestants around him, they were just as eager to begin.

X moved to the middle of the group. "As you know, this tournament will include three elimination rounds plus a championship. One gamer will be eliminated from each round. The final two will compete for the championship in the fourth game. A session may be followed immediately by another, or there might be big breaks between games. There may be little warning before it's time to play. You'll have to be ready and flexible. But you should prepare to spend a lot of time in these dorms.

"We've told you that Atomic Frontiers plans to market the *Laser Viper* game by posting videos of this tournament as an online reality show. But to do that, they can't have contestants uploading the results of every game round to the whole world. So you can keep any connected medical devices, but I'm going to have to ask you to hand over your phones, your portable game systems, VR headsets, basically anything that can go online." A lot of groans came from the gamers, but X only held out his hands. "I know. It's a pain. But you all agreed to this when you signed your contracts to participate in this tournament. Everything will be returned to you when this is over."

After they had surrendered their devices, X showed them to the dorms. Each gamer was given an individual room with a twin-sized bed, a private bathroom with shower, and a door that locked and unlocked with a thumb press to the ID pad near the doorknob. The accommodations offered a lot of privacy, for which Rogan was grateful. He'd be able to download his implant updates without anyone else noticing.

X handed out tablets. "These are about as locked down as they come. No social media. No audio or video calls. Even most news sites are blocked to keep you all focused on the games."

"If we let you spend all your time on your phones and tablets, it wouldn't make for very interesting TV, now would it?" Sophia laughed.

"What about texting home?" Jacqueline asked.

Rogan had been wondering the same thing, but Beckett smirked like she was a weak little baby for asking the question.

"Don't worry!" Sophia cooed. "We'll make sure you get plenty of time to vid call home. Trust me. This is going to be a great experience. All you have to worry about is gaming."

Beckett waved his Atomic Frontiers tablet around. "If we can't text anyone or go online with these things, what are they even for?"

"They're mostly so Atomic Frontiers can keep in touch with you all," X said. "They have your schedules, you can use them to order just about anything you want to eat or drink, and Sophia and I can send you messages if we need to. You can also reach any of us or each other, but remember that any texting to other gamers in the tournament is being monitored and may be used on the show. Questions?" Nobody had any. "Good. In your closets you'll find your *Laser Viper* game suits. Please change into them, and meet me back here in the common area. Then we'll go see the game room."

The gamers exchanged confused looks. Why would they have to change clothes just to play video games?

After they'd changed and come back together, their confusion hadn't cleared up much. The outfits were zip-up, form-fitting, one-piece jumpsuits, complete with boots and gloves, the Atomic Frontiers atom globe logo over their hearts and each gamer's name on the back. Hidden between the layers of fabric was some kind of slightly firmer material.

"What's this all about?" Takashi asked when the gamers had reassembled. He pulled at his long sleeve.

Shaylyn tugged the fabric on her arm. "It's, like, all crunchy or something."

"All of that will be explained," X said. "For now, just remember that you'll be expected to wear these suits every time you play. You'll see why in a moment. Follow me."

The five gamers were led out of the dorms, through a confusing labyrinth of hallways, and past the Sun Station One model in the atrium. Atomic Frontiers world headquarters looked large from the outside, but Rogan felt as if the place was like the TARDIS from *Doctor Who*, even bigger on the inside.

Finally, Mr. Culum greeted them before a set of double doors, hands in the pockets of his gray cardigan. "Welcome, gamers! Congratulations on making it into the *Laser Viper* Final Challenge! Behind these doors you will truly ride technology into the future with the most sophisticated, realistic, immersive gaming experience in the world. You will, to the greatest extent possible, become your own laser viper, all of you on the same fireteam in a series of short gaming sessions consisting of one mission each. Takashi Endo, you are the squad's Healer."

Takashi smiled with pride and offered a little wave to the others.

Mr. Culum went on, each gamer offering a nod or some other acknowledgement when mentioned. "Beckett Ewell, the Tank. Jacqueline Sharpe, Engineer. Shaylyn Spero, Flyer. Rogan Webber, Ranger. Tonight, you will all have exactly thirty minutes with which to familiarize yourselves with the control of your viper. Have fun, but use this time well, because the first round of the tournament will take place tomorrow."

Rogan looked at the others, sizing up his competition, even as each of them did the same. As much as Shay drove him crazy, only a fool would think she wasn't a good gamer. Takashi seemed friendly enough, smiling and bouncing around a little in excitement. Would he take the game seriously? Rogan figured he might be the first one eliminated. Beckett glared at everyone else, trying to appear tough. Rogan would have to see how the Tank rolled in the game. He wasn't sure how to read Jacqueline just yet. She might be a serious threat.

The doors opened and Mr. Culum stepped aside to allow everyone else to enter.

"Whoa!" Takashi said. "This is incredible." The reaction was shared by just about everyone on the fireteam, except for Beckett, who watched impassively with his arms folded. Beckett had to be acting unimpressed, Rogan thought, because this was . . . wow.

A few years ago, Rogan's friend Booker had an extra ticket to a Seattle Seahawks game. That football stadium was not quite as large as the room they'd all just stepped into, except this giant, empty, black-walled space had no stadium seating and had a ceiling high above them. Five technicians had been waiting a few paces inside the door holding five shiny black helmets and standing near five harnesses, each of which dangled from steel cables suspended from rigs way up in the ceiling.

"All of you are experienced gamers who have grown up with virtual reality gaming," called Mr. Culum. "But while VR has far surpassed old push-button-controller gaming, it does still have its limits. Home gamers are restricted by the size of the real-life room in which they play. Someone in a smaller room takes only a few steps before he sees the blue-green LOA lines warning him that he's approaching a real-life barrier. So if his character has farther to travel in the game, he must run or walk in place, a subtle but important reminder that his otherwise realistic game environment is artificial."

Mr. Culum motioned to Shaylyn and pointed at one of the harnesses.

"Your viper mod is the flyer. You're very familiar with an airborne viper, but flying, jumping, and climbing are more functions that provide another disconnect from the fictive dream of the game. Gamers can't feel the movement, the acceleration and deceleration of fast flight, the change in altitude. Gamers can't feel a handshake or when they bump into an obstacle. They can't feel weapons contact, the impact when they punch someone, or the sensation of changes in weight when lifting different items. Here!" Mr. Culum's voice echoed and he spread his arms wide above him. "You five will be among the first to enjoy the gaming experience of a lifetime! Here in the Atomic Frontiers gaming arena you will come closer to living your digital experience than anyone in the history of video games. Xavier will explain it all. For now, get ready. Please put on your VR helmets and allow the techs to secure your suits to the flight sim cables."

Rogan walked over to the technican beckoning him and slid his helmet on. To his disappointment, the view inside was the same as the view without, a real-time projection of the Atomic Frontiers people and the other gamers in the arena. He'd hoped to look down to find himself transformed into the Ranger.

When all the gamers were wearing helmets and connected, X put on a headset and positioned the microphone near his mouth. *"Can you all hear and see me OK?"*

The gamers didn't answer right away. It was just like that weird time before any old game when the players weren't sure if they were connected. Finally, they all confirmed they were on.

"*Good,*" said X. "*I'll be the voice of Viper CentCom throughout each round of competition. I'll offer you some guidance on mission objectives and warnings about dangers to look out for, kind of like Cortana in Halo. I'm going to step out to the control room, and then we'll get started.*"

"This is so cool," Takashi breathed.

"So we're going to, like, really fly around on these cables?" Shaylyn asked.

"Maybe if you just shut up and wait, he'll tell us," said Beckett.

"Whoa," Jacqueline said. "Calm down, Ace."

Shay and Takashi laughed.

Rogan laughed too. He admired the way Jacqueline could come up with quick, funny things to say IRL.

Beckett put his hands on his hips. "I'm going to crush you all."

This was too much. "Why don't you save the tough guy act for the game?" Rogan cut in.

Beckett pointed at him. "OK, you can die first."

"Come on, everybody," said Takashi. "We need to work together."

"*Quiet down, please, gamers.*" X's voice came over the channel. "*Your game suits are not just uniforms. They're enhanced with hundreds of micromotors between layers of fabric. These will help adjust your speed, mainly reducing speed for slower vipers. Beckett might be a fast runner in the real world, but in the game, he'll be slowed down just like his Tank. Your suits are also equipped with many environment* simulators, to give you a sense of heat, cold, or even impact. If your viper walks through fire, you won't be burned, but the appropriate areas will heat up to let you feel what is happening in the game. If your viper is hit by a bullet or punched by an enemy, you'll also feel that. But don't worry, the suits have been tested for safety dozens of times. No force will be sufficient to really hurt or injure you. Trust me. Keeping you safe is my top priority."

"What about the wires?" Shaylyn asked.

"Good question, Flyer," said X. "The harnesses will allow quite a lot of vertical movement to give you all a feel for a change in altitude. Everything from climbing to falling to flying will be simulated in the most realistic way possible, short of strapping functional rockets on your back."

Shaylyn looked around at the giant arena, full of possibility. "This is the coolest thing I've ever done."

"Instructions will come up on each of your heads-up displays about how to fire your primary, secondary, and tertiary weapons. So watch your HUDs," X continued evenly. "In general, you'll operate your weapons through a series of hand gestures. To fire your NonLethal Energy Pulse weapons, most of you will make a tight fist, a tight fist while extending your index finger to fire your Compact High-Energy Lasers, and so on. Most of the controls are the same as the home system you're used to, but there are a few differences. In a moment, I'll activate the training simulator, and you'll all have the chance to acclimate to the system. I suggest you carefully focus on familiarizing yourselves with the different functions of your suit and capabilities of your vipers. This is not playtime. It's practice time. Go get 'em, gamers."

CHAPTER 4

The giant black arena pixel-blurred, and the gamers felt themselves being pulled up into the air in their harnesses. It was a frightening sensation at first, but their uncertainty was soon replaced by wonder and excitement as their world rematerialized around them. They were standing in the familiar, dimly red-lit confines of the SR-73 StarScreamer jump-ship cargo bay where so many stages of the game began. The gamers with their helmets and wires were replaced by their laser vipers, their suits keeping them stable even though they'd been hoisted up hundreds of feet in the arena.

Beckett as Tank stood with a wide stance, raising his large arms like he was flexing his biceps. "I'm a giant! Look at me! Unstoppable!"

Shay, appearing as her usual compact flyer mod, looked the big guy over. "Went with the purple, huh? Doing your best Barney impression?"

Tank tilted his head. "Who?"

In *Laser Viper* players could customize the color schemes of their robots, allowing for individuality among the five different mods, and helping players tell one another apart on the battlefield.

"You'd be amazed at how many gamers underestimate my Tank just because it's purple." Tank gave Flyer a little shove.

"Watch it," Flyer said.

"Yeah, try to take this seriously." Jacqueline had chosen gold for her Engineer.

Tank laughed. "Oh, calm down, babies. I'm just messing around!"

APPROACHING HELE DROP ZONE. ALL VIPERS PREPARE FOR COMBAT DROP.

"*Gamers, listen up.*" X's voice came over the channel. "*We want you to get a feel for the combat drop, but this one will be a little different from those you will have in the tournament. We're going to control your fall a little so you all disperse and land separate from one another to get some time practicing on your own. For now, stand in drop position.*"

Red glowing circles lit up on the floor, and each gamer hurried to stand on one, Tank making a show of elbowing Ranger and Healer to take his place. Rogan pushed him back.

RELEASE IN 5, 4, 3 . . .

"*Ego sum maximus!*" Ranger shouted.

-----o-----

Shay wanted to make fun of Ranger's stupid line, but had no time. The relative calm inside the supersonic jet vanished.

Chaos. Howling wind. Falling.

Really falling.

The fireteam shot away from the SR-73, the sleek black arrowhead with its long, narrow forward fuselage. The jet appeared to shrink as it blasted away at Mach 5, over 3,300 miles per hour, vanishing from view in seconds. At 85,000 feet, the vipers had enough elevation to see the black expanse of space above them, the blue curvature of the world below, but that would change fast as they plummeted toward Earth.

Shay had logged thousands of hours playing *Laser Viper*, been on hundreds of combat drops, and it had always looked so real, but she had never felt it, never truly experienced a drop until now. Her stomach twisted into that cold-hollow free-fall feeling, more intense than the awesome sickening rush when the cars first dove down the hill on a roller coaster.

It wasn't completely realistic. They weren't literally falling 85,000 feet. Shay figured the cables gave them an initial fast drop, and then slowed their descent through the arena, but even that movement, coupled with the suit's motors simulating wind resistance and the view in her VR helmet, made it much more realistic than the home version.

As the altimeter in her HUD ticked off hundreds of feet per second, she laughed, tucking her legs, grabbing her knees, and rolling for a while as she fell. Somersaults in free fall. That was never possible when playing at home. She flattened out, spreading her arms and legs skydiver style. Soon her fireteam began drifting apart the way X said they would.

The light, green-colored armor of Shaylyn's Flyer was more sleek and aerodynamic than on any other viper mod, designed for speed and, with the advanced modifications she'd earned for her robot, for flight. The trade-off with every unit of the flyer mod was that their lighter weight meant lighter weapons. Shaylyn's Flyer was as leveled up as Rogan's Ranger, but her only armaments were a standard NonLethal Energy Pulse (NLEP) and a limited capacity, heavy Directed Electromagnetic Pulse (DEMP) for disabling vehicles, robots, or computer systems, both emitted from a single weapon on her right forearm. She could only fire about ten of these DEMPs before she exhausted her fourth-gen quadithium battery. But while all vipers had limited rocket capability—for braking thrusters so they didn't slam into the ground on these drops, for jump assist, and for finally soaring up into the sky to be picked up by their jump ship for exfil after missions—advanced flyer vipers could soar around indefinitely. Flyers were great for recon, rescues, accessing higher areas, or combat air support.

FLIGHT SYSTEMS ONLINE.

Instructions rolled across Shay's HUD, telling her how to fly, but the controls in this version of the game were very similar to those at home. Flying was mostly automatic. When she spread her index and middle fingers into the old peace sign, she activated Flyer's thrusters. So if she pointed both hands straight down and made the gesture, she shot straight up in the air. If she were flying forward and then shoved her hands out in front of her, she'd fly to a halt. Basically, she flew in the opposite direction of wherever she pointed peace signs, moving faster, with more thrust, the farther she spread her fingers.

Shay laughed as she moved through the air, felt the change in direction and momentum as she controlled her flight. There was a minor tug on her game suit where her harness connected to the cables, but other than that, the illusion was complete. She had the wide-open sky to practice flying, and soon found herself in total control. After a while, it was so easy, so fun. More than fun—it felt like her very best dream come to life. Her power level percentage was holding and she was steady in the sky. "You guys! This is—" She threw herself into a tight flying somersault and then came out of it to soar straight ahead. "Woo!" She laughed. "I can *fly!*"

"*No kidding,*" Tank answered. She couldn't even see him anymore. He'd fallen away from her, vanishing in seconds like a rock plunging into a dark pond. "*You're the Flyer.*"

Shaylyn laughed. "No, you don't get it. I mean . . ." How could she describe it? They couldn't be feeling quite the same thing on their combat drops as she was flying. "I'm, like, actually moving around, instead of standing on the floor at home in my basement. I mean, *I* am flying! Me. I can feel it. I'm actually . . . Woooo!!"

Following the instructions on her HUD, she kept her left hand pointed behind her, fingers spread to keep up her flight, and she reached ahead with her right hand. Squeezing her hand into a tight fist, she felt the buzz in her arm as she fired a blue-white electric NLEP off into the distance. "Look out, everybody. I am Flyer!"

-----◇-----

Like the other gamers in her fireteam, Jacqueline Sharpe had activated braking thrusters to slow the combat drop hundreds of times, but this was the first time she was actually scared. She felt the increased g-force pulling on her body as she slowed down, buildings and streets below rushing up at her at a menacing pace. Engineer landed on her feet, and she felt the ground beneath her, heard the gravel crunch.

A dull gray sky hung heavy over a city of ruins, the rubble of collapsed skyscrapers, steel I-beam frames of buildings with the walls blasted away, and abandoned cars and trucks—some of them twisted, burned-out hulks. Total destruction. "It's like something out of *Fallout 10*," Jacqueline said. "This town needs an Engineer."

Engineer vipers were another lightly armed mod. Fully upgraded, they only carried nonlethals and a single limited Compact High-Energy Laser (CHEL). The engineer's job was solving technical problems in any environment viper robots might face. Engineers were equipped with advanced processors for infiltrating enemy computers and several automated algorithms for taking over whatever systems they encountered. They carried specialized cutting tools and a supply of advanced, extremely high explosive compound, which could be used for everything from cutting through doors to taking down buildings. For hot-wiring cars or even enemy vipers, for rendering roads impassable, for secretly downloading classified intel, and for many other technical situations, the engineer mod was best.

Unlike the experience for Flyer, Jacqueline's gaming situation wasn't greatly changed. The drop was very different, and she had more control over her viper's body position, but her weapons still fired with the same hand gestures, and Engineer's technical abilities were still accessed by holomenus that projected in the air in front of her. She activated the holomenu by crossing her fingers, then flipped and tapped through them the same as she would on any website on her phone, opening up all kinds of different tools, hacking programs, and preprogrammed repair sequences. As soon as she uncrossed her fingers, the floating holomenu vanished.

Jacqueline raised the hood on a salvageable-looking car, her computer identifying it as an older model Ford Fusion. Just as quickly, her systems began scanning to identify problem areas. Dirty spark plugs. Dead battery. She knew how to fix those problems before her computer presented solutions. She quickly fixed and hot-wired the car. Laser vipers had no faces, but featured wide V-shaped lines where eyes might otherwise be, glowing the same color as their bodies. Jacqueline's glowed yellow. As she thought about all the great technical tricks Engineer could pull off, all the complex physical problems she could work out for herself and for her fireteam, the robot did not reveal her smile.

-----o-----

Rogan laughed as Ranger unleashed a wicked side kick from a series of preprogrammed combat moves. He felt his foot connect with the wall, watched the bricks fly away, opening a hole in the building he was standing in fourteen stories up. He backed up to the other side of the room, tossing away the smoking remains of a desk he'd laser-blasted. By now, the surprised or delighted outbursts from the rest of his fireteam had died down, and he imagined they were all, like him, getting serious about figuring out how to function as laser vipers with this new system. This was important business, but that didn't mean he couldn't have fun.

Rogan always felt more himself, more free, when he logged into a game or other parts of digi-space. But with the realism of these game suits and the arena, he was more alive than ever.

With his Ranger's recent upgrade to level-six armor, the lightest class of Energy Absorption-Transformation (EAT) armor available, and with both NLEP and CHEL emitters on either arm, he was one of the most powerful laser vipers in the game. Ranger wasn't as big and bulky as Tank or Engineer, but wasn't as light as Flyer or Healer—a sleek blue and silver, more streamlined, all-robot version of *Halo*'s Master Chief.

So far, everything had worked even better than Rogan had expected, but he hadn't yet tested his other latest upgrades. He looked out over the ruined city through the hole he'd busted in the wall—there would never be a better time. He sprinted forward and leapt out of the building, loving the completely real feeling of the fall. His onboard sensors picked out a number of targets ahead of him—he tucked his thumb inside his fist, squeezed, and his grappling cable launched. The end of the cable hooked onto a building down the street, and Rogan descended into a perfect, graceful swing. He felt the fall, the slight increase in tension on his arm at the bottom of the swing, the sensation of being weightless as he soared up into the air again. Another cable fired. Connection. Another swing. Rogan had played a Spider-Man game before, and he'd become pretty good at web-slinging, but that game was child's play compared to this.

He scream-laughed as he tucked into an awesome aerial flip at the top of a high swing. Rogan swung over the rubble of ruined streets, practicing firing his various weapons in the air. His scanning and targeting systems helped out a lot, stabilizing his arm and his aim. As bright ruby-red lasers exploded into the ground below him, he thought about all the years he'd been gaming and how much he'd played *Laser Viper* in particular, practicing to become the best ranger, working hard to level up and score upgrades. He felt as if all that had culminated in this moment, and as he launched into another swing, he felt more prepared than ever.

-----o-----

Beckett loved the feeling of power as he thudded down the street in a fast jog to test Tank's speed, his heavy feet shaking the pavement with each hard step. He leaned down and swung one massive robot arm to backhand a small sedan, sending the car flying out of his way.

He was a max-level tank with level-twelve EAT armor, heavy enough to stop bullets as large as .50 caliber. NLEPs couldn't hurt him, and he was resistant to EMP weapons. Every upgrade he'd earned had increased the size and strength of his armor. He could stay in any firefight longer than the others, absorbing a huge portion of the energy fired at him, channeling it to one of several glowing green energon cells throughout his body to convert the power for his own use. On both arms he packed NLEPs, DEMPs, CHELs, and plasma cannons, the latter weapons strong enough to blast heavily armored vehicles. Weapons pods could fold out of his shoulders, with three Hellfire missiles ready in each. All Tanks had bulkier backs, housing extra quadithium batteries to power their weapons, but Beckett was also equipped with one medium-range, high-explosive, avenger-class cruise missile. He packed an arsenal. He was a devastatingly powerful walking weapons platform.

Beckett wasn't like Flyer. He wasn't about to blather away to the others about every little thing he did. It was better if they didn't know all about Tank's capabilities. When the time came for him to show what he had, he would come out hard, surprising them all and playing to win. No mercy. He punched through the side of a parked delivery truck, gripping the metal hull in either hand and peeling it back like a candy bar wrapper.

-----o-----

Takashi Endo wouldn't have admitted it to anyone, but he was a little bored. He kicked a half-flat basketball down the street as he followed Tank. Healer's primary function was repairing other vipers, and Tank seemed like the best bet for finding him damaged units.

"Why are you following me?!" Beckett called as he threw a motorcycle through an abandoned restaurant. Takashi laughed.

Healer vipers were easily the quickest and stealthiest of the viper mods—they needed to be so in order to reach their team members in any situation, fast, no matter the danger. They were armed with an NLEP too, and while they didn't pack a lot of bulk, it was what was on the inside that counted. Takashi's red max-level Healer was filled with interior compartments containing critical spare parts for other vipers as well as specialized tools to repair them. Within his body, he carried extra power cells to restore vipers that had exhausted their own energy supply. In absolute emergencies, Takashi could disconnect his Healer's own limbs and install them on others. No laser viper teams ever took on missions without a Healer.

Beckett didn't seem to grasp the importance of viper repair support.

"I'm a Healer," Takashi said. Duh.

"You're weak," Beckett said.

"I can't test my repair abilities in this training round with no damaged vipers to fix."

"How 'bout I blast you? Can you fix yourself?"

"Why are you so mad?" Takashi asked. This guy was really something.

"I get it," said Beckett. "You're supposed to fix vipers and keep the fireteam going."

"Yeah!" Healer said. "It's pretty cool, and—"

"It's pathetic!" Beckett shouted. "I'm not mad. I'm just here to win, not to play nice and make friends." Beckett opened up with both CHELs, full power, cutting into the stone front of a bank and then slicing through the steel I beams in the shell of a building like a hot knife through a block of ice cream. The building collapsed behind him. "You cowards use me as a shield, there's nothing I can do about that, but I'm not going out of my way to protect or fight for you or the rest of the team."

"Okayyy . . . maybe I won't go out of my way to fix you if you're damaged," Takashi chuckled.

Beckett laughed back. "You're learning, dude! But you don't gotta worry about that. I'm a max-level Tank. I won't need help."

A pair of small explosions lit up the intersection ahead at the cross street. A steel cable lashed out and grabbed the high corner of a building, Ranger swinging behind it. Takashi watched him swing. He looked cool enough soaring from cable to cable like that, but sooner or later, something would go wrong, and Ranger would need serious repairs.

Tank seemed to be reading Takashi's mind. He leaned forward and opened the missile compartment in his back.

"What are you doing?" Takashi asked. "He must be a hundred feet up!"

"You want me to shoot *you* with this thing instead?" Beckett replied. "Anyway, X said nobody could really get hurt in the game, so he'll be fine. He just needs to learn who's best in this tournament." Beckett fired the cruise missile. It roared away, trailing white smoke. An instant later the top quarter of a building exploded.

"Whoa!" Ranger yelled as his cable disconnected and he fell out of control. "Who's shooting?!"

Takashi watched the falling Ranger desperately fire his grappling cable, catching himself before he crashed into a wrecked city bus. He was relieved Ranger had avoided full impact, because digital simulation or not, it looked like crashing full speed into the ground could hurt.

But on the other hand, Takashi was happy to have a chance to do what he did best. He moved instantly, running full speed toward the chaos to help Ranger. Finally a chance to get to work.

"Ranger! I'm on my way!" he called out.

But Ranger had used his cables to catch himself and slow his fall before he hit the bus, and he walked out of the broken vehicle with only a few scratches.

"Not bad, Ro!" Flyer swept down toward them out of the gray sky above. She whipped her hands out in front of her and flew to a hovering halt about twenty feet off the ground. "Bet you wish you could fly."

Ranger disengaged the cable and dropped smoothly to the ground. "I *can* fly. This game is awesome and I am awesome at it." He shook his head. "I only wish I knew what just happened back there."

Engineer and Tank entered the intersection. "I saw it," said Engineer. "Tank blasted the building with his cruise missile."

"What?" Flyer said. "This is a training round, Tank, not a melee."

Tank held up his big robot hands. "I had to test the missile! Why you whining about it? He's fine."

"It doesn't matter," said Ranger. "Even if he was trying to take me out, he couldn't. I'm fine."

"I guess that's good," Takashi said. "But I'm Healer, and I can't really test my viper repair abilities when nobody's been damaged."

Tank held out his big arms toward Ranger and, in seconds, fired three DEMPs before unleashing a full barrage of CHEL and plasma bursts to tear the viper up. With his EAT armor fried by the DEMPs, Ranger's chest superheated and ruptured. His arms were blasted clean off, and the wreckage of his body was thrown back against a wall.

Ranger let out one short scream. He hit the street hard, the V-shaped line of his visual sensor barely glowing blue.

"What are you *doing*, idiot?!" Flyer shouted.

"Don't be such a baby." Tank shrugged. "Healer needed to practice healing."

Takashi knelt down next to Ranger's torn-up body. "Um. I can fix that."

CHAPTER 5

"*Time's up, gamers,*" X said, just before Healer had reassembled Ranger enough to grant Rogan full movement. The game environment digi-scrambled and then re-formed into the empty black arena. The micromotors in Rogan's game suit unlocked so that he could move freely again. Shaylyn was slowly lowered to the floor. Harnesses disengaged automatically and were hoisted up near the ceiling. X, Sophia, Mr. Culum, and several technicians entered. A half dozen cambots followed to film it all.

Mr. Culum flashed a bright smile and clapped. "Great job, gamers! Absolutely wonderful. You may remove your VR headgear now."

Rogan took off his helmet and glared at Beckett. He wanted to tell the guy off right then, but X stood with his big arms folded, watching the two of them, his expression a little stern.

"What did you all think of the new system?" Sophia called. She was the opposite of stern. Cambots rolled up in front of each gamer, zooming in to film the best angles.

"Awesome," Takashi said. "When I play at home, I use my hands to reach out and grab whatever tools I need or to adjust some parts on the viper I'm fixing, but it's all digital. I can barely feel it if I have to crank a wrench or something. Today the motors in my gamer gloves and suit made it all feel real. This is the greatest game ever!"

Mr. Culum laughed. "I'm glad you think so. I've worked in computers since I was twelve years old, but I've never been satisfied with just the way things were. Why would I be? Why, when technology can take us so much further? When it can make life better?"

Mr. Culum started walking back and forth in front of the gamers, his pace quickening and brow furrowing as he became more excited.

"You were talking about the game suit allowing you most of the physical sensation of using the tools to work on that laser viper. But right now, Atomic Frontiers is developing a similar system where a doctor, say, in America, can conduct surgery on a patient in VR, actually manipulating a robot that is carrying out the surgery on a real patient elsewhere in the world. Advanced medical care, anywhere. Anytime."

He clapped his hands and his voice raised even louder. "Technology breaking down the walls that divide humanity, moving us toward the end of injustice and inequality and bringing hope and order to a chaotic world!"

Mr. Culum stopped and seemed to remember he was in his own gaming arena, not on the stage at Atomic Frontiers' annual tech reveal show touting his company's newest advancements. He looked about as if surprised to see people around him. "But, ah, yes," he finished quietly with a wink. "Well done, gamers, too."

Sophia jumped in with the smooth, even tone of a professional interviewer. The cambots zoomed even closer to the gamers at the sound of her voice. "Rogan? Beckett here shot you pretty hard. He did some real damage. How do you feel about that?"

Rogan glanced at the single lens on the long teardrop-shaped cambot in front of him, heard the faint whir as it zoomed in on him. He saw the smirk on Beckett's face but refused to let anyone think Beckett had rattled him, not in a video game tournament that was his to win.

Rogan laughed and gave Takashi a high five. "No big deal. Glad our Healer had the chance to practice."

"There should have been another way," Jacqueline said.

"Yeah, kind of a cheap shot," Shay said.

Rogan couldn't decide if he wanted his old gamer rival backing him up or not, but he wasn't going to let Beckett, and eventually the reality show audience, think he was upset about this. "It was just a practice round," Rogan said. "He'd never pull that off in the real game."

Beckett frowned. "I wouldn't be so—"

"In any case." Mr. Culum spoke loudly, with his arms spread toward the gamers. "We at Atomic Frontiers are so pleased you enjoyed our revolutionary gaming experience. This is a prototype that we plan to replicate in hundreds of abandoned shopping malls and other former retail spaces across the country, helping to reduce brick-and-mortar blight as we provide more people with state-of-the-art gaming. Thank you for helping us showcase this amazing system and for participating in the *Laser Viper* Final Challenge."

"Which begins tomorrow!" Sophia chirped. "So it would probably be best, gamers, if you all headed back to the dorms to get some rest. X will make sure you find your way back. Mr. Culum and I will see you all in the morning for the first gaming round."

"Right," X said, leading them out of the arena. "Follow me." Each of his steps were like two normal-person steps, and in moments he was pretty far down the hallway. Takashi and Jacqueline jogged to keep up with him, but the other three fell behind.

"Dude," Beckett laughed. "You should have seen how you went flying. At first you just kind of shook, freaked out while the DEMPs fried you. Then, *boom*! I nuked you, Ranger! Your head whipped back, arms shot off, and you went flying! I hope they're recording game footage. I gotta see that again."

A lesser gamer would have been mad, said something back. But Rogan was better than that. Let the guy blather on all he wanted. That practice stuff didn't even count. Real bragging rights came from winning the games.

Shaylyn pushed her streak of blue hair out of her face. "That was a real loser move, Beckett."

Rogan couldn't tell if she was putting on a show for the cameras or if she meant what she said, but he did know that he didn't want to be the guy on the reality show who couldn't stand up for himself, who had Shaylyn do his fighting for him.

Rogan was about to say something, but Beckett beat him to it. "See? This is why girls shouldn't try to be gamers. They can't handle the action."

Oh no. Rogan didn't like Shay. She was annoying. But she was definitely not weak. Or timid.

"I'm not *trying* to be a gamer! I *am* a gamer!" Shay fired back. "And I'm pretty freaking great. That's how I earned my spot in this contest."

"See? There she goes, *freaking* out. They just can't handle this." Beckett looked at Rogan like *Am I right?*

Rogan knew Beckett was way off base, but he didn't want to get caught up in this. Shaylyn spun to stare down Rogan, as if daring him to be foolish enough to side with Beckett, then turned back. She wasn't done. "Ever since I was old enough to slip on gamer gloves and a headset, it's been the same thing from guys like you. You're insecure about your own gaming abilities, and you know you have no reason to complain about my play, so to make yourself feel better, you go after me because I'm a girl."

"That's not it at all!" Beckett started. "I'm just saying—"

"I'll enjoy seeing you lose," Shaylyn said before she sidestepped a cambot and hurried ahead to join the others.

Rogan still said nothing but watched Shaylyn go. He looked at Beckett. *Wow,* Rogan thought. *For the first time in my life, there might be a gamer I hate worse than Shay.*

"I'm not your babysitter," X said when they had all returned to the commons. His sharp stare surveyed the gamers. "I won't set your bedtime, but I *will* wake you up to be sure you're ready in time for the first round of gaming. You'll find full menus on the tablets we've provided. Feel free to order whatever you want, but I suggest you get some real sleep tonight."

"Can we get any information about what the game will be like tomorrow?" Takashi asked.

Jacqueline nodded. "It would help us prepare."

Takashi smiled like he was glad to have an ally, but X quickly shut them down. "I can't tell you anything. Part of the contest is seeing who thinks the fastest and adapts most quickly. Good night," X said as he left the commons through the double doors.

Silence fell on the room, and the gamers stood around the big central table. Cameras watched them from all angles and nobody knew what to do or say.

"Well, this is weird," Takashi said. "Just left here with a bunch of strangers. No idea what to expect in the game tomorrow."

"I'm not worried," Beckett said. "It's just *Laser Viper*. I can handle anything they throw at me."

"Yeah, but this isn't just any *Laser Viper* game." Takashi took a seat on one of the ends of the couch. "So much depends on how well we play."

"I feel like I did when I was in fourth grade and my school put me on the middle school mathlete team," Jacqueline said. "I had to remember that you can figure out any challenge by breaking it down into more manageable parts."

"Mathlete?" Beckett said. "That's so dumb."

"How's it dumb to get moved up two grades for a math competition?" Jacqueline cut back. She continued as if Beckett hadn't said anything. "So, step-by-step. First, I'm hungry, and I'm going to order . . ." Her finger swiped and swiped at her tablet until her eyes widened in surprise. "Some lasagna. Which . . ." She read the screen. "I guess a service bot will deliver to my room. Step two. Sleep. Good night, everyone."

"Wait," said Takashi. "You going to bed?"

"I'm tired," Jacqueline replied.

"'Cause I was thinking we could all get a pizza," he continued. "And we could make a plan. My *Warcraft Universe* guild always does better when we decide who will do what." He pointed to Beckett. "Like Tank here could go in first, since his armor is so power—"

"Forget it," said Rogan. "I'm not trailing behind that slow-moving target. I'll lead the way."

"Yeah right, little ranger boy," Beckett said. "You think you're going to be the first to beat the boss or get the artifact or whatever, but—"

"You're both nuts," Shaylyn said. "Good luck outrunning Flyer."

"It was a good idea," Jacqueline said to Takashi over the noise of the other three arguing. "But I think it would be a waste of time tonight." And with that she headed into her room and shut the door, leaving the other gamers behind.

Later that night, alone in his room, Rogan ran his implant's software update before shutting off the light and climbing under the smooth, tightly made sheets and blanket. He wasn't a baby. At most when he was home, whichever parent wasn't working would remind him it was time to go to bed or send a text reminding him it was bedtime, or past time for bed if they'd been too deep into their game or checking messages online. Then they'd say good night and Rogan would brush his teeth, download his implant update, and go to bed.

So he didn't need to be babied, but it was strange to be so far from home, all by himself without even a good night, and he hated himself for feeling that way. He reached for his Zelda shield pendant on the nightstand and squeezed it. He wished he could have reached over to pet Wiggles, who would have understood all this perfectly.

Staying here in this dorm room shouldn't have been any different than staying in his Virtual City apartment. He shouldn't be lonely or homesick or whatever. He was better than that. Rogan forced himself to imagine that his worries were a person, one of the Covenant aliens in *Halo* or a Decepticon in his Transformers game. Then he held up his hand to them and said what his parents said whenever they were checking or replying to a message *real quick*. "Just a second." And he rolled onto his side to go to sleep.

CHAPTER 6

The next day the gamers were suited up, back in the belly of their jump ship, heading into the first round of the tournament. There was so much going on, but all Jacqueline could think about was how different this style of playing was going to be from the normal *Laser Viper* game.

Shay was thinking about the exact same thing. When playing at home, different missions were connected by the overall story, little movies in cut scenes. In one of those scenes, laser viper CentCom might receive an encrypted secret radio transmission from an intelligence operative with a hot tip on the location of some important Scorpion terrorist targets, and the player would watch his viper character say something like, "Let's go get 'em." The player would resume control of his viper when the action picked up for another combat drop.

There were no cut scenes here. For this contest, gameplay would be divided into a completely different mission for each round. And no matter how many times Takashi had asked about the nature of even the first round of the tournament while the gamers put on their suits, X, Sophia, and Mr. Culum would tell them nothing.

"Don't worry!" Mr. Culum had said. "Everything will be made clear in-game." Shay figured she'd just have to be ready for anything.

Now the vipers stared at one another, on their way to the first action that would count toward victory or elimination. Nobody said anything, and the glowing V-lines across each viper's faceplate revealed nothing about their state of mind.

"*OK, gamers. Listen up.*" X spoke to them all. "*The Scorpion terrorist network has infiltrated a Chinese warship, the Luyang III class destroyer* Tianjin. *Laser Viper CentCom believes their target is an advanced prototype power generator. We do not know who among the crew is the Scorpion agent or agents, so during this mission you will primarily use nonlethal weapons. At all costs, you must secure the* Tian Li *quantum ion fusion energon cell before Scorpion can steal it for its own evil purposes.*"

Jacqueline felt the excitement leap inside her. A technical objective. This was the perfect mission for her Engineer.

"*Gameplay is about to start, so I'm sending you your objectives. Pay attention to your heads-up displays.*"

One at a time, each objective flashed into existence in front of her as X read them.

1. Infiltrate the Luyang III class
Chinese destroyer Tianjin.

2. Capture the Tian Li (Power of
Heaven) quantum ion fusion energon
cell.

3. Prevent all outgoing
communication from the area of
operation.

4. Leave no recorded evidence of
this mission.

5. Allow no human fatalities.

FAILURE AT ANY OF THESE OBJECTIVES
WILL RESULT IN TOTAL MISSION
FAILURE!

APPROACHING HELE DROP ZONE.

"*Remember. Throughout the* Laser Viper Final Challenge, *gamers will get no respawns. If your viper is destroyed, you are out of that game round,*" X said. "*There is no tougher gameplay mode. Good luck. Go get 'em, gamers.*"

RELEASE IN 5, 4, 3, 2, 1 . . .

The five vipers shot through the bottom of their speeding jet into a blast of roaring wind, out of the dimly lit jump bay, and into the early morning sky, the horizon begining to glow. Below, all was still quite dark.

"Everyone should switch on their infrared vision," Healer said.

Tank laughed. "Thanks, Captain Obvious."

With IR view switched on, heat signatures flared in a spectrum from white to red and darker into the colder colors.

"There it is," Jacqueline said quietly. Skydiving to land on a ship in the middle of the ocean? This was the toughest combat drop she'd ever done. Let everyone else mess around, talking it up. She'd concentrate on making her landing.

"Way down there," Healer said. "Why do they have to launch us from so high?"

"Keeping our jet out of missile range or something?" said Flyer.

"They couldn't have just played a cut scene and then placed us on the ship?" Healer said.

The target was impossibly far below. Rogan held out his hand and placed his thumb at the back of the ship, his finger at the front.

"We might want to pay attention," said Engineer. "This is a hard drop."

"Hard for you chumps, maybe," Rogan said with a confidence he forced himself to feel. He threw himself into a flip and fired his landing thrusters, shooting straight down away from the others like a bullet. "Game on! *Ego sum maximus!*"

"No way!" Tank shouted. Not nearly as flexible as Ranger, he struggled to turn himself head down, but when he did, he hammered on the thrusters full power, in a nightmare fall to catch up to his rival.

"Wait!" Healer called out. "We can't just charge in there at random. This isn't a race. We need to work together!"

Flyer plummeted with ease, a perfectly controlled dive, hundreds of feet per second, her whole body shaking as she blazed straight to the ship. Nobody could fly like she could. First, she caught up to Tank, who himself had nearly come in-line with Ranger. She flew right up to him, belly to belly, and, patting him on the cheek, whipped a corkscrew maneuver away before he could backhand her. Then she increased speed, waving as she passed Rogan. "I'll see you after I get the energy cell thing. It would be nice if you could keep the enemy off my back until after I've won this game."

It was as if the Chinese sailors heard her, because the moment her words came over the channel, Rogan's IR vision flared near the ship. Something had gone hot. Very hot.

WARNING: INCOMING SURFACE-TO-AIR MISSILES DETECTED!

Flyer was closer to the ship. The missiles would be on her in seconds. Her armor was so weak, just one of those would blast her to bits. She could down them with her DEMP, but that would drain her power in a hurry. Rogan reached out, scanned for a target lock on one of the missiles, and fired his high-energy laser. The explosion below was so big, it seemed at first that Flyer had been taken out.

"Shay!" Rogan called. "Are you—"

But other missiles rocketed toward them. Rogan kept shooting. Even heavier lasers sliced down from Tank, a few of them suspiciously close to Rogan. The exploding missiles turned the air all around them into a raging storm of fire and shrapnel, but his armor held.

"I'm good!" Flyer said over the fireteam's channel. *"They've launched drones! We're going to be facing a lot of lasers, real quick."*

The ship was only two thousand feet below, and coming up fast. Rogan was a little off course and fired his rockets to adjust his pitch. His power level was down to 90 percent already. Tank had come in-line with him.

"You two *have* to slow down," Engineer said. "You're going to crash."

The two rivals flipped right side up and ignited their braking thrusters. Their trajectory was more on target than it had been, but they were still coming down too close to the edge of the ship for Rogan's comfort. He couldn't worry about that. Drones were everywhere, turning the sky into a deadly crisscross cage of red-hot laser fire. Smaller heat signatures, Chinese sailors and marines, spilled onto the deck of the *Tianjin*.

Healer and Engineer took their time, carefully targeting human combatants. Blue-white electric bolts zipped down below, slamming into one person after another, the energy flash-crackling over their bodies for an instant before the stunned enemies dropped unconscious.

In the brightening morning light, three drones chased Shaylyn in a course parallel with the ship, so close to the sea that a spray of water flew up in Flyer's wake. The small airborne enemies fired laser after laser, lighting up the mist, hunting the viper before them. She threw herself into a sort of frantic mid-flight dance to avoid being hit. They were slightly above and behind her, so she flipped onto her back. Trying to ignore how far her power level percentage had already fallen, she locked on to and shot the lead drone with a DEMP. The scrambled robot sparked and wobbled for a moment before its power cut out. It dropped speed so fast that the two behind smashed into it, sending all three robots splashing to their junkyard beneath the waves.

Rogan kept his attention on the drones. After all, Healer and Engineer could throw down cover fire against the sailors. They'd have a tougher time with the dozen remaining drones.

WARNING: SURFACE CONTACT IMMINENT.

"Here we go," Rogan called. "When we make our landing, Tank, you take out the ship's weapons. Flyer, all those antennas and satellite dishes up on top: Fry 'em! Don't let them call for help! I'll break inside and go for the power cell."

"Have a nice swim, sucker." Tank elbowed Ranger in the chest, just enough to throw him off course.

"Tank, you scumbag!" Rogan fired a cable, hoping to connect. Splash. Water. Darkness.

Tank's heavy feet smashed down hard enough to dent the deck of the *Tianjin*. He laughed at Ranger's whiny little protest. One gamer down, four to go. Sailors and marines opened up with AK-47 rifles on full auto. He could feel the bullets bouncing off him, hear the patter, like drops splashing on a raincoat. He and the others unleashed a storm of NLEPs, stunning the Chinese combatants so they fell almost as fast as their guns fired bullets.

Whipping a tight circle around the bridge tower, Flyer kept ahead of the drones, soaring up just over the top of the ship and opening up with two DEMPs. Sparks, smoke, and fire burst from the communication arrays. Flyer's power level dipped way down to 56 percent.

"Ranger!" Healer shouted as he and Engineer landed on deck. "Ranger, are you still in the game?"

"Who cares?" Tank took off on a slow run toward the bridge. The other two ground-based vipers at his side. "I don't need him."

"We saw what you did!" said Engineer. "It would have been hard enough to complete this mission with five of us. Now, thanks to you, we're down to four."

"Yeah," Healer said. "So you better stop trying to—"

Tank's big arm smashed into Healer, catching him off guard and knocking him to the deck.

-----o-----

"Um, are you guys inside the ship yet?" Rogan called to the others when he finished using his lasers to cut his way out of the torpedo loading mechanism and had stun-pulsed the security personnel who had scrambled to intercept the intruder. As soon as he had found himself underwater, Rogan had remembered that these ships could fire torpedoes beneath the surface. All he had to do was use his grappling cables to haul himself into position, laser through the exterior hatch, and then crawl right inside.

"Ro, where are you?" Flyer called.

"I started in the torpedo bay, but now I'm on the run." Out in the hallway, two sailors held a massive gun up on their shoulders.

Rogan heard a whine increasing in pitch, the weapon powering up. He stunned the operators and examined the machine. His computer identified it as a Directed Electromagnetic Pulse gun. "Be careful, everyone. They're starting to break out heavier weapons. Another second and they'd have fried me." Rogan stayed on the move.

-----o-----

Shaylyn lowered herself down before the window at the front of the bridge, marines and officers inside scrambling to arm themselves. She wound up and punched the glass hard, breaking through with one hand and firing stun pulses with the other, dropping three of the enemy right away.

"Flyer, move!" Healer called.

She felt like she was punched in the back, thrown against the steel below the windows.

> WARNING: SEVERE ELECTRICAL
> DISRUPTION.
>
> WARNING: FLIGHT SYSTEMS
> INOPERATIVE.
>
> WARNING: POWER SYSTEM COMPROMISED.
> RAPID POWER LOSS.

Internal alarms wailed. Static sparked through her visuals, and Shaylyn worried her vision would cut out entirely. The drones! In her hurry to catch up to Rogan inside the ship, she'd forgotten the remaining drones. Now she was seriously damaged, and fought to control her panic, remembering X's warning that there would be no respawns, no second chances.

Takashi watched Flyer flop down onto a dual set of 76 mm guns. Her back was torn open, her right arm barely attached. He could tell from where he stood that Flyer had a short circuit somewhere. Her battery was dying. "I can fix that!" He rushed to where she'd hit the deck.

"Tank, you take out the rest of the drones," Engineer said. "I'll go in to help Ranger."

"Forget that! You losers are on your own." Beckett ripped a heavy steel hatch off the ship's mast and ducked to head inside. An EMP slammed him hard. Another. But his advanced armor absorbed a lot of the extra energy. Still, he couldn't keep taking those kinds of hits forever. He dropped the two sailors who had carried the EMP gun, and then picked the weapon up. Its silver pistol grip and vertical white energy cell that looked like a rifle magazine fit under an enormous smooth black top. The gun's barrel was as thick as Tank's big arm. "Oh yeah!" he shouted. "Now *this* is a *gun*! All you sailors took on the wrong viper with the wrong weapon. Time to take a nap." He fired the EMP gun, his powerful arm absorbing the heavy recoil, a bright white, swirling, snapping electric blast crackling down the hallway, dropping every sailor before him. A meter on top of the weapon showed the thing was out of power. Disappointed, he tossed it aside.

Beckett stepped over their stunned bodies and hurried ahead, ducking and turning his wide shoulders to the side to fit through the low, narrow steel corridor, that tight panic feeling twisting around inside him. He was way too far behind. If he didn't hurry, that stupid Ranger would seize the objective and win. He slammed his giant armored fist through a computer access terminal in the wall, electric chaos bursting around his arm. "Winner takes all," he said quietly. "Losers get nothing!"

Beckett unleashed the full force of his lasers and plasma cannons. The bulkhead melted, solid steel curling back like burning pages in a book. "I will win this! Me!"

The ship shook. A deeper, more urgent alarm bellowed throughout. The deck began to dip to one side.

"What is going on in there?" Healer shouted. *"I've almost got Flyer fixed. There was an explosion out the side of the ship. Right at the waterline. Was that one of you? Tank? We're not supposed to sink the ship, are we?"*

"No!" Ranger called back. *"Who is sinking us?! We're on a no-casualty order. Now we'll have to make sure everybody gets to the lifeboats."*

-----o-----

Flyer sat up, a new battery installed and flight systems restored. "I'll start getting people to the lifeboats. I'm at, like, half power anyway, so I better take it easy with my weapons." She patted the other robot's arm. "Thanks, Healer."

"Gamers, the Tian Li *quantum ion fusion energon cell must be removed intact."* X's voice came over the channel. *"It is not*

submergible. The Tianjin's *engine room is on one of the lower decks. If the ship is taking on water, you may be running out of time."*

-----o-----

Rogan fought his way in a mad scramble through the ship until he finally entered a larger, more open space, full of machinery. His HUD locked on to the *Tian Li* seconds later. "I got it! It's right here!" He rushed up to the device, about the size of the big water cooler he'd seen in an office on TV. It didn't look too hard for a viper to carry.

Then he saw all the connections. Steel fittings, wires, pipes, data cables, and electrical conduits.

Tank burst into the room. "Forget it, Ranger! It's mine!" He fired two lasers, nailing Rogan in the chest, knocking him to the deck.

"You idiot!" Rogan shouted. "You keep shooting in here, you'll break the thing!"

Tank stepped up and grabbed the power cell, tugging it a little.

"I highly advise you not to try ripping the objective out of its housing," X said.

"I know!" Tank said. "But I can cut some of this away." He fired a laser to sever a steel clamp.

"Stop it!" Rogan threw himself at the larger viper, knocking him back a few steps. The two of them locked arms and wrestled around as water began running in around their feet.

Finally, Jacqueline splashed in, stepping around the two of them. "I can disconnect it. Give me a sec." It was as if this whole part of the game had been programmed especially for her. She tapped and swiped at the air in front of her, working the menus and submenus her computer systems offered her. After thirty seconds of study, she understood the procedure, and, deploying tools from both arms, began cutting, unbolting, uncoupling, and disconnecting the power system that was their objective.

Tank finally pushed Ranger aside and rushed toward Engineer. "It's mine! I'm winning this!" He took three big steps before Ranger nailed him in the back with a fierce jump kick, sending the bigger viper down faceplate-first.

Water was up to their knees now. For a moment, Jacqueline wished her viper mod came equipped with more powerful weapons so that she could shoot both of these idiots who were endangering the whole mission. She pointed at the last cable. "Listen! When I disconnect this, the engines will stop, and the ship will sink even faster. We'll have to hurry to get out in time."

"Flyer! Healer! What's your status?" Rogan called to the others.

"I hope there's not much fighting left to do, because I'm seriously low on power. We've loaded a ton of guys onto the lifeboats," Flyer answered. *"The captain is knocked out, but the first officer says they have everyone accounted for."*

"You speak Chinese?"

"Viper translation software, dummy," Flyer said.

Tank started to get up, but Rogan held his lasers next to the big guy's purple visual sensor. "I have forty-four percent power remaining. You keep fighting, and I swear, I will unload all of it in a laser beam through your head."

"I heard Engineer," Tank said. "I'm ready to go."

Rogan nodded to Engineer. "Pull it. Let's get out of here. We'll cover you in case there are any drones or anything left."

When Engineer cut the final cable, they all heard the rumbling of the engines die down, a stillness settling on the doomed ship. The water began rising faster. It was up to their waists as they waded out of the engine room. Rogan was about to remind Engineer to hold the *Tian Li* up to keep it dry, but saw she had it covered. One corridor was so flooded that they were submerged over their heads.

"*Keep holding that thing up, Engineer,*" Rogan said to her. It was weird being able to talk underwater.

"*I got it.*"

Finally, the five laser vipers gathered on the canted deck of the *Tianjin* as she sank. Lifeboats held her crew in a sad circle around their once-proud warship.

The SR-73 StarScreamer jump ship signaled it was nearly within range, and the gamers blasted off, their exfil rockets launching them up into the brilliant sunlight of the dawn, their mission complete.

CHAPTER 7

Rogan's grandpa Webber was a gamer from way back. His basement was a shrine to video game history, featuring nearly every system ever made, including an old arcade Pac-Man table game. He had the Atari 2600, Nintendo Entertainment System, Sega Genesis, Super Nintendo, Nintendo 64, Sega Saturn, Nintendo GameCube, and all generations of PlayStation and Xbox. For him, it had become less about playing the hundreds of games he owned and more about collecting rare functional games and systems that had been such a big part of his whole life.

Sometimes Grandpa Webber would fire up one of the older consoles and challenge Rogan to play. Sure, some were tough because the graphics were so bad that a gamer could hardly tell what he was looking at, and a lot of the real old games simply didn't work that well or were just lame. That was a big part of why Rogan definitely preferred the virtual reality experience of normal modern games. But ancient games were different. Many of them were really hard. Lots of times their characters would die even if the enemy barely touched them. And while in the campaign modes for *Halo: Vengeance VR*, *Call of Duty: Full Immersion*, or *Laser Viper* a gamer could get his character to a checkpoint so that if he died, he didn't have to start over, in the old games, players would begin with three or four lives and hope to find extra lives along the way.

The first *Super Mario Bros.* drove Rogan crazy. Once he'd fallen down a pit or been hit by one of Bowser's fireballs for the last time, it was the end.

Now he wondered if, after that last game round, it would be game over for him.

Rogan jumped when someone knocked on his helmet, and he felt the cool air brush his warm skin when he pulled it off. Then he stepped back.

Shaylyn smiled right in his face, that blue streak in her hair sweat-pressed to her neck. "You hiding in there?"

She'd said it as a joke, with none—or not much—of their old rivalry, but Rogan only found it annoying. "No!" he said a little too loudly. He was very aware of the cameras, since a half dozen cambots rolled around them, recording everything they did and said, from every angle.

Jacqueline was already out of her game suit, a little sweat in the armpits of her simple red T-shirt. "Nice job," said their Engineer.

"You're the one who got the *Tian Li*," Shaylyn said.

That truth burned deep inside Rogan. "Yeah, Jacqueline. That thing was a lot more complex than I thought it would be. You disconnected it fast."

"You can call me Jackie. My friends do. And the *Tian Li*?" She shrugged. "You found it in the first place."

Takashi joined their circle, a little quieter than usual, his smile forced, like a decoration left up after the party was over. "That was great, you guys."

Beckett stood off by himself, glaring at them all.

Mr. Culum stepped up to the angry Tank, reaching out like he was about to pat him on the back, but stopping just short of actually touching him. "Well done!" He smiled. "All of you are amazing. I have no doubt that we chose the exact right gamers for the *Laser Viper* Final Challenge. I've worked in the video game industry for many years now. I've been very close to *Laser Viper*'s design, and I've never seen the game played so well. I hope the experience was just as impressive for all of you."

Sophia appeared behind them, wearing a dress printed with a rainbow array of different brightly colored rectangles. "You are the first gamers in the *world* to complete a stage in the game suits. I agree with Mr. Culum, absolutely. You really are all the best!"

Rogan looked around at the others, trying to see if they were falling for all this huggy, everybody-gets-a-trophy kind of talk. Beckett folded his arms and rolled his eyes. Some of the gamers hid their true feelings better than others. Sophia didn't seem to notice Beckett's attitude, but the cambot in front of him wasn't missing anything, and Rogan thought about how ridiculous the guy would look on the reality show. He forced himself to smile for the cameras.

X entered the arena. "Unfortunately," he continued where Sophia had left off, "our job is to choose the best among you, and that means that tonight, one of you will say goodbye and leave the competition."

Sophia tilted her head a little, wearing a big sad frown. "So let's go back to the dorms while our judges deliberate. And while we wait, I'll be interviewing each of you about your experiences so far in . . . the *Laser Viper* Final Challenge!"

Back in the commons, the gamers, thirsty from fast, tense VR action in warm game suits, chugged PowerSlam Liquid Energy drinks and settled in for an awkward wait, surrounded by cameras at all times.

Sophia opened the sixth door in the curved wall of the commons. The gamers had been curious about it and gathered around to peek through. It led to a dorm room that was unoccupied, given there were only five gamers. It had been set up with two chairs facing each other and some lights shining on what must have been the "hot seat," the chair where each gamer would sit and answer questions for the reality show. Sophia flashed a grin. "Jacqueline. Let's start with you."

JACQUELINE "JACKIE" SHARPE

What does this contest mean to me? I like video games. In games, there's always a solution. At first I might not be able to activate a drawbridge or open a certain door in a dungeon. But after a while, I can figure it out. I like the Laser Viper *Final Challenge because of all the characters I've played as a gamer, Master Chief, Dr. Crexar, Mario, Link, whoever . . . the engineer viper lets me use my best skills. I love fixing things. I love making things work. My parents always talk about how important it is to be self-reliant. They wouldn't buy me an Xbox. But I found a broken one in a pawn shop for cheap. I found some videos online, and those helped me learn to fix its power supply system and replace the disc reader. It took forever, but I got it working, and for a quarter of the price of a new one. Solving tough technical problems. That's the best.*

I study a lot. I'm in some advanced classes. Sometimes people at school don't like that. I don't know why. They make fun of me or just ignore me. But when I'm Engineer, I can work machines or build something that helps my fireteam. And they ... You know. I mean, they don't make fun of me for that.

BECKETT EWELL

I'm going to win this whole thing. Believe me. You saw me. I was the best. I took out so many of the enemy. I could have destroyed the whole ship myself. Yeah, the others were there. But honestly, they just kind of get in my way. Me winning this contest will prove to everyone that I'm the best gamer in the [BEEP]ing world! Yeah, and the money will be awesome. I'm going to buy plane tickets, go see my dad, and we're gonna play so many video games. So, I don't know what you want me to say. There are no second chances. That's how I play video games. Winner takes all. Bring on the next round. Bring on the championship!

TAKASHI ENDO

When I was nine, my older brother was in a bad car accident. He could have died. I thought he was going to.... So anyway, my whole family was at the hospital all the time for a long time, and these doctors saved my brother's life. I remember when he first woke up, first talked to us again, and I remember thinking how that wouldn't be happening if these doctors had not done what they'd done.

So I want to be a doctor. That's why I chose to play Laser Viper as Healer. I know that fixing shot-up robots in a video game isn't the same as saving a real life, but I like helping the people on my fireteam. I like when they're so happy to get back in the action. I liked what Mr. Culum said about VR and robots used in surgery on real people. I'd love to be involved in that. I could control a medical robot in a village somewhere or on a battlefield in a war the same way I control my laser viper in the game. So maybe it sounds weird, but I do feel like this contest means a lot to my life. And I know medical school isn't cheap, so the prize money would help ...

SHAYLYN SPERO

The money would be nice, and it'll be radicool when this show airs. Shout-out to all my friends back in Chi-town! Oh, are we not supposed to say things like that? Sorry. I'm just having fun. Same thing with the video game contest. I'm gonna do the best I can, and I'll have a good time. I try to bring my best game whenever I play. I guess you could call me a serious gamer or whatever. Like some guys act like girls can't play or something, but while they're talking trash, I'm working on playing a better game. That's all I'm saying. Having fun. Playing a better game. The money and game credits. Oh, and, um, I totally want to beat Rogan.

ROGAN WEBBER

I want to be the best. Games are kind of my life. They are for my dad too, but we hardly ever play the same games. I've asked to play with him, to join his guild, but he says I'm too young, that I have to be a better gamer. It drives me crazy. Still, I play all the time. If I—when I win this contest, my dad will see I'm ready for anything any game can throw at me. Then hopefully he and I will take on a lot more games together.

At home, my parents are real busy. Everyone in my house has their thing, and gaming is mine.

Sorry. I'm nervous talking to this cambot.

I'm mad that I didn't get the Tian Li, *but, I don't know. I wish I knew how this contest was scored. I thought I did pretty good. I know I did. I might not have secured the objective, but I found it, and I kept Tank from destroying it. Beckett thought he was taking me out, knocking me off the ship during the combat drop. Show me another viper who can figure out how to get into the ship through the torpedo tubes.*

I usually play pretty hardcore. If you can't keep up, get off my fireteam, you know? But I feel like this part of the game was designed to require a whole team. We needed Engineer to disconnect the energon cell. I couldn't have done it. Beckett almost destroyed it. We needed Shay to fly up and scramble the ship's communications. Beckett plays hardcore too, only he almost cost us the mission. I hope the next round isn't so team focused. I don't like being forced to rely on everyone else.

A few hours after the interviews and after more than a couple nervous stop-and-start conversations among the gamers, Sophia and X returned to the commons. They both stood to the right of the giant screen at the front of the commons room. The five gamers were lined up shoulder to shoulder along a faint line on the floor on the other side. Cameras in the ceiling had rotated to the ready. Five cambots buzzed around.

"Now comes the difficult part, when we must say goodbye to one of our gamers." Sophia's smile glowed even while her words dripped with sadness. "Our judges have carefully analyzed each candidate, and they've come to a decision. When your image and name appear on the screen, you are safe, and you will be going on to the next round of the *Laser Viper* Final Challenge." She paused for several seconds and focused her gaze on each gamer down the line.

There was something very strange about being under the lenses of all these cameras, of being watched and judged by Sophia, X, and Mr. Culum. Rogan wondered what he would look like on the reality show. He was suddenly concerned with how he should stand, what appearance he should present. Another hazard of real life, magnified by being filmed for reality TV.

At last, Sophia took a deep breath, and her smile finally vanished. "The first person who is safe and moving on to the next round of *Laser Viper* Final Challenge is—"

Rogan squeezed his Zelda shield pendant, wishing with all the power of the Triforce that Sophia would call his name.

"—Jacqueline Sharpe! Our Engineer!" Sophia said. Jackie's name and picture blazed giant on the screen, and her tense face broke into a small smile. Sophia held out her hand. "Come on over here and join Xavier and me."

Jacqueline crossed in front of the screen, and Sophia reached out to put her arm around her shoulders in one of those fake half hugs.

"Good job, Jackie," Shaylyn said.

"Way to go," said Takashi.

Beckett whispered to Rogan. "In second place, Beckett—"

"The second person moving on to the next round is—" Her dramatic pause was shorter this time. "Shaylyn Spero!"

Shaylyn gasped and jumped a little. She hugged Takashi and then moved to join Jackie.

"What?" Beckett said a little louder than a whisper. "This is crap."

Rogan watched his shoes.

"The next person moving on is Takashi Endo!" Sophia gushed.

"Yes!" Takashi ran over to the others and slapped Shaylyn a high five.

"Now," Sophia said. "Rogan. Beckett. There was a lot of tension between the two of you, even some fighting in round one of the game. You are both great gamers, but the judges feel one of you has a slight edge over the other. Only one of you will be moving on to continue play in the *Laser Viper* Final Challenge. For the other, the adventure ends in just a moment." The serious face she'd put on mirrored Rogan's. He'd seen enough of these reality shows. When people saw this part of the episode, there'd be dramatic music building up, until it stopped long enough for Sophia to deliver the bad news.

"Rogan Webber. You . . . are . . . *safe* and moving on to the next round!"

By tomorrow he'd be home. His mom would put her arm around him and say something like, "It's the effort that counts." Dad would tell him how he'd done a good job, but he'd have the same look in his eyes as when he explained Rogan wasn't quite ready to join his gaming guild. His Virtual City apartment? Forget about it. He'd be homeless in Virtual City, or sitting around bored in his parents' house while they did other things. Only his fuzzy buddy Wiggles would truly support him.

"Rogan!" Shaylyn hissed. He looked up. Shay clapped her hands and then motioned him closer. "Come on!"

Sophia laughed. "It looks like one of our gamers is a little nervous. Congratulations, Rogan. You're safe!"

His feet seemed to take over automatically, and in one blur of a moment, he'd moved from the loser area to be among the winners. Takashi fist-bumped him. Jackie patted his back. Shaylyn rolled her eyes, obviously pretending to be annoyed with him. "Pay attention, Ro!"

"What?" Beckett shouted. "This is crap! I was right in there getting the power cell thing! I did better than any of these turkeys!"

One cambot rolled over to cover Beckett's outburst, zooming in to pick up the increased moisture in his eyes. The other two cambots watched the four winners.

Sophia tilted her head to one side and made a big pouty face. "Hmm, I'm sorry you feel that way, Beckett, but I'm afraid our judges don't agree. You can take a moment to say goodbye to your fellow gamers, and then you need to head to your room to pack. Xavier will be taking you home right away."

"I'm not saying goodbye to these turds!" He shouted at Sophia until his face was red, but her pitying smile didn't change. This only made Beckett angrier. "They're too pathetic to even be called gamers."

X stepped up in front of Beckett, separating him from the others like a thick brick wall. He motioned toward Beckett's room. "Come on. You're done."

Beckett backed away from everyone, wiping his eyes. "This contest is rigged! It's all a joke. You're all jokes!" He stopped just before he slammed the door to his room. "Turkeys!"

"That boy has some serious anger management issues," Shay said.

Rogan stared at the closed door to Beckett's room. At X guarding it closely, his arms folded over his chest. Beckett was out. In a few minutes he'd be gone.

-----◊-----

X and Sophia advised the gamers to relax and to celebrate their victory. It could be some time before the next game round. Sophia reminded them there were movies and shows on the server and plenty of great food and drink, all accessible through their tablets. With promises to return soon, the two adults left the commons.

The gamers stood in silence for a few moments. Rogan looked around, wondering what they were supposed to do now. If there were no video games to play, no digi-space to explore, and no school lesson objectives to meet, what was left to do?

Takashi finally produced his Atomic Frontiers tablet from his pocket. He swiped, and his taps were like drumbeats in the quiet.

Rogan met Shay's confused look.

"Chicken Does It" exploded over the speakers as the video popped up on screen. A hard *wiki-wiki* electronica rhythm, punctuated by a thumping bass beat. A guy in a feathery chicken costume, his face sticking out of the beak, sang some really fast lyrics that were hard to understand as a rapid *bok-bok-bok — bok — bok-bok-bok-beGOK* built up to a camera-shaking climax to end each mostly nonsensical verse.

"Yes!" Shaylyn immediately began flapping her arms and strutting, shouting "*BeGOK!* Chicken does it!" on cue.

"Oh no," Rogan groaned. It was the YouTube sensation of the year, with sixty-five million views in 2-D and eighty million in the VR version where people could dance around the lead chicken man and the dance troupe who wore egg costumes complete with jagged cracked-shell-piece hats. Rogan hated it.

But in no time, Takashi led a line, followed by Jackie and Shay, laughing, flapping their crooked arms and strutting, seemingly eager to get to the "*BeGOK!* Chicken does it!" part.

Maybe the others went to IRL schools that held dances, making them old pros at this. Rogan didn't know or care. He would not dance. In fact, he preferred one of the hundreds of "Chicken Does It" parodies, his favorite being "Kill the Chicken."

All that talk of chicken reminded him he was hungry, though, and with his tablet he swiped and tapped up pizza, cheesy puffs, and more PowerSlam energy drinks, more than enough for all of them. Minutes later, server bots, shorter and more squat versions of cambots with big trays on top, glided in to deliver the great feast of delicious junk.

With cold PowerSlam and the best dinner, the final four cele-brated moving ahead in the contest. Rogan plunked himself down on the enormous sofa, happy and relieved to be safe. He was not used to having this kind of uncertainty surrounding his gaming.

He was also not accustomed to celebrating with his gaming opponents. Or to how awesome arena gaming actually was. But no matter how much fun the others made the after-game party, Rogan reminded himself that they were still his opponents, that they would, if they could, be just as happy celebrating him being eliminated from the contest. Beckett had taught him not to be a jerk, but that didn't mean these people were his friends. Rogan didn't need the other gamers or anyone else. He would keep enjoy-ing these victory parties again and again, until finally he was the only one left.

Ego sum maximus.

CHAPTER 8

The next day at breakfast the remaining gamers talked about the mission the day before, their attention immediately drawn to the differences between playing *Laser Viper* in the arena and playing at home. After they'd marveled for a while about the added realism offered by the game suits, they began to notice other new developments.

"One reason I love modern video games is because the stories are so complex," Jackie said. "A good video game is like a great movie, but a movie where I'm one of the characters. I felt like that was missing from our first round."

"I know, right?" Shay said. "Like in some games, I wish the cut scenes would go on longer. This didn't have any."

"The enemy was also weird," Takashi said. "Usually, we fight a small army of Scorpion terrorists."

"And there was no end boss," said Jackie. "I was waiting for a giant robot to leap out of the sea at the last moment to try to prevent us from taking the *Tian Li*."

"It's just because it's a special tournament design," Rogan said. "There were no gamer or upgrade points available. No special achievements to unlock either. They haven't even made any music for the game yet. This isn't the normal, finished game that they would sell to the public. It's no use complaining about it."

"We weren't complaining, Ro," said Shaylyn. "But maybe finding some of the differences between the regular game and the one we're playing now could be useful in the contest. Did you ever think of that?"

Rogan was thinking up a reply when Takashi spoke. "Speaking of useful for the contest, I was dinking around with my boring Atomic Frontiers tablet last night and found out they recorded all the game footage. I think we should watch it, see what we did right last time, and figure out how we could do better in the next game."

"Good idea," Jackie said to Takashi. "Let's watch the videos. We all need to work together better."

Rogan figured it wouldn't hurt to study the strengths and weaknesses of the other gamers. "Might as well. Nothing else to do."

Shay said nothing, but watched Rogan skeptically.

They viewed the game footage, quietly at first, but as it rolled on, the group became more and more fired up.

"Nice shot," Takashi said to Rogan when his viper took out one of the *Tianjin*'s guns.

"I like the part coming up." Jackie sat on her perch on the back of the sofa seat and pointed at the screen. "Wait." Shaylyn's viper was being chased by two Chinese drones, with another enemy flying up from another direction. "Right here!"

Flyer whipped into a tight spin, swooping into position behind the single drone and using it to shield her from the other two. None of them had seen NLEPs fly so fast before. A storm of energy blasts, and the drones were quickly destroyed.

"That is some amazing gaming, right there," Takashi said.

"Not bad" was all Rogan would give her.

Shaylyn shrugged. "Well, I had help from my target lock assist, and those two were flying close together."

"Yeah, but all those moves, so fast," said Jackie. "The quick flying. The shooting."

They went on like that, reviewing which moves worked the best, sometimes acting out different parts of their previous game round, to see what they might do better. Throughout all their practice, Rogan watched the others carefully, looking for their strengths and weaknesses, thinking about how he could use them to help him get ahead in the contest. He noticed Shay watching closely too, and she met his gaze once, a look of defiance in her eyes that told him she was preparing just as he was.

In the days that followed, the four gamers transitioned from merely watching their past game performance to practicing viper movements. They walked through different patterns, from wedge formation to a circular rotating attack, being careful to remember Shay would be in the air. At first Rogan thought this practice would be boring, but they found ways to make it fun, pushing one another onto the couch or breaking out of their planned movement to just wrestle around.

"This is like a dream come true," Takashi said after practice one day.

Jackie swung a couch cushion and smacked him in the head from behind. "A dream where you get knocked down by laser cushion attack?"

He caught the thing as Jackie swung it at him again, and he used it to push her back toward the couch, where she fell on top of Shay, all three of them laughing.

"I mean, for the Healer, the laser viper mission is different. I only have one nonlethal pulse emitter, so I'm not there to run around blowing things up. I'm in the game to fix damaged robots so the fireteam succeeds. It works better if we have a strategy. That way I know where I have to go to get into the best position to fix people. When I play at home, I get stuck on teams where everything is pure chaos. The other gamers aren't very good, so I run out of parts fixing them, or they take off all over so I can't reach them in time to save them when they're blown up. Even when I play with my friends from school, they laugh at me when I talk about making a plan."

"Oh, Takashi." Shaylyn's voice oozed exaggerated sweetness. "That's just sooo nice of you." She laughed.

"Fine!" Takashi laughed. "I was going to say it's great playing with the best *Laser Viper* gamers in the country, but forget it. You're the worst."

Rogan couldn't hold back his smile. And he couldn't help but think that Takashi was a pretty good guy. If he didn't live so far away, the two of them might have been good real-life friends. He didn't have many friends IRL.

But game practice wasn't all they did, and after a while their time together started to resemble a party more than a contest. They had no idea when the next game round would be, so they stayed up late watching movies on the big screen and eating junk well past the point when their parents would have made them stop, and they never had to eat vegetables with their meals if they didn't want to. Except that Shaylyn wanted to. Weird.

One night they found a trivia game in the Atomic Frontiers system, put it up on the big screen, and had fun playing in teams. It quickly became obvious that Jackie was the one everyone wanted on their side. She seemed to know everything. After the girls had crushed the guys, Jackie slapped Shay a high five. "Not only was it great chumpifying you losers—" Shaylyn said to the guys.

"We'll beat you next time," Takashi said.

"—but it's great to be wanted for something besides chores or babysitting." Shay sighed. "I have four siblings, and I swear, at home, I'm not Shaylyn. I'm Three of Five. I love my family and all, and I guess I miss them, but it's nice being here where I don't have to clean up after everyone. That's all I'm saying."

"I know what you mean," Jackie agreed. "I have a summer birthday *and* I skipped a grade, so I'm the youngest in my classes by far. At school they mostly call me 'that smart kid' or 'the girl who reads a lot.'"

"Like reading is a bad thing?" Shaylyn asked.

Jacqueline shrugged. "Sometimes the fictional characters I meet in books feel more real to me than a lot of people I meet at school or in my neighborhood."

"I feel the same way about video games," Takashi said.

"Real life stinks," Rogan said. "Who needs it?"

-----o-----

The party couldn't last forever. Being at Atomic Frontiers was fun enough, but when they couldn't text with anyone besides X or their fellow gamers, when they couldn't watch any live-streamed games, when they couldn't visit friends in Virtual City, when all there was to do was wait for the next game and they had no idea when they might play, the dorms eventually felt kind of like a prison.

Rogan had been using one electronic device or another since he was two. He'd been playing games and visiting people in digi-space since he was eight years old. His need for news and entertainment updates, to see what other leading gamers were playing, to join in arguments in Virtual City or on old-fashioned text message boards, his need to *check* was physical. He kept picking up his tablet to log in to something, only to remember the thing couldn't log in to anything.

He was not alone with this problem.

"My guildies are going to think I've abandoned them," Takashi said a week or so in. "Worse, they're running around Azeroth leveling up and getting all the gold and weapons. Pretty soon I'll be the anchor on the team, the weak one dragging behind the others, slowing them down."

"I didn't know we'd be totally cut off from society." Shay agreed. "I belong to, like, three different gamer discussion groups. When I'm not in school, my phone is buzzing all day with updates. During the school year, the last bell rings and I get on the bus and it's, like, a million new messages. These idiot guys going on and on about how girls are bad gamers. It's not the same kind of battle as *Warcraft*

Universe, but me and three or four other girls always attack those guys, calling them out, like 'You're an idiot' and 'What's your gamer level?'" She laughed. "It's like a real war. We get some of those guys so mad, a lot of them, like older men, like over thirty or whatever, so mad that they flip out on us, drop some sexist crap. Show who they really are. Then we report them to the admins and get them banned." She dropped her Atomic Frontiers tablet on the table and tapped it hard like she was trying to stab through it with her finger. "But here, I'm cut off and can't help fight those guys."

"No texts from friends, no status updates, no new blog posts or technology articles." Takashi wiggled his fingers. "I don't know what to do with my hands."

"Good thing I never have to dust in my Virtual City apartment. The place would be a mess by now," Rogan said. "At first I thought being stuck with these offline tablets would be kind of cool, a change of pace. But now it's like . . . like I'm dead. I keep reaching for my phone, but then it's not there."

"I know, right?!" Shay said. "I keep actually checking this thing, hoping that *this time* it will connect to something. Stupid."

Jackie had been unusually quiet in the discussion. Finally she pulled them all in close. Really close. Weirdly close.

"Um, Jackie," Rogan said, "you're all great gamers and stuff, but I don't really do the group hug thing."

"You all want to get into digi-space?" Jackie whispered. She nodded toward the cambots that rolled around them. Careful to hide what she was doing from the cameras, a difficult task. She opened the right cargo pocket on her pants and revealed a pair of virtual reality glasses. It was a cheap set, something only a total noob would use, but in here, it was impressive.

"You're not allowed to have that," Takashi whispered.

"A set that small has got to be wifi only," Shaylyn said. "And Culum has everything locked out and password protected."

"I hacked the system to get this set online." Jackie smiled. "I even boosted its power supply."

"You hacked Atomic Frontiers' data network?" Takashi asked.

"You can go to Virtual City from here?" Rogan asked, amazed. "You're a genius."

Jackie frowned. "I didn't break into their mainframe or anything. I just got around their lockouts so we can connect to digispace. It's not like I'm stealing company secrets."

"You're going to get in trouble," Takashi said. "They might kick you out for this."

"Why do you think I keep it hidden?" Jackie said.

"You can go to Virtual City," Rogan said again in disbelief.

"But the cameras will see you using the headset," Shay said. "X will take it away."

"I use it in my bedroom. No cameras in there." Jackie carefully slipped the device back in her pocket, keeping it covered so the cambots and other mounted cameras couldn't see.

It was weird how close they were leaned together, worse because Takashi had been eating corn chips and his breath smelled like a dead pig fart. But Rogan ignored all that, being so excited for the chance to get out of the dorms.

Jackie met their eyes. "You guys can use it if you want. We could take—"

The double doors opened, and X and Sophia entered the commons. "Good evening, gamers! How are you all *doing*?"

The gamers jumped apart and tried to act casual.

"Is it time for the next game round?" Shaylyn asked.

Sophia tilted her head a little. "Not quite yet," she said. "But I have some other good news for you all." She was quiet then, and Rogan sensed he wasn't the only one getting a little tired of Sophia's need to draw everything out for the sake of reality TV excitement. "How would you like"—she fixed each gamer in turn with a serious stare, then smiled brightly—"to speak to your families by video tonight?"

The pandemonium that erupted in response to her question was answer enough.

-----o-----

A short time later, Rogan was happy to have his turn to call home. He would have preferred meeting his mom and dad in person in Virtual City, but he'd take what he could get.

"Hey, Ro!" Dad said. His parents were sitting at the kitchen table, family photos on the wall behind them. They were probably using Mom's tablet. "How's it going, buddy? We miss you."

"I miss you too," Rogan said. "How's Wiggles?"

Dad laughed and leaned off camera. He came back, holding the black-and-white fuzzball. "Why don't you ask him yourself?"

Dad held Wiggles closer to the tablet or whatever they were using, and Wiggles pushed his little pink nose forward, sniffing the camera.

"Hi, buddy!" Rogan said, an ache of longing in his chest. "I miss you."

Wiggles was noticeably excited, squirming in Dad's arms to get closer to the image of Rogan on the screen before him, trying to lick the camera in reply.

Dad shook the dog's paw. "Say bye-bye, Wiggles." Dad set him down somewhere off camera, and Rogan wished he could pet his best doggy friend.

"We were wondering when you were going to call," Mom said.

"Sorry. They took our phones. Now we only have these lame tablets that can't even go online." He wasn't stupid enough to mention Jackie's hacked VR set when cameras were covering his entire conversation.

"Oh," Mom said. "That must be tough. You can't even check text messages?"

"Nothing," Rogan said.

His mother raised her eyebrows. "That would be relaxing, actually. I'd love something like that, if I could get away from work that long."

The connection froze for a moment, his parents' faces stuck in those weird stopped-video expressions. "Whoops," Dad said when the image finally moved again. "Rogan, you there? Slow connection, I guess. Internet's been having prob—" Another freeze-up. His parents resumed movement a moment later. "So annoying. How's the game?"

Rogan leaned forward and smiled. "It's so cool. We use these game suits, like gamer gloves for our whole body. And we play in this huge arena so we can run all over. No more walking in place to move our laser vipers. In our first round we—" Rogan stopped when he noticed the image had frozen again. The video resumed and he continued. "We had to fight this—" When the connection locked up again, he couldn't hide his frustration. The first chance he'd had to talk to his parents in forever, and it was like he was stuck with his grandparents' internet!

"Is the trouble on your end or ours?" Dad laughed when everything started working again. "I did have a little lag playing *Warcraft* tonight. Things have been OK here. We miss you, though."

"How is it staying at Atomic Frontiers?" his mom jumped in. "They sent us photos of your dorms. Looks nice—I bet it's neat there. What's William J. Culum like?"

"He's pretty cool, actually," Rogan said. "He's really excited about Sun Station One and about this contest. About everything Atomic Frontiers does, really."

"Wow," Mom said. "It must be like hanging around with Thomas Edison or Alexander Graham Bell or Steve Jobs. Living history."

Dad spoke up. "Maybe when you get back we'll go have a stay at that hotel with the waterslide."

"Oh, that would be fun," said Mom. "Especially if we could wait until after the election. Like we could go in December when it is all cold outside, but nice and warm by the pool. And I wouldn't have so much for work."

"There're lots of options," Dad said. "But don't worry about any of that right now, Ro. You just focus on winning that tournament. That Sophia Hahn told us you'd advanced past the first round."

"We knew you would!" Mom said. "You have gaming in your blood."

They talked like that a while longer, encouraging Rogan to play his best, filling him in on all the family news from his cousin who went to camp and accidentally swamped his canoe to his grandmother thinking about selling her house in Tacoma and moving to a retirement community just north of Seattle.

X finally stepped into the vid call room. "Time to wrap it up."

"Oh, you have to go already?" his mother said. "I hope we'll be able to talk again soon."

"Me too," Rogan said. He meant it.

"We miss you, buddy," Dad said.

"We love you, RoRo," his mother added.

"Me too," Rogan answered.

And then X was back in the room, and his parents clicked out of the call, and Rogan was suddenly very aware of the many miles between him and Seattle.

X led Rogan to the hallway outside the vid call room where Takashi was waiting for his turn. "Can you wait here a second while I get Takashi set up?"

Rogan nodded and leaned back against the wall when he was alone, blinking against the sting in his eyes and the tightness in his throat. After a moment he kicked out against the wall. He wasn't going to be a whiny little homesick kid like this.

"Are you OK, Rogan?"

Rogan looked up. William J. Culum had somehow approached without his noticing. The man never looked any different, like he was his own action figure come to life. Black pants and black button-down shirt, long gray cardigan with pockets on the front. Wild gray hair. Just as he looked in the arena or on hundreds of online videos. The difference, the *big* difference now, was that he was here, in person, talking to Rogan one-on-one. And Rogan had just kicked the wall of his company headquarters.

"I'm sorry, sir. I shouldn't have done that." Rogan ducked down, licked his fingers, and started trying to rub out a faint scuff mark on the white wall.

"No, no," Mr. Culum said. "Don't worry about that. I'll have someone in facilities come fix it. I don't care about the wall. I'm more concerned about you." X came out of the vid call room right then, but Mr. Culum waved him away. "Come on. I'll walk you back to the dorms."

They walked in silence for a moment. Rogan was very aware he was in the presence of a computer god, one of the most important men in the world. He didn't know what to say, so he tried being honest. "I kind of can't believe I'm walking with you, Mr. Culum."

"I'm not *that* old," Mr. Culum said.

"Oh no! Not that! I just mean it's so exciting to be here with a legend. The changes you've made to technology . . ."

"I appreciate that," Mr. Culum said. "But for me, it's not about changing technology. It's about using technology to improve people. To help make their lives easier, safer, and most importantly to bring them together." He laughed a little. "And I know that sounds like an advertising slogan, but I really mean it. I was working with what was considered advanced computer technology by the time I was twelve, almost graduated from college by the time I was fourteen. Do you know what it's like being in college before you're even old enough to drive?"

"I can't imagine," Rogan said.

"But see, I think you can," Mr. Culum said. He smiled sympathetically at Rogan's confused expression. "It's isolating. It's lonely, Rogan. I know you haven't been to college yet, but I also know you've logged an impressive amount of game time on *Laser Viper* alone, to say nothing of other games. You have to play a lot to have such a high gamer ranking. And to be so young and have your own apartment in Virtual City. Are you there a lot?"

"Yeah," Rogan admitted. "Kind of."

"Were you so upset tonight after your vid call because you are missing your parents while you're so far away from them, or were you upset because that short vid call was one of the longest conversations you've had with them in a long time?"

Rogan's cheeks felt hot, and he knew his face must be as red as Mario's hat. He was grateful when Mr. Culum didn't look at him.

"It's OK, Rogan." Mr. Culum pushed his hands into his sweater pockets. "You don't have to answer. And I don't have the cameras on us. You'll notice we're free of cambots."

They walked without speaking for a while, the only sound the soft whisper-scrape of Mr. Culum's worn black shoes. "You called me a legend," Mr. Culum finally said. "And you mentioned your excitement. But it might interest you to know that I am excited for the chance to talk to all of you gamers. And I mean that. You are the future. This, what we're doing here with this contest, will be the beginning of many important changes. And I believe, Rogan, that sometime after this is all over, sometime sooner than you think, perhaps, technology will help make your life better, so that you never need be lonely again."

They stopped outside the dorms. Rogan smiled at the older man, wanted to pat his slightly stooped shoulders. Mr. Culum was a lot older than Rogan, but Rogan wondered if the man knew what it meant to be twelve better than most, if he knew why Rogan wanted to be a famous gamer so bad. "I'm going to win this contest," Rogan said.

Mr. Culum smiled warmly. "I have a feeling you might, Rogan. I simply wanted to tell you that I know how you feel, and I'm only a few tablet taps away if you want to talk about anything."

"Thanks, Mr. Culum. That means a lot," Rogan said. He meant it.

CHAPTER 9

"G ood morning, gamers!" Mr. Culum stood before Shay, Jackie, Rogan, and Takashi in the arena, but instead of being dressed in his usual black and gray, today he wore a game suit and held a VR headset in his hands. It was the morning after their vid calls home, and they had finally been summoned back to the gaming arena.

Rogan exchanged a skeptical look with Shay. Was William Culum going to play *Laser Viper* with them? In one way, it would be cool to play alongside one of the world's tech giants—especially after their talk yesterday—but if he intended on joining them for the tournament, things would be messed up.

As far as Rogan could tell, there were two possibilities. Either the genius creator of the game was an awesome laser viper and would totally dominate the fireteam or he was always too busy with Sun Station One and a zillion other projects so he never played and would drag the fireteam down. Either way, this wasn't good.

"I appreciate your patience while you wait for the second round of the *Laser Viper* Final Challenge. As you have no doubt noticed, the game rounds in this contest aren't unique merely because of the advanced technology of your game suits and this arena, but also because of the revolutionary advanced programming of the

NPCs in each stage. Far from mindless drones running around in the background to be shot at, I have the best AI team in the world working to program them with the most sophisticated voice recognition software and response protocols. You saw some of this in action with the Chinese characters on the *Tianjin* level. It cost a fortune to bring in Chinese linguists to make the language authentic, but if I let cost hold back technology, there would be no hyperstream data cable, no hypernet, no digi-space, no Virtual City. Instead of the world coming together to meet face-to-face in virtual reality, we'd all still be reading primitive websites and playing around with simple text-based posts and comments on social media."

"The only thing this guy loves more than technology is hearing himself talk," Jackie whispered in Rogan's ear.

Rogan frowned. Maybe Jackie was right, but Mr. Culum was a really nice guy.

"So that's why it's taking so long to get you to the next round of gaming. I'm sorry about that. My chief designer promised me the game stage was ready, but when I viewed it, I told him, 'Not good enough,' and sent the team back to work. So while we wait, I thought you might like to come with me." Mr. Culum looked at them all expectantly, saying nothing but smiling with excitement.

"Um, where?" Takashi finally said.

Mr. Culum pointed straight up. "To the stars!" He shrugged. "Well, not quite to the stars, but to space at least. I thought you might like a tour of Sun Station One."

"You mean a virtual Sun Station One," Shaylyn said.

"Well, I've long advocated for an expanded definition of real life, the phasing out of the distinction between the virtual and the so-called real. You see, with the game suits and the harnesses here in the arena, we are about to enter a nearly exact replica of Sun Station One. We will float down its corridors and visit its command center. We will interact with real-time reproductions of the people who live and work aboard the station, while they will wear special augmented reality glasses, which will show them images of us in their own environment."

"So we'll be in a sort of game environment, only it will basically be a projection of the actual station, and the people in space will be able to see us?" Rogan asked. It sounded so incredible, the next best thing to actually blasting off in a rocket.

"Exactly!" Mr. Culum said. "You get it!"

"But how will we open doors and stuff?" Jackie asked.

Mr. Culum's super excited mood deflated a little. "Ah. Well, you won't. When you touch a wall, your game suit will stop your forward movement so that you will feel that wall. But you won't be able to change the environment aboard Sun Station One."

"We'll be kind of like ghosts," Takashi said.

"Oh, way better than ghosts!" Mr. Culum said. "You're gamers. The first to go into space in quite this way. Kind of gamer astronauts! What do you say? Are you ready to ride technology into the future?"

"He really loves that line," Jackie said.

Technicians helped them suit up, and moments later, the arena digi-morphed to be replaced by a white hallway, lit by glowing white panels in the walls beside them. The corners where the ceiling and floor met the walls weren't square but interrupted, sort of rounded off, by a foot-long panel at forty-five degrees.

The gamers all appeared as very accurate digital reproductions of themselves, wearing their normal clothes. Rogan figured that having cameras around them all the time gave Atomic Frontiers plenty of opportunities to get good images for VR appearance simulations. He didn't have too much time to think about these things because they all quickly found out what useless concepts floors and ceilings were as they floated in zero gravity.

"Whoa!" Takashi laughed, flailing his arms as he rolled backward.

Jackie whipped herself into a tight roll.

Shay floated kind of helplessly. "I miss the flight system in my viper. I keep trying to activate thrusters to move around, but nothing happens."

Rogan found a handle on the wall. Or maybe it was the ceiling. He'd already lost track. Although he could still feel the pull of gravity in the arena, the environment created by his VR helmet coupled with the sensation caused by his game suit and harness created a very effective illusion of zero gravity. Up and down didn't make sense anymore.

"Grab a handle, everyone!" Mr. Culum said. "Take hold of something to steady yourselves." He waited until the gamers had themselves under control. "Welcome to Sun Station One! This is the pinnacle of solar power and space engineering. You are the first of what I hope will be a great many tourists who will visit the station this way. I brought you here and let you sample weightlessness because we have access to the arena. But since most of the visitors won't be able to experience this tour by floating around, I'm going to have X activate gravity for you. You'll notice that panel there is of a slightly darker shade than the others. Please place your feet on that panel." Mr. Culum smiled. "OK, X. One g, please."

In the next instant Mr. Culum and the gamers were standing solidly again. Rogan knew that in the real world, they'd simply been lowered to the floor of the arena.

"Of course, everyone who is" — he made air quotes with his fingers — "*really* on Sun Station One will be floating. We cannot so easily turn on gravity in space yet."

"Yet," Jackie laughed.

"Give us time, Engineer." Mr. Culum smiled.

A hatch opened at the end of the corridor, and a woman and man in dark blue flight suits glided through. They both wore slightly tinted sunglasses that glowed a little around the edge of each lens. Rogan figured this was like wearing small see-through screens that superimposed the image of Culum and the gamers over the view of what was really in front of the two astronauts.

The woman's red hair was tied back into some kind of knot or bun, and she waved as she approached the others. "Welcome! Mr. Culum wanted me to give you some time to adapt to this environment before I greeted you. I'm Dr. Valerie Dorfman, chief engineer and science officer aboard Sun Station One." She nodded to the man who floated beside her. "This is Dr. Muhammad Sharif, commander and operations manager for the station. He's the man who's going to make sure this station runs smoothly when it goes online soon. He's also the lead scientist in the development and construction of the power receiving station on Earth."

"Welcome," said Dr. Sharif. "We are excited to have you here, and we are eager to show you this station. Right now, you are standing in one of three main corridors, each of which runs through the center cylinder of the station, allowing repair access to the central power shaft and connecting the command habitat module with the energy conversion and transmission module. Currently, the final phase of construction is taking place on the energy transmission systems. You might see workers floating about. You should know that our workers are safe, but they do not like to waste time. They are not wearing augmented reality glasses or earbuds, so they cannot see or hear you. To you and to us, it will appear as though they are passing right through you."

"We're space ghosts," Takashi said.

Dr. Sharif nodded. "Yes. That's a good way to put it."

"If you'll follow us, we'll show you our command center." Dr. Dorfman spun in the air and, grabbing one of the many handles, launched herself down the corridor, flying ahead to lead the way.

"I wish we could fly too," Shaylyn said. "After being Flyer in *Laser Viper* and then floating around in here, walking seems so lame."

"Yes, I suppose it does, Shaylyn," said Mr. Culum. "But I think what you see next will thoroughly impress you."

They entered a room that looked like something straight out of *Star Wars*: a round room with computer stations lining the lower half of the wall. The upper half and ceiling were made entirely of double-thick glass, offering a spectacular view of space. There were four completely massive hexagonal reflector panels behind them, like four flat parachutes. And the word *behind* only made sense in this context because out the windows on the opposite side of the room they could see the central cylinder with the circular conversion and transmission module at the end.

And beyond that, Earth.

Dr. Dorfman made a sweeping gesture of the room. "Welcome to Sun Station One's command center. We are in geostationary orbit about twenty-two thousand miles from Earth. You're lucky you came here digitally. Our ship takes about seven hours to make the trip. On the other hand, the solar power collected by this station and transmitted to Earth as microwave energy will reach the receiver in the desert outside of Dubai, United Arab Emirates, in less than a second, with enough energy to power that entire city and more, indefinitely, and with no pollution."

"All this to power only one city?" Jackie asked.

"Dubai is a major city built in a very hot, very dry desert," said Dr. Sharif. "It uses an enormous amount of electricity for normal power needs, air-conditioning, and water desalinization. But our next step is designing and installing a massive battery system so that surplus power reaching the receiver can be stored, to put the city on batteries while Sun Station One adjusts position to transmit power to a different receiver for a different city."

"We have also constructed a network of large relay satellites, essentially reflectors in space, so that when Dubai is running on fully charged batteries, we can divert power to ground receivers near other cities. Eventually there will be dozens, perhaps hundreds of these stations, powering cities around the world," said Mr. Culum. "The video games you love so much will someday be powered by energy from a station just like this."

"But did you say microwaves?" Shay asked. "Isn't that dangerous? One time I forgot to take foil off a sandwich I was heating up. Sparks, like, everywhere. My parents were so mad."

"It's perfectly safe," said Dr. Sharif. "Think about it. We are merely reflecting the normal energy from the sun back to Earth. We cannot possibly send *more* energy than the sun is already sending to Earth all the time. I wish we could!"

"It's actually a little less power than the sun's rays provide," Dr. Dorfman said.

"Yes," said Dr. Sharif. "The physics are complex, but a certain amount of the energy collected by the reflectors is lost in the form of heat, more as it goes through our conversion system. The most power that can be sent, that could affect any one person, is no more intense than the midday sun." He laughed. "So, yes, if you are standing on the receiver panel with no sunscreen for a long time, you would eventually get a sunburn. But you run the same risk on the beach anywhere in the world."

The gamers were next led on a tour of the crew quarters, dining facility, and even the latrine with its vacuum toilets.

"Fortunately, your game suits can't reproduce what it's like to use the space potty!" Mr. Culum joked. "Those who use them are really riding technology into the future!" He looked pleased with himself when his joke made everyone laugh.

They finished their tour way down in the transmission module, in an observation room at the extreme end of Sun Station One. Out the windows before them was nothing but space and Earth in the distance.

"This is all very cool, Mr. Culum," Rogan said after the man had been quiet for a long time. He didn't take his gaze from Earth.

"Thank you for showing us all this," Jackie said. "I want to be a real-life engineer someday. I'd love to work on one of these stations."

But Mr. Culum didn't seem to hear them. "What do you see when you look out there?" No one knew what to say for a moment.

"Um, space. Our planet." Takashi looked at the other gamers like, *Is Culum OK?*

"I think . . ." Shay moved closer to the glass. "Is that Saudi Arabia there? And that over there is Africa, right?"

"Wrong," said Mr. Culum.

Rogan had earned a fair amount of credits in geography in school. He might not know every country in Africa, but he knew the continent when he saw it. "That must be Africa, though. Up above it is the boot of Italy."

"No," Culum said again. "You're talking about made-up borders and boundaries that separate humanity, lines along which humanity fights, lines that separate people who have enough from those who have nothing. You see division. Chaos." He stopped for a moment and looked at them, then turned back to gaze down at the world. "I see something different. I see the potential for a unified Earth. One people united through technology."

Culum stepped away from the window and motioned to the room around them. He continued, breathing a little heavier now, excited about what he was saying. "This station represents the greater potential for humanity to continue to evolve to something better. From the chaos of random chemicals, amino acids and such, to single-cell organisms, to more complex, more organized forms of life, to humanity, still struggling with the chaos you see out there. And now technology brings our next leap forward, allowing us to transcend petty divisions, to save ourselves from a deadly reliance on fuels that poison our world, to end our struggles, our *wars*, over those fuels and other resources."

Culum was quiet for a moment. Then he laughed a little. "I'm sorry. I'm just so terribly proud of this station and what it represents. Abundant — no, *surplus* clean energy for everyone. One step closer to eliminating the distinction between the haves and the have-nots, an end to all the pain and suffering that unfair division brings." He smiled at the gamers. "You're a part of it, you know."

Rogan frowned. "Mr. Culum, this station is great, and I love what you're saying about getting the world away from using fossil fuels, but we're just playing a video game. How are we a part of it?"

Mr. Culum pushed his hands into the pockets on the front of his sweater. He frowned. "X, can you make sure my game suit has real pockets installed? It does a great job simulating it, stopping my arms from sliding down, but it's just not the same as my real sweater."

"*Yes, Mr. Culum,*" X said over their channel from the control room near the arena.

"But you *are* a part of it!" Mr. Culum went on to the gamers. "This reality show that we're filming won't just market *Laser Viper*. It will highlight to a wide audience just how well digi-space can bring people together. With Atomic Frontiers advancements, humanity need not be bound by the physical locations of our bodies. You will help show everyone that we can be digitally freed from organic isolation. You're doing it right now. You're in space! And you know, when I was younger there were many TV shows, books, and video games about terrible futures. Dystopian fiction. *Terminator.* The Hunger Games. Tales of environmental catastrophes and evil oppressive governments. All those authors failed to consider that humanity might make it, that the future could be better." He looked out the window at Earth again. "Better than they could ever imagine."

Rogan felt like Sun Station One's ground-based receiver, absorbing at least some of Mr. Culum's energy and enthusiasm. This man had almost single-handedly created digi-space, making Virtual City possible. He was one of the richest men in the world, and yet he still cared so much, whether he was helping to provide power and communication to billions of people or taking the time to communicate with one twelve-year-old kid who missed home. It was corny to say, or even to think, but it was an honor to be around him. Rogan promised himself he would work even harder to win Mr. Culum's video game contest.

"Is this, like, a joke or something?" Shaylyn asked a few nights later, as X rushed the four gamers down the hallway toward the arena.

"I'm not laughing." Takashi yawned. "What time is it?"

"Move it!" X was awake, not wearing the pajamas the sleepy gamers might have expected at this hour, but looking almost like a soldier in dark green cargo pants and a black shirt. "If you want to advance in this contest, you need to be in the arena and suited up in the next two minutes!"

Jackie checked her watch. "Three twenty-one a.m."

The dullness of sleep and the confusion of a loud, sudden wake-up was squeezed out of Takashi by a tense fear that tingled from the core of his chest down into his legs. Rogan was down the hall ahead of him, and he ran faster to catch up, escorted as always by fast-rolling cambots.

Takashi yawned. "This is stupid," he said. "What difference does it make what time we start? Why do we have to play in the middle of the night?"

"Early morning," Jackie said.

"You know what I mean," said Takashi.

He always worried about how they were being judged in this contest. What truly mattered in the games — individual accomplishments or being part of the team? If they were judged by what they did outside of the games, would he be at a disadvantage because he didn't act as super confident as Shay or Rogan? And now, was this a test of how well they played while tired and unprepared? None of this made any sense! There had to be a way to stall to get some answers. "Where's Sophia? Doesn't she want to do interviews for the show?"

"No time!" X yelled. "Go, go, go!"

When they were through the double doors into the black-walled cave of the arena, technicians rushed to them, game suits and VR helmets in hand. Mr. Culum paced the floor, a tense urgency cracking through his usual friendly demeanor. "Good morning! Quickly now. Suit up! It's game time!"

A swarm of Atomic Frontiers techs hurried to dress them, pushing arms and legs into the suits as if the gamers were little babies.

"I can dress myself!" Shaylyn cried out.

But her protest was useless. The techs moved with the speed and efficiency of a NASCAR pit crew, each person ready to do a specific task, get one of the gamer's arms into a sleeve, slip on the gamer's VR helmet, hook up the flight and jumping harness.

Mr. Culum laughed weakly. "This game *will* start in the next minute. We are not losing this window."

"Good luck, every—" Takashi started to call out, but a couple of techs shoved a helmet down over his head. They pushed it on so fast it hurt. He thought they could have at least let him finish his sentence.

Seconds later all four laser vipers stood in the dim red light in the launch bay of the SR-73 StarScreamer.

"Wait a second!" Takashi shouted to the roof of their small cabin within the plane, like Mr. Culum or X were above them in the cockpit. How were they supposed to succeed if they had no idea what to do? "Can you at least tell us our objective? How are we supposed—"

APPROACHING HELE DROP ZONE.

RELEASE IN 0:27.

"My Heads-Up Display is different," Engineer said. "Are you all seeing the same thing? The power level percentage indicator is gone."

Takashi noticed it and smiled, because of course Jacqueline would be the first to spot a technical detail like that.

"*Listen up, gamers.*" X said. "*Your vipers have been upgraded with small but still powerful adaptations of the* Tian Li *quantum ion fusion energon cell. As a result, your power supply will be much more stable.*"

Takashi was grateful for the upgrade. One of the abilities of the Healer was to laser cut damaged pieces off vipers or weld on armor or good parts. These functions had always drained his battery fast. Hopefully the new power system would make all that work better.

"Why the rush to start the game?" Shay asked.

"Everybody listen," X said. "There isn't much time. This is a test to see how quickly gamers can react and adapt. Mr. Culum will prepare you for this round of the tournament."

The optimistic cheer was back in Mr. Culum's voice. "Gamers, here's the situation. German military scientists have developed an amazing new technology. Unfortunately, Scorpion terrorist operatives have infiltrated the staff at the lab where this technology was developed, allowing Scorpion to steal the prototype device. Moments ago, German military forces shot down the Scorpion helicopter carrying the device. However, since Scorpion infiltrators among German authorities allowed the theft in the first place, the German commandos working to retrieve the device cannot be trusted. This technology will be used as a dangerous new weapon, which will help Scorpion agents target almost any facility anywhere in the world.

"The Polyadaptive Nanotech Cloak, or PNC, is a harness worn on the chest that works with a neural interface crown, a sort of headband that fits tight to the scalp to interact via electrical impulses directly with the brain. This allows the user to control millions of microscopic robots called nanobots. These nanobots, initially stored in the harness, have limited programming to execute variations of a single program. They interlock and work together to completely cover a human body. The nanobots can change color, and working together, they can form different shapes so that they can make the wearer appear to be a completely different person. They can disguise a man as a woman, a white person as African American, a short person as a tall person. The PNC stores thousands of different patterns of appearance *and can change to look like a completely different person in a matter of seconds. It can even render the user invisible.*

"*By now, your plane is nearing the air space above southern Germany and the crash site of the Scorpion helicopter in a wooded area near Neuschwanstein Castle, an amazing castle built in the late nineteenth century. I think you'll find our designers did an excellent job reproducing a digital version of the structure. Your challenge for this level will be to locate and capture the Polyadaptive Nanotech Cloak, to seize it from whoever has it. Innocent civilians as well as German military, intelligence, and law enforcement personnel will be in the area, so there must be no fatalities. Stick to your NLEPs.*"

Flyer spoke up. "How are we supposed to find this polyada . . . poly—"

"Polyadaptive Nanotech Cloak," Engineer said. "Let's just say PNC. It's easier."

RELEASE IN 5 . . .

"*Get the PNC,*" Mr. Culum said. "*And remember it is very important that you leave absolutely no video or photographic evidence that laser vipers were there.*"

"*Go get 'em, gamers,*" X said.

2, 1 . . .

With the familiar violent air displacement, the vipers shot out of the cargo bay of the SR-73 StarScreamer, and the jet vanished in the distance.

"Crap!" Rogan shouted. They weren't nearly as high as they'd been on the previous insertion. Their altimeters showed them plunging hundreds of feet per second. "We're coming in low!"

Flyer soared out ahead of them, arms spread wide, her body in a flying T position.

"Braking thrusters!" Healer shouted. "Now, now, now!"

Rogan fired his rockets a couple of seconds after the others, so the two of them appeared to fly up above him, though the real difference was that Rogan was falling faster.

Trees rushed up at him. Small limbs whipped his faceplate, evergreen needles scraping against the outside of his helmet. He smashed into heavier branches as he continued to fall.

Hard slap to the chest.

Sharp slam in the legs.

He flipped over and over, hitting tree trunks, bashing branches, until he crashed onto the rocky ground and tumbled helplessly out toward the river.

WARNING: MINOR IMPACT DAMAGE TO ARMOR.

"Ranger!" Healer ran out of the woods moments later. "You OK?"

Rogan slowly rose to his feet, dizzy from the whirlwind crash and embarrassed after such an amateur, messed-up combat drop. He was standing in a riverbed, a long line of white and gray round rocks, like the forest had been broken open for a quarry. He picked small twigs off his body and noticed the dents in his armor. A sharp diagonal swath had been cut through the forest with busted branches, and a scarred trunk marked the path along which he'd fallen. X hadn't been kidding about their safety. He would have been killed if he had really crashed like that. Still, the simulation had been so perfect that he wondered if he would have actual bruises.

-----○-----

Jackie's drop had gone far better. She'd steered herself toward the mostly dry riverbed, and although contact with the ground was a little sharper than usual, her viper was undamaged. She immediately scanned her surroundings for hostiles. If the PNC was in the area, it was well camouflaged. This raised several practical concerns. Among them, she wondered how they would find the device if it could render it and its user invisible. She and her fellow gamers would have to be quick and clever to succeed at this round. Her radar-like direction finder showed Flyer far to the west. The other two were much closer, southwest of her position on the river. She was about to run off to join them when her sensors alerted her to a strong heat signature, something mechanical, nearby.

Her NLEP at the ready, she hurried to examine whatever it was. Sprinting at viper speed over the rocks, she reached the crash site of a helicopter. Her computer quickly identified the aircraft as an unmarked UH-60 Black Hawk. It had burned after it crashed, and a couple of small fires still smoldered. Scanning the bodies inside, she found this was one of those moments she wished *Laser Viper* weren't so realistic. Cuts and burns made facial recognition software useless. She couldn't even determine the ethnicity of the bodies. But the pilot and crew hadn't been wearing uniforms, so they probably weren't military or law enforcement. Their heavy weapons told her these weren't normal civilians.

"I've found the crashed Scorpion helicopter," she called to the others. Healer and Ranger joined her a moment later.

Healer pointed to the woods. "More bodies out that way. Some of them in uniforms with German flags on the shoulders."

"Fighting it out over the PNC," said Ranger.

"Yeah, but who won?" Healer asked.

"I've got movement to the north," said Flyer from above. *"A bunch of soldiers and . . . Zooming in . . . Yeah, one of them is wearing some kind of technical harness. I have eyes on the target. I'm going for it."*

As if they thought as one, the other three gamers took off at a run, jumping and rocket-bounding over rocks and downed trees, covering ground faster than any human ever could. A storm of laser fire convinced Flyer to join the others behind cover halfway up a wooded hill. "They're going for the castle." Flyer landed next to them. "Look at that thing. It's, like, straight out of Disney. That's all I'm saying."

"Sleeping Beauty's castle," said Healer.

"Pretty sure Disney copied this thing," said Engineer.

High on the hill above them was a perfect storybook castle. Four stories of white stone perched on top of a steep mountain, it had a dark blue, sharply pitched roof, and round and square towers at various places. The whole building looked almost as though it had been carved out of the mountaintop.

"Who cares what it looks like?" Rogan said. "How do we find this PNC?"

"That's the bad news," Engineer said. "The target and the rest of the soldiers were heading for the castle. They'd have made it there by now."

"So we go in there and get it!" Rogan said.

"Would you just calm down for once?" Flyer grabbed his arm before he could take off. "It's not that simple. If the PNC can change the target's appearance, we're going to have a tough time finding him among all the tourists."

"The castle will have tons of surveillance cameras," Healer said.

"I'll take care of that," said Engineer.

"The tourists will be taking photos and videos too," Healer said.

"That will be tougher," said Flyer. "We'll have to stun everybody quickly and make sure we destroy all their phones and cameras."

"Not just by smashing either," said Engineer. "Or they might still recover the data. All that stuff will have to be lasered. Melted down."

"You think they've programmed this game with *that* kind of specific detail?" Healer said.

"Do you want to take a chance for mission failure?" Engineer replied.

"I'll take care of the phones." Rogan nodded to Engineer. She was easily the smartest gamer he'd ever played with. "But speed will be key. If part of our objective is to keep our mission a secret, we'll only have seconds before anyone in there can snap a photo of us and post it online."

"Yeah, but the game designers will give us some time, right?" said Healer. "Like, in one of my *Call of Duty* games there's a running countdown on screen until a bomb goes off. Maybe there's a countdown like that before the nonplayer characters in the game blow our cover."

"Maybe," said Flyer. "But I don't think we can take that chance."

"Right," said Rogan, eager to get started. He had just realized that with Tank out of the game, his Ranger was now the most heavily armed viper. "Engineer, you have a big job to do. Shut down the security system and stop any outgoing communication. The rest of us will have to stun as many people as we can, as fast as possible. Even if one of us stuns our target and finds the PNC, we'll have to pick it up quick and keep going to knock out everybody else in the place so that we aren't compromised."

Healer laughed. "You guys, this is going to be hard, but you have to admit, it's so fun."

"That's the truth," Rogan said. "Flyer, you find a way into the castle from the top and work your way down. Take Healer with you. That way each of us can cover one floor. Give us some time to get in at the ground level, so that we take out as many problems at the same time as we can. Everybody know the plan?"

"That's a plan?" Flyer said.

"*Gamers,*" X's voice cut in. "*Time is running out. German police and military forces are aware that the Scorpion helicopter has crashed near your location and that the PNC is in the castle. They have been infiltrated by Scorpion. You must secure the device so that it cannot fall into enemy hands.*"

"You heard him," Rogan said. "We don't have time to sit around talking about it. Now let's go get 'em, gamers!"

Rogan and Engineer ran ahead through the woods while Flyer gave Healer a lift, all of them keeping watch for German soldiers or Scorpion terrorists who might take shots at them, staying together instead of racing one another, so that they could hit the castle and its occupants with a rapid, unified attack.

Closer to the building, they spotted a group of about sixty tourists standing outside the castle on a balcony that overlooked the serious cliff. The vipers remained under tree cover, but since the tourists were already recording pretty much everything with their cameras and phones, they'd be spotted as soon as they came out in the open.

"Flyer," said Rogan. "We're in position. Start your approach when I tell you to go."

A siren went off and the tourists looked around in alarm. Someone in uniform, a tour guide maybe, motioned with some urgency, and people began packing up.

"They're evacuating!" Flyer said. *"We have to move now or the disguised target will walk right out with the others."*

Rogan slapped Engineer on the shoulder. "Let's go! Quick is the key!"

The two of them scrambled up, alternating between climbing the cliff and the trees next to it, running, rocket-jumping, grabbing handholds and yanking themselves up. Finally, they reached the top, and Engineer vaulted over the short wall first, landing in the stone-floored lower courtyard surrounded on three sides by the castle ahead, with high walls and buildings reaching around them.

"Flyer, now!" Engineer shouted. "Go!Go!Go!"

When Rogan joined her in the lower courtyard seconds later, a mob of frantic tourists had run out onto the upper courtyard, the second stone level about eight feet higher than the first and separated by a short wall. Engineer didn't wait for him. She unleashed her NLEPs, even as she rocket-jumped to the upper courtyard and sprinted toward the stairs that led up to the big arched castle door.

He saw at once that she wasn't worried as much about the people as she was about getting inside, hopefully to disable the cameras. "Get in there, Engineer," Rogan said. "I'll take care of everybody out here."

The tourists were in a frenzy, screaming in at least half a dozen languages, and clearly no longer sure which direction to run. Some tried to go back into the castle, fleeing Ranger. Others tried to climb the wall, like they thought they'd be safe if they could get up inside the big square tower there. Rogan stunned one after another, firing an NLEP and watching long enough to see the pained, seizure-like, locked-up expression on the target's face before shooting someone else. At least with the new power system, he didn't have to keep his eye on his battery percentage, a huge advantage.

He kept hoping that one of these people would sparkle or shimmer from a disrupted PNC, or even better, revert back to his real appearance. But no luck. Just screams and unconscious non-player characters. He wanted to scream too, because he knew when he was done he'd need to check everybody for phones or even old cameras that he had to destroy, slowing him down even more.

A loud pop. A high-pitched beep. Hiss of static. *"If you can . . . hear me. Say nothing."*

The voice was hard to understand. Distorted. Not Culum or X. Rogan was about to ask who had spoken when the sound cut in again. *"—Eliminated—Tournament————Never mention. Just raise . . . right hand—you get this."*

Was it some kind of test? Rogan had taken care of all the tourists in the area, so he started lasering the phones.

Static. *"—me? . . . hand up!"*

Rogan quickly raised his right hand and waved it around a little.

"Testing the—They're always . . . watch—"

The tournament stages were all new. Rogan and the other gamers were probably the only beta testers. It made sense there'd be glitches. Whatever it had been, it was gone now. Rogan moved on. He had a game to win.

-----o-----

Outside, Shaylyn held on to Healer and rocketed into the action, heading over the steep blue roof and straight for the big, round tower that was the highest point in the castle, hoping it was a way inside and not some fake decoration that served no real purpose. She landed them on a wraparound balcony about halfway up the tower and led the way inside. "You take the first floor we reach," she said to Healer. "I'll continue down to the next."

She felt a little bad, worried she was gaming like Rogan or Beckett, rushing ahead and leaving the others behind. But this was what she was supposed to do. They had to clear the floors quickly. She emerged from the staircase onto the third floor in a weird trapezoid-shaped room. A complicated network of ceiling archways was decorated in a mind-boggling, almost flowerlike pattern of about a million colors. Big paintings of kings, queens, and knights in a medieval battle covered the top half of the walls. Red-brown wood panels and benches made up the bottom.

"I'm on the third floor," she said to the others. "It's like a throne room, I think, but no throne. Gold walls. Painting of Jesus and angels near the ceiling. Huge gold chandelier—"

"Yeah, it's neat," Ranger interrupted. "We get it. Just clear the floor and move on. We're in a hurry!"

Shout in German behind her. Hard hits, like a hammer smacking her back and shoulder.

WARNING: INCOMING SMALL ARMS FIRE.

Shaylyn spun around and shot blindly, missing the two soldiers holding handguns, and blasting minor burns in the dark wood double doors.

They shouted something and fired again.

She was knocked back, but this time aimed her NLEP, firing two quick shots to stun them both. "I have armed guards or soldiers or something on floor three," she told the others as she stomped the phones and radios of her attackers to bits on the animal-and-tree tile mosaic on the floor. "German flags on their shoulders." She ran out of the throne room to clear other, smaller rooms on her level.

-----o-----

Takashi breathed heavy, hot inside his helmet. He would have loved to take the thing off, if only for a moment, but he couldn't miss any of the game. "There's nothing here! A big balcony hallway and—"

He stepped into a giant open room, with a bunch of round golden chandeliers and knights and castle paintings on the walls. "There's just a big room. No doors." He ran around, his metal feet clomping on the polished wood floor. "Unless— What if there's a secret passage? Do we have maps for this stage? What if he's invisible? Like blending into the walls? Maybe we need to just shoot everything!"

His job was fixing vipers, not running around hunting camouflaged enemies.

WARNING: INCOMING SMALL ARMS FIRE.

A man and a woman, soldiers or maybe police, unloaded into him with rifles, round after round. The bullets smacked his viper's metal flesh hard. Other internal warnings sounded before he finally dropped the two attackers with NLEPs. "Two armed security people down!"

"*Great, Healer!*" Ranger said. "*Destroy any communication devices they have. Then move on and find that PNC guy!*"

-----o-----

Jacqueline was surprised by the look of the second floor. The first level had been like walking through an art museum, where every inch of the walls, ceilings, doors, everything was either a painting or sculpture or decorated in some flashy way. There were no plain spaces. The opposite was true on the second floor. It was like all the old cool stuff had been stripped away for the gift shop and other tourist junk.

"*Good work, Engineer,*" X said. A yellow line appeared in the air in front of her. "*Follow this to the camera room.*"

She crashed through the gift shop, overturning tables and book racks, big stein drinking mugs and ceramic models of the castle crashing all around her. A rack of shot glasses bumped sideways as they fell, as if they'd run into something. But there was nothing there.

Jacqueline froze. A pair of boot prints stood out darkly in the white powder from crushed pottery. Dust formed the faint outline of the boots and the tucked-in bottom of uniform pants, see-through, like the feet of a ghost. "Target is on—"

Her vision flashed hot red.

WARNING: Exxxrtreee-**_____

Another glimpse of laser fire in the corner of her static vision. Blast in her chest. Computer alarms. Shot to the leg. Severed arm . . .

-----o-----

Still on the first floor, Rogan stunned three armed soldiers. How many of them were there?

WARNING: INCOMING SMALL ARMS FIRE.

He stunned three police officers and half a dozen more panicked tourists unconscious and moved on to tedious camera and phone destruction. Bending down to grab a phone from a man's pocket, his head was knocked sideways. His face. Impact to his ribs. Rogan dropped into a backward roll to escape the attack, but it kept coming. A security guard held a six-foot-long gold candle tree thing right in the middle. He swung it like a battle staff.

Rogan finally ducked one attack. Jumped over his opponent's next low swing. He saw his opening and decked the guy with more than enough force to knock him out.

But the guard spun around, bringing the lamp around to smash Rogan again. Rogan didn't have time for this. Engineer was in trouble.

"Engineer!" Flyer called over their channel. *"Jackie! You there?!"*

The man spit blood in Rogan's faceplate and jabbed the lamp at his head. Rogan extended his close combat claws out from the top of his hand. He heaved with all his strength into a vicious overhand downward slash. The claws sliced the pole in half. Retracting them, he threw a hard right cross that dropped his opponent unconscious. Rogan sprinted for the stairs to go help Engineer.

-----o-----

SYSTEM RESTORE IN PROGRESS . . .

Jacqueline could finally move again. Visuals were back up, if only in black and white.

MOTOR CONTROL RESTORED.

WARNING: CRITICAL DAMAGE TO LEFT ARM.

*WARNING: CRITICAL DAMAGE TO
NONLETHAL ENERGY PULSE EMITTER.*

No kidding damage to the arm and pulse weapon. Her arm was missing! She quickly calmed her momentary panic, forcing herself to understand that only her in-game arm was gone.

WARNING: SEVERE DAMAGE TO RIGHT LEG.

*WARNING: POWER SYSTEM DAMAGED.
SHUTDOWN IMMINENT.*

Jacqueline cursed. Her viper hadn't been completely destroyed, but it might as well have been. She would be out of the *Laser Viper* Final Challenge for sure. She took a deep breath. Maybe she'd lost the tournament, but she could still help the others with the mission.

She could still crawl. When she looked at her viper body, all she saw was torn-up metal and a chaos of wiring and motors, and she could almost feel the pain she'd be in if this were real. But she wasn't totally immobilized. It would be up to the others to secure the target, but she could at least wipe the security camera footage.

When she entered the room, she immediately spotted the hard drive onto which the digital video from the cameras around the castle was being recorded. At first she thought about just shooting the whole computer with her NLEP or CHEL but blasting it might leave recoverable data, and she doubted she even had enough weapons energy left anyway. Hooking herself up to the computer, she quickly began deleting recorded footage.

Her system also accessed the live surveillance feeds. The camera offered her a view of the slight, shimmering distortion in the spiral stairwell. The light white footprint. Ranger was three feet away.

"Rogan!" Jackie screamed. "He's right in front of you!"

-----o-----

Shaylyn was behind Ranger when the laser blast came out of nowhere, slamming into the armor of his shoulder and knocking him back into her. She reached around him and fired a dozen NLEPs, hoping to hit something. Someone. But nothing.

"Come on!" Ranger shouted, shooting again and again at nothing as they ran for the second floor.

-----o-----

Jacqueline watched the crawling progress bar on her HUD menu, moving slower than the loading process on a new game using the worst internet connection. The surveillance computer was almost totally wiped and scrambled. "Come on. Come on. Finally." One hundred percent. She disconnected from the computer and turned around to try to help the others.

-----o-----

Engineer appeared in the doorway from the stairs to the second floor, motioning for Rogan and Flyer to follow. She was in bad shape. Her left arm shot clean off. Her right leg barely holding together. It was a miracle she was still walking.

"Get yourself to safety, Engineer," Flyer said. "We'll find the target."

"Healer! Where *are* you?!" Rogan shouted as he and Flyer moved into the gift shop.

"I'm on the stairs," Healer answered. *"Hang on!"*

"I can't get to safety," Engineer said. *"I can't walk. Not sure if I can—"*

Rogan stopped. "Wait. What? Can't walk—"

He was slammed in the back and thrown forward, crashing through a big crystal swan.

WARNING: INCOMING LASER FIRE.

WARNING: MINOR DAMAGE TO MOTOR CONTROL.

"Behind—" Flyer screamed.

Rogan turned around just in time to see Engineer, or what appeared to be Engineer, laser Flyer hard. One shot to the gut. Another to the chest.

Rogan aimed his NLEPs but was blasted right in the hand. The imposter was a fast shooter.

Flyer unleashed two NLEP shots. One of them hit home, and the digital disguise fizzled out, revealing a tough German commando, somehow still on his feet. He lasered Flyer again, damaging her leg pretty bad, and blasting her in the chest. But it was the last distraction Rogan needed. He took out the enemy's laser rifle with his own CHEL, and the German raised his hands in surrender.

"Who are you?" the man said in heavily accented English. "What do you want the device for?"

"Stun him!" Mr. Culum shouted over the channel. *"Stun him now and win the game!"*

Rogan didn't need any more encouragement. Seconds later, the German man was out cold on the floor and Healer finally joined them.

"Sorry I'm late!" Healer said. His viper's metal skin was torn up with bullet holes. "Ran into some company on the way."

Rogan unbuckled the PNC harness from the man's chest. He wanted to shout for joy at being the one to obtain the objective. But he still needed to get the thing out of here, and he could hear sirens coming from outside.

He looked at Flyer, who was at least sitting up. "Shay, you have to fly this thing out of here."

"That last shot took out my flight systems," Flyer said.

"I can fix that." Healer leapt at her, tools at the ready.

"I d-d—d-d-don't have much—time until shutdown." The real Engineer crawled toward them, torn up far worse than the one faked by the Polyadaptive Nanotech Cloak.

"Healer, you have to hurry," Rogan said. "Otherwise we'll have to carry Engineer."

White-hot welding sparks flew everywhere as Healer worked on Flyer. "I think she'll be able to fly now. At least for a short time.

Enough to reach extraction altitude and get picked up by our jump ship."

"There may b-b-beeeeee . . . m-more phones to destr—" Engineer shook her head.

"Right," Rogan said. "Well, that's a problem, because if we hang around too long trying to keep the secret of us from getting out, the whole German army is going to be here."

"*OK, gamers,*" X said. He sounded like the school principal coming on over the intercom. "*You have the target. The StarScreamer is on her way. Commence exfil operations immediately.*"

"Can you walk?" Rogan asked Flyer.

"No," she said. "But I can fly."

A part of him thought he was crazy, but he handed the PNC over to his biggest gamer rival. "Then take this. Get out of here. Healer, you too. I'll grab Engineer. Hopefully there aren't any more phones."

"Do you think you'll be able to extract her?" Healer asked.

"I'll put my exfil rockets on overload and hope for the best! Now go!"

Two more soldiers rushed out on the floor in front of Flyer. "Sorry, Mario." Flyer stunned one and punched the other out hard. "But this princess is heading for another castle."

As the other two vipers ran out, Rogan reached down to pick up the shredded remains of Engineer. "Nice job," he said as he strained to lift her. It was one of those times when he wished his game suit had the same strength as his viper would have in real life. But as soon as he started to complain, the cables attached to

Jacqueline must have lifted her a little, because he could manage her just fine, carrying her cradle-style, up the stairs away from the authorities closing in. Finally he reached a stone balcony and perched on the edge. In his mind, he knew he wasn't nearly as high off the ground as he appeared to be in the game, and the Atomic Frontiers people wouldn't just let him drop down to the floor. Actually, he was probably standing on the flat floor right now. He shook his head. The blurred line between the game and the arena was messing with his mind too much.

"You still in the game, Jackie?" he asked her.

She nodded slightly and made some kind of garbled computerized groan.

"Then let's do this," Rogan said. He jumped clear of Neuschwanstein Castle, slamming his exfil rockets past full power.

WARNING: EXFILTRATION ROCKETS EXCEEDING RECOMMENDED PARAMETERS.

As the computer alarms rang in his head, Rogan carried Engineer, soaring up above the beautiful wooded wilderness and fairy-tale castle below, above a tough but awesome and hopefully successful game round.

CHAPTER 11

JACQUELINE SHARPE

I would prefer not to do one of these interviews right now. I messed up. How else can I say it? I. Messed. Up. I should have reacted faster when I first noticed the target. I should have swept the whole room with nonlethal pulses as soon as I entered. I try to look at every situation logically, try to look ahead to possible dangers. I shouldn't have been ambushed the way I was. I'm very disappointed in myself right now.

Who do I think should stay in for the next round? . . . It's hard to say. Shaylyn was nearly destroyed too. Takashi saved her. Rogan captured the Polyadaptive Nanotech Cloak. He should probably move on. Shaylyn flew it out of there, but that was only after Takashi repaired her again. I don't know. These people have become my friends now, and I'd be sad to see any of them go. But someone has to be cut, and I hope it isn't me.

TAKASHI ENDO

The game started very fast. No time to plan. Why did we play in the middle of the night? Why did the game have to begin so quickly? What difference does it make what time the game starts?

I feel like I did OK. Actually, this time I saw a lot more combat than usual. Two guards on the third floor, and then this guy lit me up with a machine gun when I was trying to reach Jackie and Shay. I stunned him quick.

Other than that, my job is to fix the other vipers. I did my job. I saved Shaylyn. I would have fixed Jackie, but we were out of time. It was a weird level.

Most other times I've played Laser Viper, there have been a lot more enemies to fight. Or like on just about any Halo, the Covenant aliens keep coming, more and more. And in just about every stage there's some kind of end boss. A much larger alien or big robot or something. This is the championship tournament and the boss was one guy with a laser? I don't get it.

I don't know who should move on in the game. It would help if we knew how we're being scored. Rogan probably stunned the most nonplayer characters, and he captured the PNC. But I'm Healer and I fixed the most vipers. It's like comparing a professional football player to a dentist. Which of them should get the prize for being the best? Maybe there should be a prize for whoever can get the glitches out of the game.

SHAYLYN SPERO

How do I feel about the last round? I . . . I don't know. No, I don't think I did a good job. I was nearly blasted out of the game. Yeah, I ended up with the PNC, but I didn't earn it.

No, I'm not mad that Rogan captured the target. I helped him defeat the laser guy in the gift shop, but that's fine! I took most of the target's attack, almost like a shield so that Rogan could stun the guy out and get the PNC. He'll get all the credit prob-ably, but that's fine!

I'm not. I'm not mad. It just wasn't that fun, OK? What's the point of a video game if it's not fun? Flying around stunning tourists? I don't care how cool the castle was. What I always loved about Laser Viper *was that I had the chance to be this awesome flying robot taking out these evil Scorpion terrorists. But this last round? Weird. That's all I'm saying.*

And why do the NPCs keep screaming? Like the civil-ians panic in most games, but they just kind of get in the way while they run for it. They were weird in this round. Annoying. A little freaky.

I had the PNC in the end. I should move on to the next round. Fine. Rogan too. Yeah, he's a good gamer, even if he's, like, a total stuck-up jerk about it a lot of the time. The other two? You should probably keep Jackie. She was shot up pretty bad and Healer was nowhere around, but she still got the job done and wiped those cameras.

ROGAN WEBBER

I did my best. I don't know how this contest is scored. It's not like my grandpa's old games, not like clearing levels in Super Mario Bros. Dump Bowser in the lava and you win. So I don't know.

No. I'm not laughing at you. I'm ... OK. I guess I was trying to play it cool, but I think I did pretty great. I stunned the target. I captured the PNC. I was damaged a couple times, but that didn't stop me. Shay did all right, I guess. Takashi helped out on repairs, had a couple of tough fights. Jackie. She's the one I need to be worried about in this competition. It's weird when your viper is damaged, how the suit slows you down or how even though, of course, her hand was still in her suit, you can't see it in the *game. It's kind of freaky, if you really want to know. But Jackie's hardcore. She crawled into that camera room with extreme damage to her viper. Still accomplished her mission. So, I guess she deserves to go on to the next round. All three of them are kind of cool, but this is gaming, this is* Laser Viper, *and what do you want me to say? We can't all win. As much as I hate to see the others disappointed, I want—I need—to win this.*

"Super!" Sophia Hahn stoop up from her chair behind the cambot and started walking around to him. "That was perfect, Rogan. All that bold confidence." She clapped her hands and nearly bounced. "That's the kind of thing the audience loves." The cambot shut off its bright light and buzzed away to the door leading from the interview room to the commons, eager to find someone else to film.

Rogan smiled from the praise. Sure, Sophia was always gushing, with super nice things to say about all the gamers. But her words had felt especially great just then because he'd been worrying a little that he wasn't providing her and Mr. Culum with the right kind of entertainment for their reality show. And if the point of waking them up in the middle of the night for the latest game round was to see how well they could handle playing while tired, if they were being judged by criteria other than basic gameplay, then maybe pleasing the cameras was important.

"Ms. Hahn?" Rogan asked.

The cambot zipped back in front of him. She turned her sparkling smile toward him. "Please, call me Sophia."

"Sophia." Rogan nodded. "How did you get this job, working here at Atomic Frontiers, with Mr. Culum?" Whenever people asked him what he wanted to be when he grew up, his answer was always something about video games, computers, or other technology. "I mean, it seems like the perfect job."

"It was a long process. I wish I had time to explain it all to you." Sophia tilted her head a little. "But it feels like I've been here forever. Atomic Frontiers is a natural fit. Technology has always been a part of me." She refreshed her smile and motioned toward the door. "Now, shall we join the others?"

-----o-----

The atmosphere in the commons later that morning after their interviews was less than energized. The gamers were fried, sitting slumped on the big couch and staring into space, wishing they could give up on fighting to stay awake, but too eager for the game results for them to go to their rooms.

"Well," Jackie said after a long, long silence. "It's a good thing this place is full of cameras. This should make some great TV."

Rogan and Shay looked at her for a moment, then at each other, before the two of them burst into laughter.

"Come on, Takashi," Shay said. "That was at least kind of funny. Worth a chuckle."

"Sorry," Takashi said quietly. He motioned for them all to move closer. Rogan was already sitting by him so he only leaned in.

Takashi beckoned again for Shay and Jackie. All three cambots rolled up around the back of the sofa to try to get in on the conversation, but they could only get so close. When the gamers had all huddled up, ducked down to use the back of the sofa as a privacy shield, Takashi spoke barely above a whisper. "I don't want the cameras and microphones to hear. This game. In the castle. Something is wrong. The castle level made no sense. I think—"

"OK, gamers!" Sophia's chip-chipper voice rang out from the main door to their common area. They all rose up to look over the back of their seat. X towered next to her, as always. "Sorry to keep you waiting!" She leaned forward with her hands clasped together on her knees. "Oh, look, Xavier. They're all huddled together. Sharing little secrets like best friends!"

She stood up straight, letting out a long breath, patting her right hand over her heart as though she couldn't hold in all the emotion that threatened to gush from her. It did gush in her voice. "This is the hardest part. Unfortunately, we will have to say goodbye to one of you, and our judges have made their decision. So, gamers"—she moved her hand back and forth along the line on the floor next to the giant screen where they'd all stood for the first elimination—"if you'd all get into position, please?"

They all looked at Takashi like they were hoping he'd finish whatever he'd tried telling them, but he only shrugged and led the way to the mark.

"Perfect!" Sophia clapped. "Three of you will be advancing to the next round of action-packed *Laser Viper* gaming. But for one of you, the journey of a lifetime ends now. The first gamer who will

continue in the *Laser Viper* Final Challenge is . . ." She looked at
them all, dragging the experience out in a dramatic pause. "Shaylyn
Spero!" Shay's giant portrait popped up on the screen a second
before Sophia called out her name. "Come on over here! You're safe!
Congratulations!"

Shaylyn lit up like someone had thrown a switch and activated
her happiness. She pushed a blue lock of hair out of her face as she
jumped up and down. She hugged Jackie, hugged Takashi, and
then, after hesitating with her old archrival, hugged Rogan before
running to stand beside Sophia and X.

"Perfect!" Sophia said again.

Rogan remembered the cameras and kept smiling, wondering
why Shay had been declared safe before he had. He'd played better
than her. But maybe they were giving more points for the one who
brought the PNC in. He'd be safe next, for sure.

Sophia exchanged a look with X, like the two of them had been
holding on to a huge secret for months. "The next gamer who will
stay with us to game another day is . . ." A cambot slowly rolled by
in front of the three gamers still in jeopardy. "Jacqueline Sharpe!"
Jackie brightened and nodded to the two guys before joining Shay
in the winner circle.

Now Rogan figured they were just keeping the best for last.
Unless the judges were impressed with how Takashi had fixed
Shay's flight system. He'd watched plenty of reality shows on
which the eliminations made no sense. Maybe he wasn't as safe as
he'd thought. All the same doubts he'd experienced during the first

elimination session surged again, only amplified by the feeling that he had disappointed Mr. Culum.

Sophia's mega smile transformed, almost like the morphing of the Polyadaptive Nanotech Cloak into a new appearance, into the saddest frown a human could make. A double depressed sad clown. "The person whose name I'm about to call is a terrific gamer. You *all* are. But we have to say goodbye to this next person, who will *not* be moving on to the next round of the *Laser Viper* Final Challenge. I'm so sorry . . ." Again with the longest pause. "Takashi Endo."

Takashi's shoulders slumped, his face dimmed with disappointment.

Sophia clasped her hands over her chest. "Takashi, please say goodbye to your fellow gamers and then return to your dorm room to pack your belongings."

Rogan thought Takashi might offer a high five, a fist bump, or even a handshake, but he was surprised when the guy pulled him in close for a hug. "Something is wrong here," Takashi whispered in Rogan's ear. "Be careful. Look out for the others."

Then Shay and Jackie joined them in a big, weird group hug. Rogan's family weren't big huggers, and he couldn't wait to escape. Fortunately, X gently eased them apart and pulled Takashi away. No shouting tantrum. No threats. Instead, Takashi went quietly to his room. Rogan watched him go. Takashi was a cool guy. He'd have to find him in the *Laser Viper* war room sometime after this big tournament so the two of them could team up again.

"Congratulations!" Sophia pulled the three remaining gamers to the space in front of the three giant portraits on the big screen. Three cambots rolled up in front of them. All the ceiling and wall-mounted cameras in the common area pointed at them. "Rogan Webber. Shaylyn Spero. Jacqueline Sharpe. You are moving on to the next round of the *Laser Viper* Final Challenge!"

They might have freaked out more, jumped up and down, celebrating, if they weren't so tired from being yanked out of their beds in the small hours of the morning. They were happy, though, and they congratulated one another.

"*Enjoy* this time, gamers," Sophia said. "You've earned it. Take some time to celebrate." She looked at the three remaining gamers and laughed. "Maybe after you get some sleep!"

The two adults slipped out of the room, leaving them alone. After another round of congratulations, they went to their rooms.

Lying in his bed, Rogan thought about the tournament and about Takashi's warning. What did he think was wrong? Was that what he had tried to tell the group just before Sophia had come in to conduct the elimination? He had been talking a lot about how the last round had been strange, and he was right. The gaming in this contest wasn't like normal gaming. The pacing and objectives, and the whole idea that if their vipers were destroyed they were simply out of the game, was unlike anything he'd ever played. And what was that sound and voice that had cut into the middle of the action? What a weird glitch.

He yawned and laughed a little. Maybe everything just seemed a little off because he was so tired. He should be grateful that he was still in the contest. He thought about being *Laser Viper* Grand Champion, about the $250,000 and one million game credit prize, about being able to forget his e-viction notice and flat-out *buying* his own airship apartment above Virtual City, about how proud his parents would be when he got home. With the afterimage of robots and laser fire floating behind his eyelids, he drifted off to sleep.

CHAPTER 12

After long naps, the gamers were awoken late in the afternoon, more gently than last time, to another surprise. As they emerged from their dorms into the commons, they saw Mr. Culum seated at the central table, which had been set with plates, cups, silverware, and several different dishes. He pressed his lips together, holding a hand to his back as he rose from his seat to greet the gamers. "I would be honored if you would join me."

"Wow! Really?" Shay said.

Rogan could hardly believe it. A whole meal with the greatest technology genius of modern times?

"Sounds great, Mr. Culum," Jackie said. "We usually eat—"

"Pizza and cheesy puffs." Mr. Culum laughed. "I've noticed."

Rogan moved to the table first, eager to get started—

"I've wanted to give you gamers the opportunity to experience my healthy way of eating," Mr. Culum said.

—until he saw what was on the table. Forget pizza or burgers or even Hot Pockets.

In a few minutes everyone was seated and had been served. A pressed bean-mash patty for the main course, served on a gluten-free rice-based bun. Quinoa salad with white chunks of tofu and some kind of little twiggy things on top. The best thing available was a fruit cup, though even that contained enough cantaloupe to ruin the dish for Rogan's tastes.

"Go ahead and dig in!" Mr. Culum said happily. "My lifestyle, working with computers and technology, is inherently unhealthy. All that sitting. But I do what I can to stay fit through the healthiest diet possible. Some people may find it strange, but—"

"Wha—" Rogan spoke through a mouthful of the bean patty thing. He forced himself to look happy as he struggled to keep from gagging. "Mmmmm." When he swallowed he coughed a little and took a drink of his soy milk. "S'good!"

Shay had known him long enough to understand that Rogan, the world's leading connoisseur of Hot Pockets, probably wasn't converting to Culum's diet quite as fast or wholeheartedly as Rogan was letting on. She held a napkin over her mouth to hide her laughter.

"Technology has made tremendous progress in increasing food plant yields so that we can better feed humanity. But still population outpaces food production. And raising food animals is hardly the answer. Cruelty considerations aside for the moment, the livestock industry continues to contribute to deforestation, creation of greenhouse gas methane, and other problems." He held his hands up. "It is probably not surprising to hear me say I believe technology can help us to overcome these problems. But I did not come here to lecture. I simply wanted to sit down and spend some time with my semifinalist gamers. Very soon, you will compete for the chance to participate in the championship round. And I'm sure you're excited about that, but I also want to make sure you're all doing OK. I know that the last game round started abruptly, and that was a bit stressful. I know you've been away from your homes and families for a while now. How are you all doing?"

Cambots moved up close to the table, recording it all.

Jackie laughed. "Is this a test?"

"Not at all!" said Mr. Culum. "If the cameras are bothering you, I can have them shut off. We'd miss some great material for the reality show, but I care more about all of you than the show."

"It's fine," Jackie said. "I don't mind the cameras. I'm great. Actually, my family always takes the time to sit down to meals together, so this is kind of nice. And I love quinoa!"

"Me too!" Rogan lied.

Shay pretended to cough to cover her snort.

"Are you all right, Shaylyn?" Mr. Culum asked.

"Absolutely," Shay said. "I was just thinking that this meal with the four of us—well, the four of us plus the cambots—is kind of small. I do miss my family. But it's a large family and meals can be really crazy sometimes."

"A little calmer with your Atomic Frontiers family, then." Mr. Culum smiled. Then he turned his attention to Rogan. "Ro, how are you holding up through the tournament?"

Rogan's family never sat down to meals like this. And he wasn't used to someone asking him how he was doing—really stopping and asking him and listening to what he said. "I'm great, Mr. Culum." He shoveled a spoonful of quinoa into his mouth, chewed a little, and forced a swallow. "Honestly. This is the best. I'm really great."

The dinner conversation rolled along like that, relaxed and easy, less like a competition or an interview, and more like fun.

-----o-----

"Congratulations on advancing another round, Rogan. That's wonderful." Rogan's mother smiled warmly when they were given video conference time two days later. "I'm so happy for you. Your dad's proud too. He's in a meeting right now, but you can bet he can't wait to tell all the programmers and developers about his pro gamer son."

"Mom, he can't tell anyone about the tournament before the reality show goes online. It's in the contract and everything."

She nodded. "He knows that, hon. Don't worry. The big secret is safe with us. We're excited. That's all. When the show is finally on, we'll have a viewing party and everything."

When Rogan first heard about the *Laser Viper* Final Challenge, he had figured his parents would be interested, but he never thought they'd be this excited about it all. He never expected a party. He frowned. What if he was eliminated after the next round? Then his family would watch the show about the tournament, knowing he had already lost.

It was as if his mother read his thoughts. "You just focus on doing the best you can. Have fun. You and your dad. Gaming is your life!" She looked down for a moment, and although Rogan couldn't see her phone off camera, he recognized that slight dulling of her eyes, the distance between what she was thinking about and where she was. Twitter update or text message. She seemed to realize Rogan was waiting. "Sorry. I'm being horrible." She tapped at her phone. "This is a . . . Just a second." Finally she looked up and smiled. "Sorry. Crazy news day. Have you heard—" Her expression froze on screen.

"Oh, come on," Rogan said. He wondered how this place could have state-of-the-art gaming equipment, how Atomic Frontiers could build an entire advanced space station, but not be able to get a decent connection for a simple video call.

"—basically about that." She sighed. "More connection problems? That's been a big problem across the—" She froze, mouth open and eyelids lowered in a weird expression. He would have laughed if the situation weren't so frustrating, if this weren't the only chance to talk to his mom for who knew how long.

The video resumed and Rogan asked quickly, before the system could freeze up again, "How's Wiggles? Does he miss me? Will you give him a treat for me?"

Mom laughed. "Wiggles is fine. He absolutely misses you. He goes to your bedroom to check for you every night."

"Will you pet him so he doesn't get too lonely?" Rogan asked.

"I will pet him. And I will make sure he gets plenty of treats."

Rogan tried to tell her about the most recent gaming round, about how he and Shaylyn had been gamer rivals for so long, and how he'd totally come out ahead, and how he never thought they'd find the target in the woods and the castle. But the connection kept stalling, and finally they were both ready to give up. They said their goodbyes, and Rogan, discouraged and a little lonely, disconnected early.

"How was your crappy call home?" Shaylyn asked Rogan when he returned to the commons.

"Mom might as well have sent me a photograph," said Rogan.

"Mine froze up a lot too," Jackie said. "I asked X about it. He said they were working on the problem."

Shaylyn sipped her Orange-a-Tang PowerSlam energy drink. "How does it feel to be the last dude, Ro?"

Rogan shrugged. "Fine." He didn't care who he was up against, boys or girls. But he did care that he basically couldn't call home.

His irritation must have showed, because Shay zeroed in on it the way their vipers might establish a target lock. "You don't look fine. Only guys have been cut from this contest so far. I think you're worried you'll be the next one to go home." The cameras must have picked up on the tension as well because two cambots approached.

Rogan wanted to appear as if he didn't care what she said, but the harder he tried to be casual, the more uncomfortable he was sure he looked. "I'm going home only after I win this thing."

Shaylyn didn't appear convinced. She kept up her snarky smile. "So I'll probably be leaving with Jackie, since she'll be up against me in the finals after you lose next round."

"Can you two please leave me out of this?" Jackie said.

Rogan would have continued the old adversarial banter, were he not feeling so weird about that messed-up vid call. He flicked his hand like he was brushing away a fly. "Whatever. I'll be in my room."

Jacqueline followed him, catching up to him just before he reached the door. She handed him her hacked VR headset and its cheap gamer gloves, using her body to block anyone or anything that might be watching. "You looked kind of down, like maybe you'd like to get out of here for a while."

Rogan watched Jackie, wondering if this was a trick, if she was trying to get him caught with the VR set so he'd be in trouble and maybe kicked out of the contest. But no. They'd spent a lot of time together so far in this tournament and he was starting to get to know her. She was just being cool, being Jackie.

"Thanks," he whispered. She was right.

Minutes later, Rogan was in his bathroom, an ever greater separation from the constant camera presence than his camera-free bedroom. He set out the two small, cheap VR room sensors, slipped on the glasses and gloves, and adjusted the headphones over his ears before turning it on.

Then . . . he was on his way to Virtual City.

Even though heading into digi-space was as routine for him as checking for implant software updates, this time his hands were clammy and his heart pounded. He knew he was really in his private dorm bathroom, but he felt like he was making some daring escape from Atomic Frontiers headquarters. There was an old virtual reality gaming classic called *Escape from Alcatraz* which, even though it seemed pretty primitive by now, still managed to thrill when you played it, and this was like that times a hundred.

And yet, for all the excitement of sneaking around, Rogan found himself, seconds later, on the corner of Nintendo Avenue and 834th Street on a regular day in Virtual City.

Normal traffic rolled by. A Ford Model T. A Back to the Future DeLorean. A car shaped like a big unicorn with wheels where its hooves should be. The usual thing. He took in a deep breath, and somehow he could smell a difference in the air, even though he knew that should be impossible.

"It's good to be home," he said, and started the long walk toward his apartment. The room sensors that came with this crappy VR set barely worked and didn't pick up his in-place walking very well, so his movement felt a little like one of those terrible dreams in which he was trying to run but his legs wouldn't function. He thought about hailing a cab, but then figured it'd be best to avoid spending any game credits, just in case Atomic Frontiers could somehow track the transaction to figure out he'd been to Virtual City. After all, they owned a lot of the taxis here.

It didn't matter. It was simply great to be back in his other hometown. His legal residence of record may have been in Seattle, but he felt far more comfortable here in Virtual City than down near Pike Place Market or over by the Space Needle. Virtual City had a Space Needle that was so big, it literally reached up to space.

But after he'd walked several blocks, he started to notice something was not quite right. Ad screens were common all over the city, like Times Square in New York, except the whole town was like that. But instead of the usual ads targeting each individual user's interests and online search patterns, most of the signs were now scrolling information updates about the disturbances. *Technical difficulties expected to subside soon. Aberrations are a minor temporary fault that will soon be corrected. All interrupted transactions will be refunded.*

A few more blocks down the street, a massive protest was well on its way to becoming a riot. People of all kinds—Russians, Chinese, Canadians, vampires, knights in armor, superheroes—were all throwing a fit, demanding the system be repaired.

"I was planning on proposing to my girlfriend!" one man shouted. "Then the restaurant we were in digi-scrambled and her whole account was deleted. No reason. I've never met her in the real world. I don't know how to find her!"

A tall woman-giraffe hybrid towered above the others, complaining about her critically important investor meeting that had been interrupted. "It's hard enough to line up people to attend in the first place. When everyone in the building freezes until people log out, they don't usually come back!"

"This is the end!" A man with a long beard and flowing robes held up a wooden staff and shouted in a vain effort to get people's attention. "For it was foretold in the second chapter of the Book of Digitization: 'And lo, these shall be signs unto you, of the coming compocalypse. Accounts shall freeze and avatars shall be deleted. And in the digital city, neighbor shall turn against neighbor, even as the fabric of their digital existence crumbles around them. And no backup of your data shall save you! No software patch will redeem you. Behold, the end times. . . .'"

"What's going on here?" Rogan asked an orange-skinned lizard man.

The lizard man flicked his tongue. "Oi! Where you been, mate?"

"That's hard to explain," Rogan said.

A man in a business suit and dark sunglasses rushed up to him. "Rogan Webber, I don't think you want to be here right now. You need to get back to the dorms."

Rogan took a step back. "What? How do you know where I am IRL?"

"I don't have time to explain. Log out of digi-space and get back to the dorm." The man took another step closer to him. "Now."

It wasn't super weird for someone in Virtual City to know his name. After all, the name floated around above him in his bio-bubble for everyone to see. But some stranger in Virtual City knowing where he was in the real world was scary, and for a long moment Rogan froze in terrified indecision.

"Log out *NOW!*" the man shouted.

Rogan yanked off the headset and held down the power button to force a hard logout. He sat on the edge of the bathtub, squeezing his Zelda shield pendant and trying to catch his breath. It was the first time he could remember feeling more comfortable in real life than logged in to digi-space.

CHAPTER 13

B ut there have been protests before," Jackie whispered at the table the next day after Rogan had huddled them all together to return the VR set to Jackie and tell them what had happened. "Riots and stuff."

"But that's not the weird part," Rogan said. "How did that guy know"—he glanced up at the cameras—"What he knew?"

"Maybe he didn't," Shay said. "There are a lot of crazies. He wasn't, like, totally specific."

They let the conversation drop and were happily surprised about half an hour later, when X came to take them to their next round of gaming.

"We're already starting the next round?" Jackie said. "That's fast."

"I'm not complaining," Shaylyn said.

"Let's do this," Rogan said, leading the way in pursuit of X toward the arena.

After the usual enthusiastic greeting from Sophia and Mr. Culum and a quick briefing, the three remaining gamers launched right into their next round of *Laser Viper*, this time, weirdly, without a combat drop from the SR-73 StarScreamer.

In moments they stood next to the Thames River in a game-simulated London at midnight. The square, castle-like buildings of Tower Bridge were lit up nearby over the river, and the ninety-five-floor skyscraper the Shard reached for the sky upstream. The three of them stood outside the walls of the fortress known as the Tower of London.

It wasn't much of a tower. They'd been shown a hologram of the entire fortress before starting this round of the game. The low castle structure had double walls laid out in a square that looked a little pinched together on the north side. A lot of different buildings were situated directly inside the inner wall, but the section that really stood out was the square White Tower in the center, three or four stories tall, with small towers in each corner.

Their objective was in a secret British military research base, the entrance to which was located under the White Tower. The best British military technology was developed there, including the device the three vipers were supposed to steal before Scorpion infiltrators got their hands on it. Rogan thought the scenario of Scorpion operatives infiltrating a foreign security force in order to steal an important piece of technology was getting old, but he supposed what Mr. Culum said was true. His engineers were doing all they could to get the incredibly detailed games programmed in time for each contest round and didn't have time to worry too much about the story.

The amazing device the vipers were supposed to rescue this time was the Velox Mercury X. It was the size and shape of a gallon paint can, but with a metal X fused to the top where a can's lid would be. It was capable of transmitting almost a thousand terabytes per second, enough for every digital TV show and movie on every Netflix cloud server in less than one minute. If Scorpion stole the Velox Mercury X before the laser vipers secured it, they could use it to hack computer systems and spread a devastating computer virus over a widespread area.

The three gamers were in an arena, wearing suits that put them in a simulated environment disguised as advanced fighter robots who were disguised as people. Rogan had to take a moment to run through it all in his head to get it straight. The Polyadaptive Nanotech Cloak, powered by the *Tian Li*, generated perfect alter identities for each of them. Bio-bubbles showed up on each viper's HUD to help the gamers spot one another. Anyone else would see Rogan as the uniformed Lieutenant Ericson, a twenty-four-year-old communications technician assigned to the base, Shaylyn as stocky Staff Sergeant Benton, in charge of the base's armory, and Jacqueline as water treatment specialist Corporal Carson, a compact man with flecks of white in his hair and wrinkles around the eyes.

"Problem number one," Shay said in Sergeant Benton's deep voice. "This is just weird for me looking and sounding like some guy. You know what I mean? It's going to take some getting used to. That's all I'm saying."

"What's the big deal? Just stay away from the beautiful women NPCs, and you'll be fine," Rogan said.

"Like this old guy could get a woman to notice him," Shay added. "Problem two. How are we supposed to get in there?"

Bright spotlights beamed on every inch of the fortress. "The place is lit brighter than the sun."

"Problem number three," said the man who was really Jackie. "In real life, London has about half a million surveillance cameras watching everybody everywhere. If they've set the game up like that, we might have a real challenge sneaking over the wall undetected."

Rogan watched the fortress. "If we move fast enough, maybe it won't matter if—"

"That's, like, your plan for everything, right?" Sergeant Benton spoke in a man's voice, but still sounded like Shay. "Charge in as fast as possible? Try to be the first one to reach the—"

"Just because you're always behind, always blown up in the first half of the—"

"Stop it!" Jackie grabbed the others by the arm and pulled them closer to her to get their attention. "Arguing won't get us anywhere. We are a team or we fail." She let go of their arms and spoke more quietly as a group of enthusiastic partiers passed them. "Farther down the path, there's more tree cover. It's not going to completely hide us, but it might be the best we can do."

"Should we go invisible?" Rogan asked.

"No way. Someone will see us disappear out here or reappear in there," Shaylyn said.

Jackie shook her head. "It's risky, but I think we should do it. Movement draws attention. It's why people wave. If we're standing still out here and blink out of sight, they might not notice. But three grown men leaping over that giant wall is more than enough movement to make people see us."

Rogan held out his hands, palms up to Shay as if to say, *See, I told you so.*

They started exploring and finally passed a big gatehouse, which stuck out from the rest of the wall much closer to the public walkway. It had round towers in the corner, one of which must have enjoyed a lot of shade in daylight hours from the nearby tree branch.

"There," Jackie said. "We go invisible, then rocket-jump up onto that tower. One more leap over the inner wall should get us inside."

They watched the walkway, waiting until they couldn't see anyone around. Then they flipped through their HUD menus to adjust their PNCs, and vanished. Their human disguises were replaced by only the faint wire-frame outline of their laser viper attack robots. "*Well, Flyer,*" said Rogan quietly. Once in invisibility mode their communication was internal only, silent to anyone but the vipers. "*You wanted action. Here we go. You want to fly ahead and scout the area for us, warn us if anyone's coming?*"

The outline of her body gave a thumbs-up. "*You got it.*" And she was gone, up over the wall, and out of sight. "*I have a heat signature on a security guard way down at the other end of the castle. Another couple up on a roof. But nobody right around here.*"

"*In real life, these would be the guards assigned to protect the crown jewels,*" said Engineer. "*So let's not be thinking they're like average mall cops. Plus, they said our PNCs draw too much power, so our weapons won't work with our disguises active. Hold back and wait for us.*"

Rogan rocket-jumped up to the tower on the gatehouse, grabbing the parapet at the edge and hoisting himself up effortlessly.

Engineer joined him a moment later. "OK," Rogan said. "*It's a lot farther to the inside when you're up here in person than when looking at a map.*" Engineer didn't wait for him but moved across the roof, walking carefully, not running, probably to keep the noise down. She led the way, climbing up atop a small square tower in the opposite corner and from there leaping to a big, round building on the inner wall and then down to the ground. Ranger and Flyer joined her.

"*Stop!*" Jackie grabbed Ranger's arm. She risked one more step to take hold of Flyer as well. "*Nobody move.*"

"*What's the problem?*" Flyer asked.

Engineer's sensors were lit up with infrared lasers, crisscrossing lines of light, waiting for someone to set off an alarm.

"*Trip beams,*" Jackie said. "*Everywhere. Cross one of them, and security will be on us in moments.*"

"*All I see is the yellow line in my HUD, directing me toward the objective,*" Ranger said.

"*My viper mod has better scanners,*" Jackie explained. "*Trust me, there are a lot more lines. If we run into the wrong one, it will be total mission failure.*"

"*I'll just go above them,*" Flyer said.

Jackie shook her head, a nearly useless gesture while invisible. "*Some of the beams are up off the ground. You'll fly right through them. You both need to follow me. Exactly. Step where I step. Walk the way I walk.*"

"*I can barely see you,*" Ranger said.

Flyer shoved him. "*Then we'll stay close together.*"

So the three gamers made an awkward procession, almost bumping into one another as they took big steps, small steps, high steps, and ducked down low across the grass toward the big castle building in the center of it all.

But although their movement was weird, it was short, and basically easy. In no time they were up a set of wooden stairs to the entrance of the White Tower.

"I'm going to guess the door is locked," Ranger said.

"Good guess." Jackie smiled and deployed a specialized tool from her left wrist, a small cylinder with hundreds of micromotorized metal filaments on the end, like a frayed wire brush or mop, visible only to her, appearing in a sort of transparent green in her field of vision. Carefully easing it into the lock, she let the device perform its function, the motorized filaments probing the lock's interior, manipulating the heavy tumblers within.

A quiet metallic scrape.

A dull click.

She swung the door open, and the gamers stepped into the dimly lit ancient structure, a cold, heavy quiet hanging from the stone walls.

-----o-----

Inside, the yellow line visible only on their HUDs turned to the right and led them through a large open hallway, the walls of which were adorned with displays of old battle armor and weapons. Around another corner to the right and they passed through a door into a great stone chapel.

"*You picking up any more security sensors?*" Flyer spoke in a whisper, even though they were all still locked into internal comms. The place inspired that kind of respect. With round white stone columns rising up into arches beneath a dome and only a few lights illuminating the simple chapel, the place felt like it might sound with ancient echoes of hymns or like the ghost of an armored knight might step out from between the columns.

"*We're clear,*" Engineer said. The yellow guide line led to the corner on the left side at the other end of the chapel. "Secret elevator is right up here."

"*Let's drop the invisibility,*" said Rogan. "*If they see us opening and closing elevator doors, it will look weirder if they see nobody there than for it to be three guys who work in the base.*"

The three gamers reverted to their former digital disguises and stepped over the red velvet rope that cordoned off the chapel. "Getting into the elevator might be tricky," Engineer said out loud in Corporal Carson's voice. "Judging by infrared scans, it's hidden behind this stone wall, thinner and lighter than the rest of the wall, but still not something we can easily get through."

"Who're you lot, then?" A thick Cockney accent cut the quiet from behind them, echoing menacingly off the walls. The three gamers spun to face a tall, thin man with the beginnings of a beard and a private security contractor uniform, gripping the handle of his holstered gun. "Nobody's s'posed to be in here a' this hour."

"We work down below," Rogan said in his disguised voice.

Engineer switched to internal comms. "*It's a secret base. He might not know about it.*"

"Wha? Down in the dungeons? Come off it, mate. You lot are in big trouble." He reached for the radio clipped to his belt.

Rogan charged the guard, wound up, and cracked his fist hard into the man's jaw. The guard's head spun to the side, followed by his body. Red blood splattered the white wall, and the man collapsed to the worn stone floor.

Engineer and Flyer looked at him, their digi-disguised faces impassive but their arms open in surprise. All three of them could easily see the guard's life signs readout, but the abrupt brutality of Ranger's attack had surprised the other two.

"What?" Rogan said. "Weapons don't work while our PNCs are on. Couldn't let him call for help."

"We should hide him," Flyer said. "Maybe behind one of the armor displays?"

"No time for that," said Rogan. "Who knows when this guy is due to check in. We do this mission fast and get out of here before he's missed."

In any other normal video game, they would have just taken the guy out, and his body would disappear after they'd walked out of range. This *Laser Viper* tournament had been different. NPCs who would be completely out of the action in other games were still a factor in tournament play.

"Let's at least hide him behind the altar." Flyer was already dragging him to the hasty hiding spot.

Engineer opened the stone covering in the corner, revealing the steel doors of the elevator behind it.

"Locked," Engineer said. "My viper's computers are labeling this as a retina scanner. I know we look like people who work in this base, but I doubt the disguise is good enough to fool the scanner."

"Don't you have explosives for this?" Rogan asked. "Just explode the door?"

"That would set off every alarm in the tower," Flyer said.

"Half the alarms in the city," said Engineer. "I have some highly corrosive acid that might eat its way through these doors, but I bet it would still set off alarms. And it would blow our cover."

"Well, I guess they wouldn't have programmed this scanner in, if it didn't work," Rogan said. He leaned down to position his eye before the lens. "How does it work, do I just—" He pressed a button at the base of the panel.

"*Identify for retina scan*," said a flat computer voice.

A red beam flooded Rogan's vision. Did he need to keep his own eye open? Would the PNC-generated eye stay open for the scan? His Ranger viper didn't even have eyes.

"*Error,*" the computer said. "*Retina scan incomplete. Please stand by for base security.*"

"*Leftenant Ericson.*" The woman's voice coming from the speaker was sharp. "*What are you doing on the surface? At this hour?*"

Rogan didn't know what to say. Flyer elbowed him. "Um, we just went out . . ." The only thing he had going for him now was that his voice disguise included a British accent.

"You went out to get a pint." X's voice came over the channel. *"You couldn't take it down there and needed a break."*

". . . out for a pint," Rogan said. "We needed a break."

"Well, leftenant," said the woman, *"if you think I enjoy a fortnight monitoring security on the graveyard shift, you are sadly mistaken. All of you — yes, you too, Sergeant Benton, Corporal Carson — are in serious trouble. Now because our scanner is on the blink, I have to check you in myself."* The elevator doors slid open and the gamers climbed in. *"Have your bloody IDs ready as soon as you step off the lift."*

"Don't worry about it, gamers," X said calmly over their channel. *"I'm sending your Polyadaptive Nanotech Cloaks special programming to produce identification cards. Act like you are reaching into your pockets, and when you bring your hands back up, your disguise will appear to be holding a card. Just don't hand the card to her. The PNC has a very limited range for producing an illusion."*

When the elevator finally stopped and opened, the three of them stepped out into a rectangular room with concrete walls, floor, and a low ceiling. Fluorescent tube lights hummed above them, casting a dull glow over the British flag and some wooden, high-backed benches by the walls. A large oval-shaped steel hatch with a heavy door was bolted to the concrete at the far end of the chamber.

A military officer stood waiting for them in a uniform of a shade of gray slightly darker than the walls, captain insignia on her shoulders, shiny black boots, red-gold hair pulled back tightly, and a Glock 17 9mm handgun holstered on her belt. The name on her chest read STAR.

"You know the regs." Captain Star folded her arms. "ID cards. Now." The three disguised gamers held up their illusion IDs. The captain barely looked at them. Apparently the cards were only a formality, and she waved them away. She pointed at Flyer. "Sergeant Benton, I am still waiting on that inventory of the armory. You have enough time to be gallivanting about London but can't get your work done?"

Flyer was about to respond, but Captain Star kept going. "And you," she said to Rogan. "You're supposed to be on duty in the communications room at zero one. Less than an hour! If you fall asleep at your post, I will catch you, and you will be punished." To Engineer she added, "One more slipup from you, and I'll have you do a level-four purge of the secondary *and* tertiary water filters, along with a complete changeover with the filters in operation now, all by yourself."

"We're really sorry," Rogan said. He saw the captain's expression harden further and remembered the military games he had played, adding, "Ma'am."

Captain Star seemed to relax a little after that, and Rogan was impressed with how interactive this game was, that they'd figured out how to make this NPC react to his remembering to talk military.

"I'm on duty in the security room. I need to get back there. But I promise, any more violations from any of you, and you'll be demoted and reassigned." She spun on her heel and left through the hatch.

"Where do we go from here?" Flyer asked quietly.

Engineer didn't hesitate but rushed to a computer terminal. A computer data probe emerged from her human-looking finger, plugging into an access point. She stood there for a long time.

"Jackie?" Flyer asked after a while.

"Hold on," said Engineer. "Some serious firewalls on this system. I'm running hacking protocols. It's pretty much automatic, part of my mod's onboard computer package. But I can't just attack their system with full force or I'll trip alarms."

"I get it," Flyer said. "But if we are in here much longer, that angry woman is going to come back."

"Bingo," Engineer said. "I have the layout of the entire facility. Sending you the map now."

A blue-green 3-D holographic image of a series of interconnected rooms popped up at the side of Rogan's HUD. They had entered on level two of a three-level compound that consisted of modular rooms deep under the Tower of London and the Thames River. Most of the rooms were pressed right next to each other like in any other building, but some, like the screening room they were in now, were connected via giant steel tunnels, pipes with flat floors welded in.

Level two appeared to be where the crew lived. Through the tunnel was the kitchen and conference module, followed by the rec room and library, then the barracks followed by a latrine module.

A vertical tunnel from the kitchen/conference room led down to one section of level three, the Queen's Quarters, probably a private living space for the royal family or other important officials in the event of emergency. The other section of level three was accessed by a ladder going down from the latrine at the back of floor two. That was the largest part of the base, with adjoining modules for a laboratory, workshop, and a large room for an electric generator, air filter, and water purification.

Level one, the closest to the surface, consisted of three separate module rooms connected by tunnels. Main security was in the center, and from there a tunnel led to the communications room, and another led to the armory.

"Good work, Jackie," Flyer said.

Rogan switched to internal comms. "*The Velox Mercury X must be in the communications room or the laboratory. I'm supposed to be on duty in about twenty minutes.*"

"*Which means you have less than twenty minutes until the real Lieutenant Ericson shows up,*" said Flyer. "*I'll go to the armory. I guess it's possible the target is locked up there, but maybe I could keep them from getting to their guns in case something goes wrong. Anyway, Captain Star is probably watching us right now, and she'll be less suspicious if I go to my post.*"

"*I guess Corporal Carson works down in the engine room,*" said Engineer. "*I'll search the lab on the way there.*"

"If Captain Star is watching us on cameras, she might wonder why the two of you are going to work in the middle of the night," Rogan said. "And why we're standing here, saying nothing out loud."

"*Then we'd better hurry,*" Flyer said. "*Might have to stun Captain Star.*"

Suddenly there was a high-pitched beep. Static pop and hiss. "*—another signal infiltration test. Gamers, if you can hear this, do not say anything. Clap your hands twice.*"

The three gamers looked at one another. It sounded like Takashi. Rogan had spent enough time stuck in the dorms with that guy to recognize his voice anywhere. Finally, all three of them clapped twice. They'd all heard it.

"*Continue the mission like normal,*" the intruder voice said.

"*What are you three waiting for?!*" X exploded onto the channel. "*You're wasting time!*"

"Right. Let's get moving," Rogan said out loud in Lieutenant Ericson's British accent.

Putting aside their confusion, the three gamers went through the tunnel into the kitchen module, a slightly larger concrete room with all the basic appliances one would expect, only the rectangular table there was much larger than any of their tables at home, and could easily seat sixteen. Not wanting to draw any more attention to themselves, they were careful to abide by the instruction printed on plaques by every entrance and exit: STANDING ORDERS: CLOSE ALL HATCHES AFTER USE.

From the kitchen they entered a somewhat cozier room, with floor-to-ceiling bookshelves on every wall except for a break in one wall for a TV and an ancient PlayStation 4. Here, there were puffy couches and chairs, and two tables for playing cards and games.

"*This is where we split up,*" Flyer said internally. She nudged Engineer's arm. "*You going to be OK on your own?*"

"As I'll ever be," Jackie said out loud. She left the other two at the ladder leading up to level one, and she continued through the next hatch into the dark barracks. Fortunately, she could easily see in the dark as she walked down the central aisle between the two rows of bunk beds. Near the middle she spotted the real Corporal Carson, the man she was imitating. She hoped Captain Star had no cameras watching the barracks, or that if she did, they couldn't see in the dark.

Jackie froze when she opened the door at the end of the room and the man in the closest bunk grunted, smacked his lips, and rolled over. Confident he was still asleep, she closed the hatch, passed through the latrine, and headed down the ladder into the laboratory.

-----o-----

"What are you doing up, Sergeant Benton?" Captain Star said to Shay as she emerged from the hatch into the security room. It was an impressive setup, with nine screens on one wall, rotating camera feeds from the ceilings of nine different rooms in the compound. On another wall, a computer screen displayed the status of alarms and other security systems and environmental controls.

It took Shaylyn a moment to remember that Captain Star was an advanced NPC and was expecting an answer. "I thought . . . I mean, I felt bad for breaking the rules. I figured I'd get that inventory done for you as fast as I can."

"Don't think this will get you out of your standard duty shift," said the captain.

"No, ma'am," Shaylyn said.

Ranger, disguised as Lieutenant Ericson, emerged from the hatch in the security room floor next. "I'm on duty soon. I might as well get started early."

Shay gave Ranger a small nod and went through the hatch and down the tunnel to the armory. A big cement room just like the others, the walls were lined with steel cages filled with weapons, and another row of gun lockers ran down the middle, splitting the space into two aisles. Her viper's system identified the weapons as she looked at them. A dozen old M4 rifles. Fifteen Glock 17 9mm handguns. Ten Uzi submachine guns. Six third-generation Compact High-Energy Laser rifles with modular power cells and high-resolution targeting scopes. A case of twenty-four fragmentation grenades. A case of twenty-four thermal grenades. Another twenty-four EMP grenades. More weapons on down the line. But no Velox.

"Oi! What do you think you're—" The voice that had come from behind her halted as soon as she turned around. Staff Sergeant Benton—the *real* Staff Sergeant Benton—stood right in front of her, gaping at an exact image of himself staring back at him. "Who are you, then?" He didn't hesitate but began drawing his gun.

-----o-----

Rogan entered the communications room. "I know I'm not due to come on duty for a while, but I was already awake. You can go to bed."

"Hey, thanks, mate," the man sitting at the desk behind the computer said. "I had to keep slapping myself in the face to stay awake." He stood up, stretched, and patted Rogan on the shoulder. "Blimey!" He shook his hand in the air a little. "You been working out, have you? Rock solid, mate."

When he was gone and had closed the hatch behind him, Rogan scanned the comm room. From this place the operators had access to radio communications on all frequencies from FM to civilian band to shortwave. A large video camera and professional microphone setup was ready before a wooden desk in front of a British flag backdrop.

Rogan figured this whole facility was supposed to be like one of those nuclear bomb shelters he'd seen in *Fallout*. From here, government officials could communicate with survivors on the surface.

He carefully checked the whole room over, searching for the Velox Mercury X, watching the clock, worrying about when the real Lieutenant Ericson would be reporting for duty.

-----o-----

Jackie quickly descended to level three. In the dim standby lighting, she headed for the switch to light up another plain concrete box, this one lined with workbenches and shelves along the walls, a larger worktable in the center. Computers and other scientific tools everywhere. Instantly, her viper's onboard scanners began identifying hardware and equipment. Microscopes, electron microscopes, burners, beakers, graduated cylinders, hundreds of different chemicals, scales, thermometers, circuit boards and electronic components of all kinds, charts with complex figures, computers in every corner, and some custom devices her own computer didn't recognize. The lab was a scientist's dream, but it wasn't Jackie's dream, because even after searching every cupboard, the Velox was nowhere to be found. She sighed and hurried to search the adjacent workshop, worried she was taking too long and the alarm would sound any moment.

-----o-----

Shaylyn didn't think but cranked back her fist and cracked the real Sergeant Benton in the jaw. His head whipped to the side and he flew back into the wall. Shay was about to send an internal comms call to the others and run to stun Captain Star in case she was watching it all on camera, but although Sergeant Benton wasn't the biggest man, he was tough, because he came back with a hard jab to Shay's chest.

A sickening crunch-crack. Sergeant Benton stepped back, clutching his hand, his face twisted in pain, his thumb and fingers at horrific wrong angles.

In all the games she'd ever played, Shaylyn had shot people, killed people, cut enemies down with swords, exploded whole buildings, but she had never been in so realistic a fight. And judging from the way she felt, punching this NPC, physically throwing her fist, her game suit putting slight pressure on her knuckles, the micromotors in her suit abruptly stopping the forward motion of her swing when her punch hit home, she never ever wanted to be in a real fight.

The hatch to the armory was closed, but would that be enough to muffle the man's eventual, inevitable screams? She doubted it. And though there was a chance Captain Star wasn't watching the armory on camera right now, there would be no chance she wouldn't hear the shouts.

Shaylyn had no choice. She had to drop her disguise so that she could power her weapons and stun this man.

The real Sergeant Benton's expression changed from pain to shock as the computer-generated duplicate of Sergeant Benton digi-melted away, revealing a sleek, aerodynamic robot that raised its arm and fired one blue-white electrocrackling stun pulse.

-----o-----

"All right, Murphy, you can get some sleep now." The real Lieutenant Ericson spoke while closing and latching the hatch behind him. He turned to face his doppelgänger. "I'll take over from— What the—"

The real Lieutenant Ericson froze as Rogan's digital disguise faded out to reveal the Ranger viper. In the next moment Rogan dropped Ericson with an NLEP, then sprinted for the security room.

He made it to the end of the tunnel and cranked the wheel to unlatch the hatch to the security room, knowing it was already taking him too long, that Captain Star would have more than enough time to call for help.

But when he rushed into the security room, he found Flyer standing over Star's unconscious form. "Way ahead of you, Ranger. As usual. Any luck in the communications room?"

"No," Rogan said. "I checked every inch of the place twice. The target isn't in there."

"Engineer?" Flyer said. "What d'you got?"

"I'm still searching," Engineer said. *"There's a lot of equipment down here. The rooms are huge."*

One of the panels at the security station beeped. *"Excalibur Base, Excalibur Base, this is tower security."* Ranger and Flyer looked at each other for a moment. *"Excalibur Base, this is tower security. Captain Star, please respond."*

"We have to answer them," Flyer said.

"How?! They want to talk to the captain that you just stunned unconscious," Rogan said, panic swelling up inside him.

"Use the PNC!" Engineer said. *"That's what it's designed for!"*

"Right." Rogan crossed his fingers and hurried to flip through the menus on his HUD. "Shay, head down there to help her."

"Excalibur Base, respond or we'll be forced to declare Code Black and initiate final emergency security protocol."

"Hurry!" Flyer said, heading down the ladder.

Rogan found the right section of the menu and activated his Polyadaptive Nanotech Cloak to become Captain Star. "Just go help Jackie find the transmitter thing," he said in the captain's British accent. "I've got this."

He hoped he had it. He searched the board for what might be the transmit button. Finally he guessed and flipped a switch. "This is Excalibur Base."

A sigh came over the open channel. *"What is your status?"*

"Everything is fine," Rogan said. How could he sound more official? "We just had our regular shift change. Is there a problem?" That was good, Rogan thought — pretending to be concerned about security would make it seem less likely that anything was going wrong down here. He smiled. Most of the games Rogan played were all about shooting or racing. Hardly any of them had complicated interactive voice features like this.

"We have a breach. One of our guards didn't check in on time. We found him knocked unconscious in the White Tower. We're going to Condition Two. It doesn't look like the intruder has infiltrated Excalibur Base, but protocol calls for an extra squad to be sent down to reinforce you."

"I don't think that's necessary," Rogan tried. "I'm watching the cameras, and nothing's out of the ordinary."

"I know. But you know how it is. Orders are orders. And it's better to be overcautious than unprepared."

"Right," Rogan said. "Um, I'll have some tea on for your men."

The man on the line laughed. *"Understood, Excalibur Base. Tower security, out."*

As soon as Rogan had clicked out of the call with security, he looked up at one of the screens and saw the armed soldiers enter the elevator. "Shay," Rogan said. "Forget going down to level three. In less than a minute, we're going to have a whole army squad down here."

"On it," Flyer said.

"Jackie," Rogan said. "They're onto us. We're running out of time. Have you found it yet?"

-----◇-----

A trembling, cold fear cut up through Jacqueline. She'd searched the laboratory and workshop very carefully but had found nothing. What was this? In the entire history of the Zelda games, over two dozen adventures, there had never been a dungeon harder than this. Was she supposed to search for secret passages?

"It's not down here," Jackie said to the others. "It doesn't make sense!"

"Keep looking," Flyer called back. *"You must have missed it. It has to be down there."*

"I'm going to need some help," Jackie said.

"I'm a little busy up here!" Flyer shouted.

-----◇-----

Having floated down the ladder shaft from the security center on level one to the library on the second floor and then flown through the kitchen and into the tunnel to the screening room, Shaylyn arrived just as the elevator doors opened and seven soldiers in camouflaged uniforms stepped out.

"What *is* that thing?!" one soldier shouted.

A second soldier wasted no time with words but drew what Shay's computers identified as a Glock 17 9mm handgun and pulled the trigger, the shots exploding louder than a truckload of dynamite inside the tightly enclosed concrete chamber.

WARNING: INCOMING SMALL ARMS FIRE.

A round hit her shoulder, like someone had punched her. She fired two NLEPs, stunning one soldier but missing the other.

The whole squad fired. Her game suit made it feel as though dozens of hammers were hitting her.

WARNING: MODERATE ARMOR DAMAGE.

"Where's Healer when you need him?" Shay said to herself. She flew at the squad feetfirst, kicking two of the soldiers in the head, stunning another two as she passed. She zapped one of the last two standing, but the other soldier smashed right into her. He would have tackled her, but she flew up into the air, spun around, and slammed him into the concrete wall, breaking his hold on her.

He fell to the floor and reached for his weapon, but Shay stunned him before he could shoot. She took two more rounds to the back from the two she had kicked before she whipped around to stun them as well.

"It's an attack! Get to the armory!" a man shouted from deeper in the compound.

"The gunshots woke up the barracks," Shay called to the others. "They're on the way up to level one."

"*Got it covered*," Ranger said.

-----o-----

Jacqueline had checked over most of the generator room. Nothing but pipes, filter chambers, and electrical conduit. She shook her head. She hated getting stumped on games. Once she had nearly thrown her Xbox at the wall when playing *Halo 10* and was unable to figure out how to activate a bridge over a deep canyon. When playing at home, she could at least pause the game and look up the strategy guide online. No option like that here. Worse, the other two were handling all the hard stuff, and she was on her own, down here, accomplishing nothing. If she didn't start doing something, and soon, she'd be going home after this round.

"One more scan," she said to herself, switching her vision to infrared in case it might help her recognize something she hadn't noticed before. If the target device were transmitting, it might pop hot on her scanners.

Giving her eyes a moment to adjust to the flood of colors in her field of vision—whites and oranges for warm objects, down through purple and deep blue for cooler temperatures—she didn't locate the target, but she did see a big square in the wall at the back of the room. It was a yellowish green, starkly different from the blue that made up the rest of the concrete wall.

Back in normal vision, she felt around the edge of the square, and there it was, a small piece of concrete that swung open on a hinge to grant access to a handle, which Jackie pulled, to open a door to a secret vault.

And inside, on a shelf in plain sight, was the Velox Mercury X.

"I found it!" she called to the others. She picked up the device and started her way back. She was in the game once again.

-----o-----

"That's great!" Rogan said when he heard Engineer's news. He and Flyer had just stunned the last of the base personnel. "Let's get out of here."

"Excalibur Base, this is tower security." The voice came over the speaker, more urgent this time.

Rogan checked the feed for the camera covering the chapel in the White Tower on the surface. Three heavily armed and armored squads were staged there now, a few of them carrying High-Energy Armor-Piercing lasers. Even if the three vipers rushed out of the elevator, all guns blazing, they'd be melted down in seconds by all that firepower concentrated on the small elevator space. "Hey there, gamers," Rogan said. "I think time's up. They're onto us. A ton of soldiers at the gate. Anyone have any ideas about how to get out of here?"

"Excalibur Base, this is tower security. Our squad did not comply with orders to immediately check in. Standard operating procedure requires we assume you are compromised. Be advised, we are commencing final emergency protocol."

Rogan called to the others, "They just radioed down here, saying something about final emergency protocol."

"What's that?" Flyer said.

The piercing *Oh-ooooh-gah! Oh-ooooh-gah!* wail of an emergency Klaxon filled the confined chambers of the entire compound. A recording of a calm female voice came over the speakers. *"Warning. This facility is compromised and scheduled for flooding in sixty seconds. Evacuate immediately and surrender to security personnel on the surface. Warning. This facility is* compromised and scheduled for flooding in fifty-one seconds. Evacuate immediately . . ."

"OK, I figured out what the final emergency protocol is!" Rogan said.

"Yeah, no kidding!" Flyer said. "Everybody get to the elevator!"

Rogan started down the ladder from level one to level two. "They have the elevator covered. They'll blast us as soon as the doors open."

"Then what are we going to do?" Flyer asked.

"Warning! This facility is compromised and scheduled for flooding in twenty-six seconds. Evacuate immediately and surrender . . ."

"The generator!" Engineer shouted. "Get down to level three right now!"

"We can't go deeper!" Flyer said. "We have to—"

"Now!" Engineer shrieked.

Rogan had joined Flyer on level two. He grabbed her arm and pulled her out of the library and through the barracks to the hatch in the floor in the back of the latrine. A ladder there led down to level three.

". . . scheduled for flooding in eleven seconds. Evacuate immediately and . . ."

"The base is under the Thames," Flyer said as she and Rogan reached level three. "The whole place will flood, like, instantly."

When they reached the final room on the bottom level, they found Engineer on top of the semitrailer-sized electrical generator. She opened a hatch on her chest, pulled out a glob of gray-white clay, placed the Velox Mercury X device inside the cavity, and resealed her chest. She didn't waste a second but fashioned the clay into a ribbon around a large pipe above the generator. Before it was halfway around, and just as he and Flyer joined her atop the giant machine, she pulled them both down so they all lay flat and away from the pipe.

"*. . . scheduled for flooding in five, four . . .*"

Shrapnel blasted everywhere.

WARNING: MINOR IMPACT DAMAGE.

Engineer pointed to the shredded remains of the pipe near the ceiling. "Up the exhaust duct—"

"*Flooding.*"

White water everywhere. Flyer soared up through the narrow exhaust pipe, the raging flood shooting up right behind her.

Room filled. Rogan upside down. Head smacked the wall, the floor, the generator. His body seized up hard, his game suit locking in position while the current bashed him around.

WARNING: ENVIRONMENTAL ELECTRICAL OVERCHARGE. MODERATE DAMAGE TO ARMOR.

Rogan fought the urge to hold his breath. The game simulator threw his body around and the images inside his VR helmet completed the illusion, but he forced himself to remember he wouldn't drown. He was in the arena. There wasn't really any water.

"*Can you hear me? You guys?*" Flyer called to them.

"*Hang on!*" Rogan called back. "*Water's rushing around in here like crazy!*"

He deployed his close combat claws and punched a steel piece of machinery as hard as he could, piercing deep and stopping his tumbling movement. He was in one piece, but Jackie hadn't been so lucky. She'd been closer to the exploding pipe and she didn't have the kind of armor with which Ranger was equipped. Her leg was sheared off at the thigh. Pockmarks from shrapnel scored through her back. Her right arm was twisted around and useless. Right then, Rogan missed Healer's confident *I can fix that.*

"*Ro?! Jackie?!*" Flyer tried again.

Rogan spotted the exhaust vent in the ceiling above. Would his grappling cables even work underwater? There was no better time to test them out. Reaching up with his left arm, he fired the cable, making a secure connection partway up the shaft. He was anchored with the cable but knew that when he pulled his claws out of the machinery in front of him, the water would push him all around. He had to hurry. If the damage to Engineer was allowing water to get to the Velox Mercury X, the mission could be in big trouble.

He fought the current, trying to adjust his shot with his other cable to compensate for the force of the water. He fired, and the line whipped out, catching Engineer in the back. A second later, he retracted both cables, pulling the remains of Engineer and himself up to the exhaust vent. They bumped around at the torn-up edge of the shaft before he maneuvered both of them into the narrow space. When he had pulled Engineer up next to him, her arm locked around his neck.

"I'm barely functional," Engineer said. *"But I can hold on."*

Rogan looked up the exhaust conduit and spotted Flyer coming back down. *"I've got Jackie. She has the target. Get to exfil elevation!"*

Flyer shot up out of the tube. Rogan put his exfil rockets on overdrive and blasted off right behind her. A few red-hot laser beams cut across the black of the London night sky as the three laser vipers soared up above the ring of police cars and emergency vehicles, lights flashing around the Tower of London, but the three of them were clear in seconds.

"Good job, gamers!" X said. *"The StarScreamer is inbound to recover you."*

"oo!" Rogan couldn't help exclaiming as he removed his VR helmet at the end of the game. His flight harness disengaged automatically from his game suit and retracted to the ceiling, and he took a moment to get settled on the solid floor of the arena.

The girls removed their helmets too.

Shay shook out her blue-streaked hair, almost as if she were trying to get water out of it at the pool.

Rogan laughed. As convincing as the game illusion was, he'd expected to be dripping wet as well. Instead he was only a little sweaty from running around in the warm game suit. "That was awesome! I've played some flooded castles in *Lost Cities* and had to swim in *Call of Duty*." He sidestepped a cambot that was already buzzing around him and went to join the others. "But when that room flooded?! Whoa! I've always wondered what it felt like to take a spin in the washing machine." He laughed. The other two laughed with him, but Rogan noticed Jackie wasn't as enthusiastic. He wondered if she worried about being cut from the tournament since, once again, she'd been damaged so badly at the end. He had kind of saved her, and therefore saved the mission since the target was inside her viper's empty explosives chamber, so he was pretty sure he was safe.

But as the three of them stood there, he remembered how the others had done. Flyer, not Ranger, had fought off the tower security soldiers who had come down to check out the base. She had stunned most of the base personnel. And Jackie had actually found the Velox data transmitter in the first place, as well as their way out.

Could he be the one in trouble in the contest? But no. If he hadn't pulled the busted-up Engineer out of there, they would have lost.

All three of them had played crucial parts in this round. They'd succeeded in the mission as a team.

The double doors slid open in front of them, and Mr. Culum led Sophia and X into the arena. The first two smiled enthusiastically. The third did not.

X seemed . . . what? Rogan wondered. Worried? Nervous. The big guy shot a look at Mr. Culum, but then, cracking his knuckles, turned his attention to the gamers.

Mr. Culum clapped his hands. "Gamers! Gamers, gamers! In all my years in the business, I have surveyed thousands of video games. I have played hundreds myself and watched the best players in the world take on hundreds more. Your ability to adapt to different types of gameplay, from tough combat drops, to landing on that single Chinese battleship way out in the middle of the ocean, to the fierce firefights claiming the Polyadaptive Nanotech Cloak, to this, the careful subterfuge, barely escaping the base security measures."

He laughed, shaking his head in what seemed like disbelief.

"And all three of you have kept your objective in mind! A lot of gamers with twice your age and experience would have just shot

at everything, every piece of tech and every NPC they saw." He paused for a moment. "I like games that make players think. That's why I got into the computer and gaming industry in the first place. Because I wanted to challenge people to think more, to expand our idea for what is possible. That's why I'm experimenting with *Laser Viper*, turning it into a game like no other. The greatest game the world has ever known!"

Six cambots circled around him.

Sophia took advantage of his pause to congratulate the gamers as well. "I was as impressed as Mr. Culum," she said. "All three of you did such a great job." Her shoulders slumped a little. "Unfortunately only two of you can move on to the championship round. So Xavier will escort you back to the dorms. As usual, I'll call each of you into the interview room one at a time for our customary after-game talk. And by the time we're done, the decision will be made. But for now, you should all be very proud of yourselves! Super good job!"

Back in the dorms, the commons was decked out like a party—like the first time they had completed a mission and really felt like a team. A bowl of cheesy puffs, a tray of taquitos, all kinds of candy, a pizza, and an iced tub filled with cans of PowerSlam covered the table. Upbeat adventure music, the kind of sound that played in the background of action movies, echoed from speakers around the room.

On the giant screen, clips from the game showed off the best action of the last round. Rogan punching out the guard in the White Tower. Shay landing a perfect flying kick to take down two soldiers. Jackie prepping the cutting charge and exploding the generator exhaust vent.

"Xavier thought you deserved a celebration." Sophia spoke loudly to be heard over the music.

The gamers exchanged confused looks. But Rogan wasn't about to complain. He flopped down on the couch and popped the top on a Tangernado!-flavored PowerSlam, ready to relax, to celebrate with his fellow gamers, with his friends.

"Shaylyn?" Sophia said, standing next to the open door of the interview room. "You're up first."

Shaylyn said nothing but went with Sophia. When the door closed behind them, the party atmosphere felt diminished, not only because they were missing Shay, but because the beginning of the post-game interviews signaled they were one step closer to one of them going home.

SHAYLYN SPERO

Before I answer your question, can I just say that this is, like, the most fun I've ever had. The Flyer, like, barely ever gets into hand-to-hand fighting. In most games I fly recon or provide cover fire from the air. Fly rescue or carry other vipers up a cliff or something. I don't want to brag, but I had some awesome moves in this round. Like, boom, boom, boom, the bullets kept hitting me, but I took down that entire platoon or whatever. Gaming at home? If my laser viper gets hit, my gamer gloves vibrate a little bit. Like my little brother's baby rattle. But today, although obviously I'm glad bullets weren't really ripping through me, I could really feel where each one was hitting my viper. It's like I was the viper. And I was a pretty good one, all ninja and stuff. That's all I'm saying.

What? Oh yeah. That's, like, the hard part. I came into the contest to win it, to beat all the others and become the champion. But that's become harder and harder, you know? Because I've spent a lot of time with these people, and they're really cool, actually.

Yeah. I guess. Even Rogan. Even though he's still, like, a jerk sometimes, thinking he's all that.

But he is a great gamer. So is Jackie! And Takashi too. Beckett? Well, he might have been if he could have kept his temper under control. But I don't know who should be going home this time. Of course I want to move on to the championship. But I . . . I don't know . . . I wish all three of us could move on. Like, you know what I mean?

Back in the commons, Rogan and Jackie waited for their turns at talking head interviews.

"If the second-to-last gaming round in the tournament was that intense, I can't imagine what they have in mind for the championship. What could top that?" Rogan fingered his Zelda pendant.

Jackie moved closer to him on the couch, to the one place between the table and the sofa's high back, the only place in the whole complex besides the bedrooms and bathrooms where cambots could not go. That wouldn't stop the cameras mounted in the ceilings and walls, but maybe they were far enough away, and the music was loud enough, to cover their conversation.

She spoke quietly. "What was that stuff at the beginning of our time in the underground base? Clap your hands twice?"

"Oh yeah," Rogan said. "Forgot about that. Some kind of side quest, maybe? An Easter egg type thing? A voice cut in like that once for me on *Call of Duty: Alien Wars*. Turned out it was an alien trick. Maybe it was supposed to be a secret Scorpion message?"

"With Takashi's voice?"

Rogan chomped a cheesy puff and thought it over. "It sounded like him, but who knows? Maybe that was part of the Scorpion trick." The two of them munched treats in silence for a while. Then Rogan asked, "What do you think it was?"

Jackie shrugged but said nothing.

"Jacqueline?" Sophia chirped, returning to the dorms with Shay. "Let's go have a chat."

JACQUELINE SHARPE

Any of us. All of us, really. It was a team effort in this last round. We had a big base to search. It took all of us. Shay kept the soldiers off our backs. I found the device and our way out. Rogan helped get me out in the end. If any of us hadn't been there, the other two would have failed.

That's why I don't want to see anyone have to go home. They're my friends, and they deserve to be in the championship as much as I do. So I won't say who I think should move on to the finals with me.

But I really want to win this. I know not a lot of kids my age think about stuff like this, but I want to go to college someday. My parents said they'd pay for it if I keep my grades up, but one thing I learned rebuilding my Xbox is that I like relying on myself. My cousin has a PlayStation. He barely cares about it. Doesn't take care of it. Always wants something else. Me? My Xbox is my baby because I earned it.

I like earning my own stuff. When you're a kid, you have nothing. You live in a house your parents own, sleep in a bed they bought for you, and you have to do what they say. Like, it's the law. When you're twelve, you can't go out and get a job and buy an apartment or something. You can't even buy an apartment in Virtual City without parental consent. Everything comes from Mom and Dad.

I love my parents. That's why I don't want them to have to pay for my school. I want to take care of myself. They love helping me, but they're proud of me when I take care of myself too. That's why I want to win this contest.

And, also . . . it's fun. Yeah. Man, it feels good to be a gamer.

ROGAN WEBBER

It's such a close call. I'd be happy to stay on with either of them. I know I started this contest with a lot of attitude. Shouting Ego sum maximus all the time. I was almost as bad as Beckett. OK, maybe I was a lot like Beckett.

I want to win this. I have to win this or I'll lose my Virtual City apartment. I don't think it's bad to want to be the best, but what's different now is that it's not like I'm playing against random gamers online. A lot of real life has come into my game. Jackie and Shay are my friends.

If I am picked to play in the championship, it will partially be because of them. We took on that last gaming round together.

What? No. Come on. It's impossible. It's not fair.

Fine. If you force me to pick one who should move on with me. I'd have to choose . . . Shay. But just because she has been bugging me for a long time about who is the better gamer. If I beat her in the final round, I'd finally prove that's me.

"We have come to the time that you three gamers, and all of the viewers at home, have been waiting for." Sophia's dress and its light horizontal pleats looked almost like the folds of an accordion. A loose silver silk sash hung from her left shoulder, diagonally across her to a knot at her waist, and a large silver Atomic Frontiers electrons-orbiting-the-globe logo broach was pinned near her right shoulder. Somehow the light glinted off the broach and dazzled her smile. "In a moment, I will announce the two of you who will move on to the championship round of the *Laser Viper* Final Challenge. This has been, without a doubt, by far the most difficult decision our judges have had to make. All three of you are excellent gamers, and you should be proud of your accomplishments. But two of you have a slight edge that has earned you a place in the championship. The first gamer who is safe, and moving on to the next exciting round of gaming, is . . ." Her smile beamed as she looked the three of them over. The giant screen, blank between them, would soon display the first finalist. "Shaylyn Spero! Congratulations!"

Rogan's shoulders slumped. Why couldn't he be called first? Just once.

Jackie hugged Shay. "Great job. You deserve it. Good luck."

Shay fist-bumped Rogan and took her place beside Sophia and X. Rogan clenched his fists and glanced down a few times, but mostly he was confident. Mostly. Out of the corner of his eye, he saw Jackie bite her lip.

"Now . . ." Sophia swapped out her cheerleader face for her serious look. "It's time. Rogan Webber. Jacqueline Sharpe. One of you . . . will be moving on to the championship round. One of you . . . will unfortunately be going home." She folded her hands in front of her. "The other finalist in the *Laser Viper* Final Challenge . . . is . . . Rogan Webber!"

Rogan heard a small sigh from Jackie, but turned to meet her sincere smile. He was a little surprised by her tight hug.

"Congratulations, Ro." A sob shook through Jacqueline. "Good luck."

"We'll miss you," Rogan told her. He meant it.

Jackie smiled through the tears and waved at Rogan and Shaylyn. "You two are the best friends I ever had. And Takashi." She sniffled. "We'll game together again."

"Rogan?" Sophia sang. "If you've said goodbye to Jacqueline, please join Shaylyn over here. We want to get some great publicity photos of the first ever *Laser Viper* Final Challenge finalists."

X had already stepped up to Jackie, signaling it was time for her to go.

"Bye, Jackie," Shay called out.

Jackie headed toward her room, but then stopped suddenly and turned around for a second, long enough to fix the other two gamers with a serious stare. She clapped exactly twice, and a moment later vanished into her room to pack. Rogan and Shay both knew what she was hinting at.

Cambots swarmed around them, recording video and snapping still photos. Their faces smiled larger than life on the big screen. Shaylyn and Rogan exchanged slightly competitive grins, the long-time bitter rivals now secure with a spot in the championship. Each knew the other would never back down.

"I hope you two are excited," Sophia said. "Take some time to celebrate, but also get some rest. The final game is coming soon, and I promise you, it will be like nothing you've ever imagined."

CHAPTER 15

Over the course of the next three days, Shay and Rogan relaxed and watched movies and a little game film. Cambots continued buzzing about, and mounted cameras made sure they were always being watched, never alone. But the environment in the dorms was weird. When they'd first arrived it had been full of activity, tension, and conversation. Now it was often quiet enough for them to hear the tiny motors that aimed and focused the cameras.

After Jackie was sent home, Rogan had worried that he and Shay would soon be arguing like old times. But since there was no one else with whom to hang out, and since their old bitter rivalry had been mostly replaced by a mutually beneficial partnership, neither wanted to say or do anything that might set the other off. The result was a calmer and friendlier atmosphere than Rogan would have thought possible.

The two of them were eating dinner one night, seated on opposite sides of the table, both having selected big plates of spaghetti with a side of meatballs. Rogan broke the silence. "I've been thinking about something." He stopped, twirling his fork around and around in his spaghetti. Part of him wondered if it might be better not to bring this up, to talk about some gaming thing instead. But this had been on his mind a little since Takashi left, and a lot since Jackie went home. "I don't want you to make fun of me."

Shay frowned. "Why would—"

Rogan's fork clanked down on his plate. "I just don't want you to make fun of me."

"OK," Shay said sharply.

"Because other people, like other vipers in the war room, or people around Virtual City, would make fun of me for talking like this." Rogan took a deep breath. "I love video games."

Shay opened her mouth like she was going to speak up, but she stopped herself.

Rogan continued. "I love them because in a game there's no question about how I should be, how I should act. In a Batman game, I know I have to fight bad guys until I take down Joker. In *Laser Viper*, I'm Ranger and, except for the weird gaming stages in this contest, I know my job is mostly to fight."

"Okayyyy." Shay held out the word like, *So what's your point?*

"I don't get the real world. I don't spend a lot of time IRL. Everyone in real life knows all the coolest shows to watch, how to act, what to wear, what to say, and who to say it to. I don't."

"Really?" Shay asked. "In digi-space you always seem like—"

"A jerk?"

She pressed her lips together for a moment. "Like, confident. That's all I'm saying. I don't really fit in so great at my school. Like, I'm OK at volleyball, but not a part of the inner circle. But from our time together in *Laser Viper* and in the war room, I always, I don't know . . . I pictured you there in Seattle with, like, a million followers. In real life, I mean. Like, I thought you'd be up in the Seattle Space Needle, and all the other kids rushing to buy tickets to come up and hang out with you."

"No. We don't actually get to the Space Needle much." Rogan laughed. "It is cool, though. I guess what I'm trying to tell you is that I've always been a failure at real life, and I thought if I could win this contest, I could be someone awesome in Virtual City, like Mario Alverez."

"Oh, he is so cool. So cute."

Rogan rolled his eyes. "Can you not?"

"What?"

"Never mind. I still want to win the contest."

"Yeah. Not happening. Sorry, Ro."

He turned his fork around and put a meatball on it, like he was ready to fling the food at Shaylyn. She held her hands up in surrender, and he lowered his weapon. "But this is real life, right? You and me and Jackie and Takashi."

"And Beckett?"

"It's like Jackie said before X took her away. I don't really have a lot of friends outside of digi-space. But we've been hanging out together here, in the real world, for a long time, and . . . well . . ."

"You haven't been a failure in real life with us," Shay finished for him.

He was grateful she said it. He'd really set himself up for her to take him down hard.

"I'm still going to beat you in the tournament, but"—she sighed as dramatically as something out of Shakespeare—"you're all right, Ro. You're even, I guess, if I had to be totally honest, but I'll call you a liar to your face if you ever tell anyone I said this, but you're even . . . kind of cool. Maybe real life isn't so bad."

The two rivals smiled at each other. They went back to eating in friendly silence.

After dinner, they vid called home, and Rogan was happy to talk to his mom and dad. They didn't talk about anything special, but somehow speaking to them reminded Rogan of how much he missed home, and at the same time, how comfortable he was starting to feel on his own on the other side of the country. It was a paradox, Rogan knew, but it was true all the same.

On the morning of the fourth day after the previous game round, X came to the dorms for the two gamers. Both Rogan and Shay were puzzled when he told them they didn't need to bother with their game suits, and doubly puzzled when they were taken down a different series of corridors, not through the atrium with the Sun Station One model but to a section of the giant compound neither of them had seen before.

Finally they entered some kind of medical lab with oxygen masks, IV towers, defibrillators, and various pieces of complex scanning equipment. Advanced computers stood by at the head of two long, narrow tables in the center of the room under bright lights. The top half of the side wall was a window, on the other side of which were the smiling faces of Mr. Culum and Sophia Hahn.

Mr. Culum reached forward and tapped a button before speaking into a microphone. A click, and his voice came through into the room, slightly hollowed out the way speakers could do.

"Good morning, gamers! It's great to see you again. You are no doubt wondering why you have been brought here instead of to the game arena. I can tell by looking at you that you're both a little worried, no doubt wondering what all this equipment is for. Well, you have nothing to fear. I promise you that. In fact, it's time to get excited. I can't wait to tell you all about it! But not from up here in the control booth. I'll be right there!"

He and Sophia walked off to the side and down a few stairs, emerging a moment later through a door and into the lab.

"Good morning from me too, gamers!" Sophia said in an *aw shucks*, cutesy-teasing kind of tone that went perfectly with her festive green-and-gold dress. "How are my favorite finalists doing today?"

Shay and Rogan exchanged a look.

"Fine," Shay said.

Culum spoke up. "From the day that little white dot first bounced off a white bar in *Pong*, to Pac-Man's first chomp on a pellet, to Mario stomping his first Goomba. That remarkable moment when the first gamers joined the world of *Neverwinter Nights,* the first fully graphic multiplayer online role-playing game. The explosion of virtual reality play on console and computer game systems. Then establishment of the hyperstream data network, digi-space, and Virtual City. Today is also a milestone in gaming history, the ultimate gaming accomplishment!" He nodded at Sophia who smiled back.

"Throughout the history of video games, in car racing games from *Pole Position* to *Forza Motorsport* and shooters from *Doom* to *Call of Duty* to *Space Marine*, no matter how varied in their content, there has been one universal constant in all of gaming: the quest for better graphics, more intuitive game control, greater realism.

"Today, gamers, you will be privileged to be the first ones to experience the ultimate realization of that quest," Mr. Culum said.

"You have something better than the suits?" Rogan asked.

"Better than that giant arena?" Shay added.

Mr. Culum looked as though he might dance. "The gaming you embark on today will make that and other VR systems, and especially old-fashioned button-pressing gaming, seem completely primitive." He swept his arms around the room. "Welcome, to full Neurolytic Transduction Control. Or NTC."

Sophia elbowed him playfully. "Or NeuroCon."

Mr. Culum shrugged. "Patent and trademarks pending. The point is that with Neurolytic Transduction Control there are no more gimmicky controllers of any kind—you are simply quite literally *in* the game." From each table he held up an inch-thick, four-foot-long, silver cable with a complex plug on the end. "With this simple connection you will no longer control your laser viper. You will *be* a laser viper."

Shay actually took a step back, as if she were preparing to flee the room. But Rogan noticed X standing a few paces away, looking intently at the both of them. "It's OK," X said quietly. "You'll be safe. I promise you."

"You look worried," Sophia said. "Don't be. Like X said, NeuroCon is one hundred percent, completely safe. Atomic Frontiers technology is here to make life better for everyone. And you gamers are so important to us. I feel as if we're family, or closer even than that!"

Rogan and Shay exchanged a look. Sophia was laying it on pretty thick.

"It works quite simply," Mr. Culum said. "We connect to the software update and maintenance port on each of your deep brain tissue electrical stimulation implants."

Rogan's insides twisted cold. How did Culum know about his implant? What did the thing have to do with gaming? He looked at Shaylyn.

"*You have one too?*" they both asked at the same time.

"ADHD," Shay said.

"Epilepsy," Rogan said.

"Takashi has one too," said Shay. "He told me. He didn't say what it was for."

"It could have been for the treatment of any number of conditions," Sophia said. "It's completely normal."

Rogan frowned. This was all too weird. "Yeah, but what are the odds that out of the five top gamers in our age group, three of them have . . ." Then he figured it out. "I bet all of us have implants."

"All for this?" Shaylyn asked. "But why? My doctor says all my implant does is stimulate the impulse control and focus centers of my brain."

Mr. Culum held up a finger. "That's all it does for now because that is all it is programmed to do."

"Well, it's not like my phone," Shaylyn said. "It doesn't download games and play movies."

"But it could," said Mr. Culum. "If they knew how to program it. With a large software patch and a revolutionary data compression system Atomic Frontiers has developed, your implant can make a safe, passive scan of your brain's entire neuroelectrical pattern, all your brain waves, all of your conscious and unconscious nerve signals, transmitting an exact real-time copy of that information into our gaming computers, while at the same time information from the game is being relayed directly to your brains in the exact same way your brains are taking in sensory information right now in this room. The end result is that you will effectively be put into the game."

"Sounds dangerous," Shaylyn said.

"What if the system crashes while we're connected to it?" Rogan asked.

"Then the game would end abruptly and you'd wake up safe and sound right here," Sophia said. "It's just a copy of your current thoughts and responses to sensory stimuli that interacts with the game. The real you is just fine." She patted one of the two medical beds. "Safe right here."

"Wait," Shay said. "You want to make copies of us?"

Mr. Culum laughed again. "No, no. Not copies in the sense you're thinking. There's not a hard drive on Earth large enough to contain a complete copy of all your thoughts and memories. Think of this like live-streaming. The idea is to live-stream you into the games. If a politician's speech or some breaking news is being streamed or broadcast live and your computer or television is destroyed, the real event is just fine, right? That is kind of what's going on here."

"And it's how you are both going to embark on the gaming experience of a lifetime!" Sophia said. "What we'd like to do today is let you try this new system, to familiarize yourself with it in an easy simulation environment so that you're ready. Ready for tomorrow's championship game round!"

"What do you think, Ro?" Shay asked him quietly.

"What he was saying sounds like it makes sense," Rogan said. "And my mom's always talking about how we have to fight negative stereotypes about brain implants."

Shay rolled her eyes. "Oh yeah. I've heard it all. Whenever people find out about my device, it's all 'Frankenbrain' and 'cyborg.'"

"Exactly," said Rogan, looking at the cables and connector plugs on the two tables. "Maybe we're being like those idiots, afraid of a perfectly safe technology."

"I understand your hesitation," Mr. Culum said. "And we can take all the time you need to get comfortable with NeuroCon. Nobody is forcing you to do anything. I'm here for the two of you." Mr. Culum turned around and brushed aside some of his bushy gray hair. With the flick of a fingernail, he peeled back an inch-diameter circular synthflesh cover to reveal his own data port. "Trust me, gamers. I have tested this system myself. It is completely safe."

"You have an implant?" Shay asked, surprised.

The brain implant technology had only been approved and in widespread use for about ten years, and it didn't work nearly as well when installed in adults as it did in young brains that could still grow around the implant. It was almost unheard of for someone as old as Mr. Culum to have one.

"Your brain didn't reject it?" Rogan asked.

"We at Atomic Frontiers are a little better with technology than people elsewhere. We're always significantly ahead. Exponentially so." Mr. Culum smiled and held his hands out before him, beckoning Rogan and Shay. "Now, gamers. Are you ready to ride technology into the future?"

If Rogan had any remaining doubts about the new technology, they were assuaged by his trust in Mr. Culum. The man was a little weird. Geniuses often were. But what he lacked in normality, he made up for by caring about people, especially his gamers. That was enough for Rogan.

"You're sure about this?" Shay asked Rogan as the two of them lay back on their tables.

Rogan didn't answer right away. It wasn't like Mr. Culum was asking them to undergo brain surgery. It was only a software update. He ran one of those every night. He'd meant what he'd said the other night at dinner about making friends, but he'd also meant what he'd said about wanting to win this contest. If Culum had a cool new way for him to do that, he'd do what it took. Rogan looked over at her. "If you don't think you can beat me in the finals, it's OK to back out now."

Her eyes narrowed. She tried to keep from smiling. "I hate you."

"Save it for the game," Rogan said as he faced the strange, uncomfortable sound and feeling of the connector being inserted into his implant's external port. "Where I will beat you."

"Connections secure," X said.

"Initiating system" came the sound of Mr. Culum's voice over the speakers from the control room.

"Dream on, Rooooooogggaaaaaaa . . ." Shay's voice, stretched somehow and garbled, followed Rogan as he felt the brief sensation of falling. X standing next to him, the lights above, Shaylyn on the other bed, everything around him pixelated and digitally dissolved. ". . . aaaaaan."

Rogan nearly fell down. That was the first thing to adapt to, the fact that he was standing, not lying on a bed.

Next he was startled to find himself back in the cavernous arena, only he was much taller than he had been the last time he stood there. He looked down at his Ranger hands, their weapons and grappling system built into the forearms. No surprise there. He was used to looking like a laser viper, to moving around, making the image of the viper move with him.

What was new was *feeling* like a laser viper advanced combat robot. He could not have easily explained the difference in the way the new version of the game felt to someone who had not experienced it. He imagined it was like trying to explain the color blue to someone born blind. But the sensation of being inside his game suit was gone. The flight and jumping harness wasn't there. His head wasn't stuffed inside a tight, hot VR helmet.

Instead, he felt a bit naked at first, being aware of the absence of clothes, but of course a laser viper didn't need clothes, and in his head he knew his real body was lying safe in the med lab in jeans and a *Mario Kart Turbo* T-shirt.

He watched Flyer moving around, checking herself out the way he had been looking at himself. The line of green light gleamed on her visual sensor plate. "Ro? This is amazing." She tapped her left arm. "Like, I could feel my hand through my game suit when I did this, but this is like I'm hitting my own arm." She was quiet for a moment, looking around the arena. "Kind of a lame practice level. No burned-out city like before?"

"I guess they wanted to spend more time programming the actual game instead of a practice level?"

Culum's people had whipped up a sort of obstacle course, like in Army movies. Except this was a super obstacle course with much taller barriers, at least one of them fifty feet tall. Big plastic rings hung from the ceiling, wide enough for a person to fit through. Flight practice for Shaylyn, maybe. A couple of small swimming pools. An old van and a few cars parked all around.

"So I guess we're supposed to try out this new game mode?" Rogan said. "See how this works?"

"*That's exactly right, Rogan,*" X cut in on their channel. Rogan jumped, being caught up in the new experience, forgetting for a second they were always being watched. X continued, "*You're going to find a lot is different. No more hand gestures to activate weapons and other systems. This is all thought control. So, have fun. Test your weapons, your grappling—*"

"I wonder," Shaylyn said. She shot up into the air like a bottle rocket on the Fourth of July. Straight up so fast, she nearly struck the ceiling.

Instantly, Shaylyn knew she was about to have more fun than she ever had before. She'd had dreams of flying. She'd loved the way her game suit and harness, combined with her VR helmet, had created such a realistic illusion of flying. But this wasn't an illusion.

She was flying! She felt every twist and turn, the heavy feeling as she soared up into the air, the fluttery-flip sensation in her stomach when she dropped altitude. No more pointing her hands opposite of the direction she wanted to fly. Now she thought about moving and she did. Moving through the air was as natural to her as walking.

She laughed as she flew. How often had she watched a sparrow or some other bird sweep up from the ground to land on a wire? How often had she dreamed of becoming a pilot, of sitting at the controls and safely taking a sleek aircraft into the sky? This was better than any of that! Sure, it was just a game, but it was like Mr. Culum said, a game unlike anything she had experienced before.

She landed on top of a fifty-foot-high wall, instinctively able to activate some kind of auto balance system so she was completely stable up there. "Rogan! This is the greatest thing I've ever done! Come on!" She fired an NLEP at him, simply imagining the blue-white energy pulse out of her forearm. It spark-smashed into the floor near Ranger's feet.

Rogan jumped back and then sprinted forward. Right into a low wooden barrier. The wood splintered and he burst through, spilling onto the floor.

"What are you doing, dummy?" Flyer said.

"So fast." If Rogan had hit that wall at that speed IRL, he would have ended up with crushed bones and deep cuts. He'd probably be knocked out. Or dead. But Rogan could never have achieved that high a velocity. Ranger could have outrun the fastest car right there if he hadn't crashed, if he would have been prepared for the ability to move that quickly.

The game suit did its best to create the illusion of speed, and it was good for slowing down Beckett so that he moved like the slower Tank viper mod. But the micromotors within the suit couldn't force Rogan to run faster. If they had, they probably would have torn his body apart. Now, though, with his mind sort of freed up in the game, operating this viper robot, there were no limits. Now, Rogan could run, maybe over a hundred miles per hour, and he could *feel* what it was like to run that fast.

Flyer swooped down to land next to him, offering a hand to help him up. "You OK?"

"Yeah," Rogan laughed. "I just wasn't ready. Watch this."

He sprinted again. Jumped to the top of a twelve-foot-high barrier. Feet on top. Leaping into the air. Grappling hook to the ceiling. Fast swing to within forty feet of the far end of the arena. He swept around in a smooth, fast arc before disengaging the cable. Barely thinking about it, he pulled his heels up, tucking his legs in far tighter than his human body ever could, and spun into a series of rapid backflips before touching down neatly on his feet.

"How did you know how to do that?"

"*Your vipers are augmented with preprogrammed sequences for movement and fighting,*" X said. "*With the game suits, you had to select different programs from a menu on your Heads-Up Displays. Now you can access those programs by thought alone.*"

Flyer whipped into a blur-fast jumping spin kick, clocking Rogan in the chest and head three times before knocking him back to the floor. "So I basically know karate?"

"*Your viper is programmed to know it, and a lot of other techniques, yes,*" said X.

Rogan got back to his feet, tempted to retaliate against Shay's little display, but not wanting to reveal how much her blows had hurt. "Is that safe? I mean, you're reprogramming our brains?"

"Can you just program us with everything we need to know so we can forget about school?" Flyer asked.

"*Your brains aren't being programmed. You are simply able to access programmed sequences in the game, at the speed of thought. Mario is programmed to raise his fist to break through bricks. If we had you connected to Super Mario Bros., you'd be able to do that, not by pressing a button but by thinking about it,*" X said. "*It looks like the system is working great, and you're getting the hang of it. We want you to challenge yourselves, test out what you can do as laser vipers.*"

For the next hour, Rogan and Shaylyn had more fun gaming than they ever had before. They tested their considerable speed. They fired weapons at different targets. They punched holes through cars. Rogan laughed as he swung through the air like Spider-Man, with Shay zipping around cutting tight corners and testing her incredible flight capability.

They even had a friendly martial arts fight, suddenly able to cut loose with fast-as-lightning kung fu moves, karate chops, aikido throws, jujitsu strikes, judo takedowns, and other kicks and punches. With their computer-assisted attacks and defenses, the two of them moved so fast, an observer would have seen only a blur, heard a rapid clank-scrape-clang of metal on metal.

Miraculously, the two rivals kept up a friendly, even match, Flyer compensating for Ranger's superior strength with more speed and flexibility, and by taking their sparring match up in the air, where she could claim the advantage.

After the shortest hour either of them could remember, X interrupted them. *"That's all the time you have for practice, gamers. We're about to commence system shutdown. You will want to stand still so it's less of a shock when you find yourself resting on the tables in the med lab."*

> PREPARING SYSTEM SHUTDOWN . . .
>
> CALIBRATING THOUGHT CENTER
> RELOCATION . . .
>
> DISENGAGING GAME ENVIRONMENT . . .
>
> SHUTDOWN IN 5, 4, 3,
> 2222222222222 . . . .

The practice arena level digitized out around them, and again there was a short, dizzying moment, like falling into a dream. Or in this case, coming out of a dream.

Rogan and Shay opened their eyes, felt the scrape-click of the game system connection being removed from their implant ports. They turned to smile at each other.

Then X stood over them, a hint of that strange expression once again on his face as he looked at Rogan and Shay. "You're both ready for the final challenge now."

CHAPTER 16

Back in the dorms the energy was the highest it had been since Jacqueline left. Rogan and Shay had the service bots roll in with some PowerSlam, and they talked and laughed in amazement about the training round.

"Culum's a weird guy, but he's right," Shay said. "This technology is going to change everything. Everyone will be lining up to get the implants if it means they can do what we did today. We weren't people in game suits controlling characters in a game, we *were* people in a game."

Rogan flopped down on the couch. "That's the weird thing."

"What?"

"Well, that all of us in this tournament have implants." He looked up at her. "I thought we were here because we're the best, because we'd earned our chance. Not because of stupid devices in our brains."

"It's not like that," Shay said. "We *are* top-ranked gamers in our age group. It's just that the brain implants are required for this new system. Of course he needed people who were both great gamers and who, like, also have the hardware."

"Then why not tell us all that right away?" Rogan said. "Too much—" He stopped himself as a cambot approached. He pulled Shay down to hide by the couch and whispered, "Too much weird stuff is going on."

"Takashi's voice telling us to clap twice?" Shay whispered back.

"And the guy coming after me in Virtual City. Knowing who I was and *where* I was in real life."

"*And* that stuff Takashi was saying about how the game rounds are so weird, completely different from the normal *Laser Viper* game."

"Right. Game levels with more noncombatant NPCs than enemies to fight?" Rogan said.

"What are you saying?" Shaylyn asked.

"I don't know," said Rogan. "Nothing, I guess. It's just strange."

She stood up and talked out loud with all her old attitude. "Maybe you're just nervous about the championship."

"Maybe." Rogan was serious. He didn't know what to think.

-----o-----

That night Rogan went to his bathroom to brush his teeth, wash his face, and update his implant before bed. Reaching for the update cable, he saw it.

"Jackie's hacked VR set," he whispered. But how did it get in his bathroom? It hadn't been there earlier that day. Or, if it had, and he'd missed it, he was certain it hadn't been in there the night before when he ran his updates. Jackie had been gone for a while. Who had brought these in?

He was shaking now. Before he realized how silly the gesture was, he hid the headset under a hand towel. Then he walked around his room, checked the closet, and even under the bed to see if he was alone.

Returning to the bathroom, he leaned back against the closed door, breathing heavy, his heart pounding, looking at the towel as though it covered a terrible creature instead of a hacked piece of cheap hardware. Was this a signal from Sophia and Mr. Culum that they knew he'd broken the contest rules and gone to digi-space a while back? But then why didn't they just tell him about it? Kick him out?

Maybe they were trying to make him freak to make better reality TV. Maybe the set was a part of the contest, like if the contest were about more than gaming. What if there were puzzles to work out both in digi-space and real life?

"Or maybe I'm still in digi-space," Rogan whispered to his reflection in the mirror. He pinched himself and felt the sting. "But that doesn't tell me anything. I'd feel that if I were still streaming into a simulation through my implant." He splashed water on his face.

If he started thinking like this, doubting what was real and what was part of the game, he'd lose his mind.

"No," Rogan whispered to his reflection in the mirror. "Jackie took her VR set with her. Unless she left it for me. But then who brought it into the room?"

For just a moment, he thought about going to ask Shaylyn. That's when he pulled the towel off the device. He figured if the glasses and gloves were in his room because he was in trouble for using them before, then he might as well use them again. More importantly, whether this was all a form of the contest that took place in real life or if it was a digi-space imitation of real life, there was a good chance Shay was in her own bathroom right now with a VR headset just like this one. Perhaps she had already turned hers on and moved way ahead of him.

Rogan set up the sensors, slipped on the gloves, put on the headset, and hit the switch to activate the hacked system. Last time he'd used them, he had materialized in Virtual City someplace Jackie must have picked. He expected to arrive there again.

But instead of pixelating into the flash and glamor of Virtual City, he ended up in a place that more closely resembled the burned-out ruins he and his fellow gamers had trained in when they first arrived at Atomic Frontiers headquarters.

He stood on a cracked and buckled street in front of stores that had been shot full of bullet holes. And yet, at the end of the block was a beautiful shining skyscraper, undamaged and gleaming in the sun. Across the street was a hobbit hole from *The Lord of the Rings* and some boxy pixelated wooden bungalow that looked like it had been taken block by block straight out of an old version of *Minecraft*. One of those flying laser gunships from Terminator flew overhead before an X-wing starfighter soared through and blasted it to fiery rubble.

This time, there had been no login menu for him to access his own account. Instead a different avatar had been preselected. His pop-up holodisplay told him he was "Boy 8472, Age 12." A completely generic identity. He didn't even bother pulling up a picture of it.

The same chaotic mix continued down the street to the limit of his avatar's line of sight. This city had suffered lots of battle damage, but in digi-space, new buildings and streets could appear in seconds, so rubble could easily lay next to riches. But that wasn't the only juxtaposition. As Rogan walked along, he spotted buildings, vehicles, and characters from dozens of different video games, TV shows, and movies.

That kind of mix could be found in Virtual City too, but that place had limits. Virtual City had become a collection of different neighborhoods, with stone castles in one section, copies of celebrity homes in another, blocks of apartments, super tall buildings grouped elsewhere, and more. And Virtual City had plenty of copyright characters from all corners of human imagination, but the use of those elements cost a lot of money or credits, so most people stuck with basic avatars or those based on self scans.

By the time two Supermans and Cyborg Mario flew by overhead, Rogan had figured out where he was. "Hackerville," he said quietly. The hidden, illegal, dark side of digi-space. To access this place, a person had to have mad computer skills or be able to pay someone who did. Someone trying to get in here had to be brave, and it helped to have few, if any, moral reservations. In Hackerville, there were no restrictions on violence, no protection for young people, and certainly nobody cared about copyright. That's why he'd run past Mega Man blasting a kid and his dog with his Mega Buster, a sniper shooting up a real live *Mortal Kombat* match on a plaza a few blocks to his right, Donkey Kong throwing barrels at the whip-carrying Simon guy from the *Castlevania* games.

It was risky hanging out in Hackerville. Every once in a while, the FBI, Atomic Frontiers' safety and welfare officers, or other official enforcement agencies raided these places, arresting users who couldn't effectively mask their sign-on signature and who had illegally copied licensed material or were up to other crimes. A lot of people had ended up with fines, forfeiture of digital property, and long-time bans from digi-space.

Everyone called the place Hackerville, like it was the only one, but in truth, this illegal VR town had been reborn hundreds of times. Every once in a while the servers running the town were seized by law enforcement or shut down for some other reason. It never took long for the place to be reestablished though, and so police and other hypernet security elements spent less time trying to shut down Hackerville, focusing instead on sending in undercover agents to catch more serious law and user agreement breakers.

A shiver rolled through Rogan at the thought of being banned from video games and Virtual City, being confined to real life, worse than jail.

"Ex-ter-min-ate!" A blue-green laser beam crossed in front of him. Another behind. Six Dalek avatars straight out of *Doctor Who* rolled into his area, blasting everything and everyone. Rogan's first instinct was to light up the shooters with CHELs, but he remembered that Boy 8472 didn't have Ranger's weapons. Unlike safe Virtual City, Hackerville had weird, often unpredictable combat rules. When avatars were destroyed, sometimes they respawned at their origin points and sometimes they were completely erased. Like everyone else, he ran in a panic.

Rogan rushed around a corner, sprinted across the street, and leapt up onto the hood of a burning *Halo* Warthog fighting vehicle. He missed the superior gameplay of the arena, where he would have rolled over this vehicle to clear it faster. With this cheap, hacked VR set, all he could do was run and jump. So 8-bit.

Tomb Raider's Lara Croft carried a plasma rifle, running toward the Daleks beside a classic Arnold Schwarzenegger Terminator, the flesh on half its face having been ripped away. The Terminator avatar carried a phaser rifle from Star Trek, unleashing a red-hot phaser beam toward the Dalek force.

Lara Croft shot at a Dalek. "Remember, there's a creature inside!"

"Aim for the eye stalks," the Terminator said in Schwarzenegger's heavy accent. "It's the Daleks' most vulnerable point."

Rogan left the battle far behind him. He hated running away, but he had no chance unarmed against that kind of firepower. Looking at the chaos of fleeing people all around him, it was clear that everyone else was thinking pretty much the same thing.

Except a hooded man in the ragged dark robes who'd followed his every move, every turn, for four blocks now. The man was fast and carried a pair of silver handguns just like Agent 47 from the *Hitman* games.

Rogan turned on the speed, sweating so much as he ran in place in the real world that he wanted to slip his glasses off and wipe his face.

He didn't dare take the time out. He had no idea who his pursuer was. Some random punk trying to act like a tough assassin? Or was this the next stage of the *Laser Viper* Final Challenge, a strange test to see how the finalists reacted to combat when they were unarmed? Was it a totally different phenomenon that he didn't understand? Whatever was happening, whoever was after him, he'd beat it.

"*Ego sum maximus*," Rogan whispered as he jumped to grab the bottom rung of a fire escape ladder on the side of an old, two-story brick building.

The man was at least a block behind him. "Stop!" he shouted. A gunshot echoed down the street.

Rogan continued his scramble up the metal ladder, across a steel landing, and up another ladder. A bullet ricocheted off the bricks six feet from him.

"This guy is a seriously terrible shot," Rogan muttered to himself, reaching the top of the ladder and vaulting over the little wall onto the flat tarred roof.

"Come back!" the man shouted from below. "I don't want to hurt you!"

"Shooting at me," Rogan said. "Doesn't want to hurt me?" It wasn't that he was afraid of Boy 8472 being shot or even erased. It wasn't his avatar, and generic characters like this were easily replaced. And he certainly didn't fear being injured. VR bullets couldn't hurt him even when he was in his game suit. He just didn't want to be killed and taken out of this Easter egg level or whatever it was. He risked a look over the wall at the edge of the roof to spot the Agent 47 wannabe still down in the street.

Rogan smiled, waved at his would-be attacker, and took off running along the edge of the roof, careful to let his attacker keep him in sight.

"Rogan, stop!" the man yelled.

Rogan ran as fast as he could, straight for the end of the build-ing. Again wishing he had the greater precision and control of his game suit or the new NeuroCon system, he jumped up on the wall at the edge and launched himself for all he was worth. In the arena or wired in with the NeuroCon system, the impact on top of the next building would have been a lot to deal with. All Rogan did was finish a jump on the cool tiled floor of his bathroom.

Finishing the jump to the next building was as far as he would flee. He ran a few more paces on the next building for show, drifting to his right, away from the street and out of his attacker's sight. Then he doubled back and dropped to a low crouch by the wall at the edge of his new building. There he waited.

And waited.

After all this, was his attacker quitting?

A second before Rogan gave up and rose from his hiding place, the man came flying over the alley between buildings, finishing his jump right in front of Rogan. In the next instant Rogan was on him. A noob would just punch the guy, but Rogan knew better and went straight for the enemy's guns. It worked. He took his pursuer completely by surprise, knocking the guns away before jackhammering him in the gut with a fast series of four hard, low punches. When the cloaked figure bent over from the assault, Rogan threw his whole body into a vicious uppercut.

Ro's attacker flew away before slamming down on his back. In an instant, Rogan gathered and aimed both of the guns. "Prepare to respawn, digi-turd."

"Rogan, relax. It's me." The man sighed and pulled down his hood.

It was Beckett Ewell.

Rogan fought the reflex to pull the trigger and shoot his round-one nemesis right there. "That's not helping you," Rogan said. "What's going on?"

"You have to come with me."

Rogan shook the guns a little. "You're running out of time, Beckett. Or whoever you are."

"No, *you're* running out of time," Beckett said. "You have *no* idea how much danger you're in."

Rogan wished Beckett could see him roll his eyes. "Oh, why? Because I'm sneaking onto a VR set in the dorms? Because I'm in Hackerville?"

Another voice came from behind him. "I left my VR set for you, Ro."

Rogan stepped back from his captive, spreading his arms to keep a gun trained on Beckett while he also aimed at the new-comer. Jackie. She must have found another way onto this roof. Takashi was right behind her.

What was happening? "Who are you people? What have you done with my friends? Someone better start explaining, or I'm going to start shooting," Rogan said.

"I didn't have my guns drawn to shoot you, man," Beckett said. "I was trying to keep you safe in that firefight back there. I was trying to stop you so I could talk to you."

"Why? Who are you?" Rogan said.

"We are exactly who we appear to be," Takashi said. Before Rogan could ask for proof, Takashi continued. "Remember right before I left the dorms I whispered to you that something was weird about the games? You know there is no way the cameras picked that up. No way anyone could impersonate me and tell you that."

Beckett kept his empty hands raised and began rising to his feet. "Right after we first met, when we left the airport in that SUV, I made you climb over me in the back seat instead of moving over to make room for you. Remember? No cameras for that. You have to believe us. I know you hate me, but you gotta listen to us. We're telling the truth."

"Truth about what?" Rogan demanded.

"The truth about Atomic Frontiers and the so-called games," Jackie said. "And we have to tell you fast, Rogan, because there's a chance Culum can detect your presence here. The longer you're here, the greater your risk of being caught."

"The game is real, Rogan," Beckett said. "When we were running around in game suits, we weren't playing a video game, but operating laser viper combat robots in real life."

"That fancy mind-streaming NeuroCon system doesn't put you in a game. It puts you in a robot. Somewhere in the world. That's why Culum had us steal the Velox Mercury X transmitter. He needed that high-capacity data transmission capability to more fully sync you in real time with your robot body."

"How do I know this isn't just part of the championship round? Like, both Shay and I are facing really good copies of all of you, or maybe Culum's got you three playing these parts as a consolation prize?" Rogan ran his fingers through his real-life hair, almost pulling his VR headset off. This was maddening. "What if I've been in one long NeuroCon simulation, living inside an ongoing video game ever since they connected my implant to that machine?" He was speaking to no one in particular now, his mind whirling with world-inside-game-inside-world possibilities.

"Rogan, we've seen the news," said Takashi. "The Chinese navy has cranked up tensions over the sinking of their ship. An actual, real-life ship."

"There was nonstop coverage of the so-called terrorist attack on that German castle," said Beckett.

"Until they broke in with coverage of another terrorist attack on the Tower of London," Takashi added.

"You're just saying that stuff. Doesn't mean it's true. I don't even know if you are really who you appear to be," Rogan said. But a sharp, cold fear was worming its way through his mind and body. That thing with Beckett in the SUV was true and there was no way anyone else could know about it. This couldn't be real, could it?

No. Impossible. But the nonplayer characters in the challenge had been so realistic, the gameplay and objectives so unlike any other games.

If it *had* all been real, that meant—Rogan put his hands on his knees, steadying himself—that meant they'd really sunk a Chinese warship. All the people they'd hurt.

Had anyone died?

He thought of the people in that underground British bunker, how quickly the place had flooded. If it was all real, were the knocked-out soldiers OK? Did they get out of there in time?

"There's no way we can get you to believe us," Jackie said. "In a way I'm glad you're skeptical. But now we have to wrap this up before you get caught. Listen, Ro. Mr. Culum and Atomic Frontiers are dangerous, and they're up to something big."

"Mr. Culum is one of the nicest people I've ever met in digispace or IRL," Rogan said. "Sure, he's a little weird with all that 'ride technology into the future' stuff, but he cares about people. He's been good to me. To all of us."

Jackie shook her head. "We don't have time to explain it all right now. You have to trust us. You and Shay are in danger. If your laser viper robot is destroyed while your mind is still uploaded to it, you will probably suffer serious brain damage. It will probably kill you. Xavier is working undercover for a secret group that's code-named Scorpion and trying to stop Culum and Atomic Frontiers."

"That's right," Beckett said. "Scorpion are the good guys."

"Be ready," said Takashi. "Try to *secretly* get word about this to Shay. Scorpion is about to make its move to get the two of you out of Atomic Frontiers HQ. Until then, trust us, and trust X."

"But don't blow his cover!" Beckett said. "You have to keep going along with everything like you were before. Don't let Culum know you suspect them."

Before Rogan could protest any more, Jackie squeezed his hand, but he felt nothing in the cheap gamer gloves. "You've got to log out and hide that VR set now. But remember, when you're in your viper, *stay alive*. This is *not* a game."

CHAPTER 17

B y the time X came to get Rogan and Shay up for the champion-ship round, Rogan had hardly slept. He'd spent some time shaking and alone in his bathroom. Then he carefully hid the VR set and paced his room until he decided to risk going to tell Shay about what had happened. He hoped it was all a game, and she'd been playing too. But he stopped himself outside the door to her room. He was being watched by cameras all over the commons, and there was no way he could explain a midnight visit to Shay's dorm room.

It was all so confusing, so frightening. For the first time in a very long time, Rogan thought he wanted a break from video games. In the end, he slept two, maybe three hours.

After a short breakfast, Shay and Rogan followed X. The man had always been purposeful, but his march to the med lab today was so rapid and big-stepped they almost had to jog to catch up. He stopped at one point, and turned to them like he was about to say something.

Rogan held his breath, hoping X would give him some sign of what was really going on, but when two cambots rolled up, X shook his head and kept moving.

"Shaylyn!" Sophia cried as they entered the lab. "Rogan! This is it, you two! You're the two best *Laser Viper* gamers in America, maybe even the whole world, but Atomic Frontiers is looking for a champion . . ."

She kept going on with the usual stuff about how they were both amazing, they'd both done a fantastic job, and while it would be so hard to say goodbye to one of them after this round, it would be wonderful to recognize a champion.

Rogan watched Mr. Culum carefully, looking for any trace of evil or danger. But he was the same nerdy old man, the same kind and enthusiastic genius. Even his clothes never changed. Mr. Culum said a lot more of the same stuff about the greatness of his new game system, changing the world, nothing would be as it was, and blah blah blah.

Neither of them listened. They were both too nervous, excited, and focused on the upcoming game to pay attention to the speeches, though Rogan figured their anxiety came from different sources. Shay hadn't given any sign that she'd been to digi-space last night. She was the same old competitive gamer.

"Listen up!" X finally said loudly. "For this game round, because Flyer is so much faster and because the judges feel that Rogan has earned a bit of a head start, Rogan will begin the round a bit earlier. Shaylyn will be held back for a while."

"What?!" Shaylyn shouted. "That's not fair! So you've already decided on the winner?!"

Rogan couldn't say he was happy about this either. If he were in Shay's position, he'd be furious. Beyond that, he was looking forward to a fair contest, the chance to play his best, and hopefully to beat Shaylyn fairly, leaving no doubt about which of them was the best gamer. But this way, she'd always have that "head start" excuse to hold over him.

And if this wasn't a game, he'd need her help.

Mr. Culum waved his arms in front of him. "No, no, no! It's not like that. I can see how that would be upsetting. It will all become clear in the game. The point is that each viper mod has its own set of specific functions, and although you will both be part of the same mission, you have different roles within the mission, and you'll be judged by how well you accomplish the goals for your part of the mission."

Sophia beamed at her. "I admire your passion, Shaylyn. Way to stick up for yourself! But I promise you, Atomic Frontiers is absolutely dedicated to fairness in the *Laser Viper* Final Challenge."

Mr. Culum held up the silver data cables, ready to connect the gamers to the game. "All that said, who's ready to begin?"

-----o-----

After the dizzying pixelation, Rogan didn't know what surprised him more: the fact that he was sitting in the back of a stretch limousine or that the face staring back at him in the reflection off the inactive wall screen was that of a woman. But it wasn't just any woman. He was Sun Station One chief engineer and science officer Dr. Valerie Dorfman.

Rogan moved his hand in front of his face, and the woman in the reflection matched his movement. "Wow" was all he could think to say. His voice came out much higher than Lieutenant Ericson's, Captain Star's, or his own. He — she — was no longer wearing the plain blue jumpsuit she'd had on when floating around the station. Shiny red hair fell in loose curls down over her right shoulder. Black makeup stuff had been stuck in her eyelashes over her deep green eyes. She . . . He . . . was sitting there in a long, dark blue dress with kind of shiny trim stuff that looked like a fake belt. Suddenly he knew how the girls must have felt when they were digi-disguised as dudes. It took some getting used to.

But this had to be a game. If it were all real, why would he possibly be disguised as Dr. Dorfman in this prom dress? Whatever super-secret mission was involved with this game round, he hoped nobody would ask him about fashion.

"OK, Rogan. This is X. The game system is up and running. How are you feeling?"

Rogan caught the limo driver's eyes in the rearview mirror. He turned away from the driver and covered his mouth. "X," Rogan said quietly. "What's going on?"

"Relax, Ro. The driver is an operative for Project Laser Viper. You can speak freely."

"Right. Fine. Just tell me why," Rogan said. "What's the mission? And where's Shay?"

"Shay is inbound to your location on the StarScreamer. Her viper will be in the area soon. We're going to do this one a little bit different, Ro. We're filling you in with the needed details as the mission rolls along."

"Seriously?" Rogan asked. "How am I supposed to do whatever it is you want me to do if you don't tell me what I'm supposed to be doing? Where am I, anyway?" Rogan looked out the window, and in seconds his system labeled the six-lane freeway he was on as Sheikh Mohammed bin Rashid Boulevard. Dubai. United Arab Emirates.

Rogan shook his head. No matter how weird he felt appearing as a woman in a dress, he had to admit it was cool to be able to instantly google just about anything right in his head. The programs and abilities he could access in this game with just a thought were like magic, and he wished he could have these abilities permanently.

The road curved a little as it passed the Dubai Mall, and out the window Rogan had a view of a ridiculously tall tower. His system instantly labeled it as the Burj Khalifa, 2,722 feet tall.

"That's the site of your next mission," X said. *"When it was completed back in 2009, it was the tallest building in the world. Now it's in third place, but it's still impressive. Now check out your purse. It's real and not a product of your PNC. In it you'll find a couple thousand dollars in cash, an equivalent amount in United Arab Emirates dirhams, several high-limit credit cards, and some gently used makeup to help sell the illusion of your cover when the purse is searched."*

Rogan peeked into the shiny sequined handbag. X wasn't lying.

The man continued. *"There's also an ID and a VIP pass to an exclusive party on the one hundred fifty-fourth floor. You will be attending a reception that will kick off a conference about the future of the United Arab Emirates. The UAE and other Middle Eastern countries are working to shift away from total oil dependence to other energy supplies and sources of income. You might recognize Dr. Valerie Dorfman from your tour of Sun Station One. You are scheduled to offer* a presentation on the second day of the conference about SS1, and about the final phase of construction. As you know, the real Sun Station One is scheduled to go online very soon, so we thought it would be the perfect addition to the game."

"A presentation? But I don't know anything about that stuff," Rogan objected in a woman's voice.

"Relax," X said. "Even if you had to deliver your presentation, we'd be able to feed you enough information to get you through it. But this mission will be over long before that."

"What is the mission?" Rogan asked.

"One step at a time," said X. "Part of what we're testing is the gamer's ability to adapt to unexpected and changing situations. And, um, working alone. Right now, just get yourself into the reception. Whatever happens, no matter how strange or unexpected it might be, act like you belong there, and try to have a good time."

After stopping to show credentials at several checkpoints, the driver brought the limo to a special entrance in a secure parking facility. Rogan appreciated the realism and detail as the limo rolled past cars his system recognized as a gleaming red Ferrari, a Pagani Huayra with gull-wing doors, a five-million-dollar Bugatti Veyron, a couple of Lamborghinis with a top speed of 240 miles per hour, and a Koenigsegg ZX Diamante, the exterior of which was finished in carbon fibers coated with a diamond dust resin. Other lesser BMWs and Porsches filled the spaces between these incredible vehicles. He wondered if this was an accurate representation of Dubai, if people were really this rich.

"*OK, Rogan. Here you go. Remember, your disguise works perfectly, but it is keyed to your movements, so smile and step out of the car. Try to remember you're supposed to be wearing high heels, so take small steps.*"

"Yeah, haven't had much practice with that," Rogan said.

The driver opened the back door, and Rogan slid out of the car directly onto a red carpet that led through a set of glass doors into the building.

A man with black hair, brown skin, a sharp business suit, and a smooth smile stepped up to greet him.

"Welcome to Dubai and the Horizon Conference, Dr. Dorfman," the man said. "I'm Essa Al Tayer. If you will follow me, my assistants will check your identification and quickly scan your bag. Then they will lead you to a direct elevator to the reception."

Inside, a man in long white traditional Arab robes ran Valerie Dorfman's purse through a scanner. After he was reunited with Dr. Dorfman's purse, Rogan was led into a shiny elevator with a young man in a straight suit and white gloves. There were 154 buttons on the panel and not a single fingerprint. The man punched the top left button and the elevator started its ascent.

A projection on the inside of the white doors counted up the numbers, about a floor per second, and the height in meters continued to increase.

Off to the side of his field of vision, Rogan caught a flash of blue-white light, a digital pixelation distortion in the air. "*Ro—*" A voice, not X's or the elevator operator's, was cut off by static. "*Rogan . . .*"

A 2-D image projected on the door made the lift appear to rise above one of the Egyptian pyramids . . . the Eiffel Tower in Paris . . . Central Park Tower in New York . . .

Another flash. More digital distortion in the air. Then a blue-white see-though holographic image of Takashi flashed into existence next to him. *"Rogan, if you can hear and see me, say nothing but put your hands on your hips."* Rogan hesitated for only a moment, but then did as the image asked.

A digi-ghost hand pushed Takashi aside and he vanished, replaced by Jackie. *"We're getting better at hacking into the Atomic Frontiers's laser viper system. Culum can't see or hear us, but he knows everything you do and say, so be cool. We're working on a way to get you out of there. But you have to keep playing along until then. Above all, keep your laser viper functioning."*

Beckett's head materialized, as if he'd leaned into the projection field from wherever he, Jackie, and Takashi were transmitting. *"If your viper dies, you die."*

Jackie nodded, looking right at Rogan. *"We have to cut our signal off soon, or we risk detection. I know what you're thinking, Rogan. But this isn't some clever twist that Culum has sneaked into the final challenge to test you. It's not a game. It never was. It's life or death. Good luck, Ranger."* The ghost image pixelated and winked out with a static hiss-pop.

The elevator operator had been staring off into space, but he'd begun to notice Dr. Dorfman acting strange. The video projected onto the elevator door showed Wuhan Greenland Center tower in China, and finally the Burj Khalifa, as the recorded narrator pointed out in the two-minute elevator ride that it was the third tallest building in the world, behind Saudi Arabia's Jeddah Tower and the colossal 5,500-foot Sky Mile Tower in Tokyo, Japan.

Rogan emerged into a bright room with white walls and a white ceiling. Pale upholstered chairs and sofas were spaced near small round wood tables. About as many guests were dressed in Western-style tuxedos and dresses as were in the long white robe-looking clothes that the Arab men wore. Servants in simple black dresses or suits flowed through the reception, carrying trays with hors d'oeuvres or fruit juice.

Was this real or a game? It wasn't like it was the 1990s and his grandpa's video games anymore. Games had looked real for a long time. But this *felt* real. Still, that could be part of the illusion. Rogan wondered if he could switch to internal comms.

"Is Shay here yet?" Rogan asked, relieved when nobody else in the room seemed to hear.

"She'll enter the game pretty soon," X said. *"Everything is fine. Trust me. Now just try to have a good time. Blend in."*

Had Rogan imagined it, or was there a little more emphasis when X had said "trust me"? No, he thought, this was all just part of a realistic, complex video game. There was no way this could be real. Unless . . . if game suits could tell a computer how to move characters in a video game, why couldn't they control a computer in a robot the same way? If that had all been real, then that super-high-capacity data transmitter might make hyperstreaming his whole consciousness to his viper possible.

Either way, real life or video game, he had to keep going, play to win—or to stay alive.

His gaze moved past two men in flowing Arab garb, and his system showed red triangles near each man's hip.

WARNING: COMPACT HIGH-ENERGY LASER WEAPONS DETECTED.

"Don't worry about it, Rogan. It's just standard security. With any luck, a lot more of these guys will turn up."

Rogan sauntered over to the windows, away from the secretly armed men near the elevators. He grabbed a champagne flute of mango juice from a server on the way, figuring he could just hold it, the way everyone else seemed to be carrying a drink.

"You'll actually be able to appear to drink that, no problem," X said. *"A modification has been programmed into your laser viper for this purpose. Just try to take small sips. It's not like the viper has to take normal, human-sized drinks. You could dump all that juice along with the whole glass down the hatch all at once. The liquid will be boiled off in a special processor in the Ranger's belly."*

"Right," Rogan said quietly. If this were only a video game, would they bother with a detail like the practical way to get a robot to appear to drink? "I suppose the steam comes out of my—whoa." He had stepped up to a bank of floor-to-ceiling windows to take in the view out over Dubai. Rogan had flown in real airplanes. He'd been in the most realistic gaming combat drops. He was no stranger to heights, but he'd never been this high in something that was still attached to the ground. Dubai's buildings were tall.

From the ground, they looked at least as tall as the highest ones in downtown Seattle, but from up on floor 154 they seemed fake, or like little toys, LEGOs maybe. Cars had become tiny dots, smaller than ants, crawling along the freeway. In the hazy distance beyond it all, the Persian Gulf stretched out to the horizon.

It was a lot more detail than was usually programmed into even the best video games.

"Magnificent view, isn't it?" A man in a tux had stepped up next to Rogan, looking Valerie over a little too closely. Remembering to blend in, Rogan kept smiling. "Though I prefer the view of the Red Sea from the outdoor sky terrace on the Jeddah Tower, even higher up than we are now."

"It's hard to believe people could build something like this," Rogan said.

"Really?" said the man. "I should think these simple skyscrapers seem like stacking a child's wooden blocks compared to Sun Station One."

"Um . . ." Rogan wasn't sure what to say.

"*The real Valerie Dorfman returned to Earth only two days ago for this conference,*" X said.

Rogan went to internal comms. "*Wait. The real Dr. Dorfman or a game simulation version of Dr. Dorfman?*"

A long pause.

Mr. Culum laughed. "*Great question, Rogan. I'm sorry for the confusion. I can see why trying to sort out this gaming stage's backstory might throw you off. Don't worry about it.*"

That wasn't an answer. The question was actually very important.

Rogan knew Sun Station One was real, that Atomic Frontiers had actually developed the technology and provided most of the funding for the project. But did that prove all of this was real? It would be easy to program this reference into the game. Was this all too sophisticated to be a game? He didn't know. But like Holo-Jackie had said, he had to keep going.

He noticed the man watching him, waiting for an answer. "Well." Rogan searched his mind for something, anything, to say on the subject. "When we're building the space station . . . like . . . if we drop a wrench, it just floats there. If one of the guys building this floor of the tower had dropped a tool—"

The man laughed. "Yes! Yes, he'd probably kill somebody!" He spoke so loudly that Rogan stiffened, wondering if the laser-toting Arabs had heard and what they might do. The man shook Rogan's hand, holding on a little too long. "I'm Dr. Herbokowitz," he said with a small note of triumph in his voice, as if Valerie Dorfman should know him.

His onboard computer quickly floated the man's bio-bubble on his viper's HUD.

DR. CARL HERBOKOWITZ. AGE 47.

EXPERT IN GEOLOGY AND PETROLEUM ENGINEERING.

LEAD ADVISOR, UNITED ARAB EMIRATES ENERGY TRANSITION TEAM.

"Dr. *Carl* Herbokowitz! Of course!" Rogan said, noticing the appearance of six more Arab men with hidden laser weapons in the room. Two of them were casually edging their way through the crowd, heading in Rogan's direction.

Had they seen through the Polyadaptive Nanotech Cloak? How could they? If this were a game, they'd be programmed to fall for the disguise. If it were real . . . there were a lot of lasers. But Dr. Herbokowitz clearly thought he was talking to beautiful Dr. Valerie Dorfman and not an advanced fighting robot.

"You might wonder why an oil man like me would be talking to the so-called clean energy enemy," Herbokowitz said.

Apparently this guy loved nothing more than to talk about himself. Rogan didn't know what to do but found a preprogrammed flirtatious laugh. Ranger's head tilted back as Valerie giggled. Rogan scanned the crowd and spotted a total of twelve laser-armed men spread throughout the room. Their heart rates were slightly elevated and their hands were damp with perspiration. When he focused on their eyes, he saw most of the men searching the room, carefully looking over each guest.

Essa Al Tayer emerged from the elevator corridor. "Ladies and gentlemen, distinguished guests all." He paused until the room quieted. Then he smiled, spread his arms, and held them out to the group as though offering a gift or a blessing. "It is my great honor to present to you the secretary-general of the Supreme Petroleum Council, deputy supreme commander of the armed forces, chairman of the executive council of the Emirate of Abu Dhabi, and the crown prince of Abu Dhabi, His Highness Sheikh Ahmad bin Mohammed Al Abdullah."

"*He's the second in command of the whole country,*" X said.

Rogan set his juice on a small table and joined the other guests in applauding the important arrival. He saw that the armed men didn't seem to be after anyone in particular but had taken up positions around the room to protect the sheikh. He let out his woman's laugh and sighed with relief.

"OK, Rogan. *It's time for your mission,*" X said. "*That's the man you have to kill.*"

CHAPTER 18

The crown prince? Are you serious?" Rogan asked out loud while everybody was still clapping. It was the first kill order to go out in the whole tournament. If the appearance in the elevator had really been his real gamer friends and all this was really real, then he'd really be killing a real person. "No way."

Dr. Herbokowitz leaned close to who he thought to be Valerie and whispered in the viper's digital illusion ear. "Unbelievable, isn't it? His estimated net worth is something like twenty-six *billion* dollars. They say he just bought a Porsche 920 Super Spyder X, and then had the whole body plated in pure gold. The whole thing had to cost over ten million." Either this Herbokowitz guy was a programmed distraction or he was blathering on about the real world. Either way, Rogan really wished he'd shut up.

The ruler smiled and held up his hand. "Please. The honor is mine. Welcome, all of you. Please get to know the people who are with us for this important event. Relax and enjoy yourselves, for tomorrow we begin the serious task of planning for a better future."

Everyone clapped again. Rogan switched to internal comms. *"No way. I will not shoot that man."* The string quartet in the corner resumed playing, and gradually the conversation returned to its former volume.

The voice that answered freaked Rogan out. It was Mr. Culum, not X, and he did not sound happy. *"The crown prince is working with Scorpion, Rogan. He's a major source for Scorpion terrorist funding."* His voice was sharp, just short of shouting. *"You will shoot that man or you will fail the mission and lose the championship!"*

Rogan stayed on internal comms. *"First, it's impossible. There are a dozen guards all over this place. Second, I —"* He was about to say he didn't want to kill a human being, but he'd "killed" thousands of video game people in the years he'd been gaming. The other gamers had warned him not to make Mr. Culum and Atomic Frontiers aware that Rogan knew this wasn't a game. *"I'm just not doing it!"*

"Are you feeling all right?" Dr. Herbokowitz asked.

How could Rogan get rid of this guy? "Dr. Herbokowitz," Rogan said in Valerie's voice. His only hope was to get the guy talking to buy himself some time. "May I call you Carl? Carl, tell me about why you're here. What's your project all about?"

Herbokowitz seemed pleased that Valerie was interested. He launched into an explanation of some technical oil stuff.

Rogan was relieved when X came back on. *"Rogan, you have made it this far in the* Laser Viper *Final Challenge. You beat out* Beckett *and* Takashi." He spoke their names slowly, as if trying to drop a hint. Or was Rogan imagining that? *"You beat out* Jacqueline. *Remember when you two used to talk?"* This was maddening. He felt sick. *"If those three were still in the game, they would trust me. I need you to trust me."*

That's what the other gamers had told him to do. Trust X. "Fine," Rogan said out loud but quietly.

X continued, *"Now tell Dr. Herbokowitz you think the process he was just describing might be useful for Sun Station One's earthbound power receiver."*

Rogan passed the message to Dr. Herbokowitz.

"Do you really think so?" Herbokowitz asked. "Because I had this idea about . . ."

"Just get close to the crown prince, drop the PNC, power your lasers, and fire. The sequence will take seconds."

"Um . . . excuse me, please, Dr. Herbokowitz," Rogan said, beginning a weave through the crowd, hoping X would get him out of this. A mission to kill. If this were real, and he lasered the man, not only would he be committing murder, but his viper would instantly be shot down by the others. If it was destroyed, while Rogan's mind was still inside it—This wasn't fun anymore.

Sheikh Ahmad stood near the end of a tan sofa before a shiny black column a few paces in front of the windows with their brilliant view. He laughed and made a small bow to a woman while another man waited for his attention.

"You can do this, Rogan," X said. "One quick laser blast. A head shot. Then get to the elevator. The Ranger easily has the strength to force open the doors. If the elevator is on your floor, jump up through the emergency hatch in the ceiling of the car, and then get down into the shaft. Drop down to level one twenty-four, the more popular of the two public observation deck tours. Change your appearance there to the French man we have on file. Translation software will

turn anything you say into French, but try not to talk much, because the software doesn't work perfectly. The goal is that you rush out with the rest of the terrified tourists when the alarms go off."

Sheikh Ahmad had moved on to discuss energy policy with the man who had been waiting to speak with him. "Of course, when Sun Station One goes online, the UAE will become totally independent of oil for its own energy needs, using our oil production solely for profit from exports. Then, with Sun Station Two and so on, we will guide the world through the transition to solar power." He shrugged. "Again, because of forward-thinking scientists like you, the UAE is in a position both to help other countries meet their growing energy needs and to help the UAE profit and grow."

One of the security guards who had been standing by a low table began edging closer to Sheikh Ahmad as well.

Rogan went to internals. *"If these guys shoot me, am I going to feel pain?"*

"A very minimal sensation," X said reassuringly. *"Just enough to let you know you're under fire so you can take action to get to safety."*

"Are you sure I'll be safe if my Ranger is destroyed while I'm still connected to it?" No response. *"X? Hello, Control. Can you hear me? If Ranger dies and my mind is still inside it—"*

"I'm here, Rogan," X finally said. *"Um . . . Mr. Culum and Atomic Frontiers promise you'll be fine."*

Was that code talk? If Mr. Culum and Atomic Frontiers were the bad guys, if he was supposed to trust X but not Culum, then was that really a warning? More than anything, he wanted out of this. He wanted to hit the switch and stop it all. Or was this part of the test?

What if this, the warning from the other gamers, the whole question of whether this was a game or real life, was all an illusion? Maybe Shaylyn was playing the exact same game right now, but separately, and the loser was whoever first asked for the game to be shut off.

If this were all a game — worst case, he lost. If this were all real — worst case, he died.

"I want to stop this," Rogan said out loud. "I don't care if I lose the tournament. Shut it off. I'm done."

No answer. Confused looks from party guests around him.

"X?" Rogan asked. He waited. "X? Control? Did you hear what I said? I quit the tournament."

Mr. Culum came on the channel. He was even angrier than before. *"The only way for this game to end is if you take out your target. Now! Shoot him!"*

Rogan was shaking. If this was just a gamer tournament, they would let him stop. This was no video game. It had never been a game. It *was* life or death.

Sheikh Ahmad had noticed Rogan, or rather, Dr. Valerie Dorfman. He motioned for her to join them. "Ah, Dr. Dorfman. I was just discussing energy production with Dr. Anton Lopez."

Rogan stepped closer but eyed the exits. He would just run. That would be the safest way. But if Atomic Frontiers was dangerous enough to have set up all of this, if they were that ruthless, what would they do with Rogan's body? He could make this robot escape this tower, maybe, but how could he ever escape the robot to get back to his own body, or get his body out of Atomic Frontiers headquarters?

Burn. Stabbing pain. Rogan felt his chest and shoulder catch fire as he was knocked back by a laser blast. Another beam shot past his head. Another pegged his hip. Rogan screamed.

WARNING: POLYADAPTIVE NANOTECH CLOAK FAILURE.

WARNING: PRIMARY AND SECONDARY ROCKET THRUST FAILURE.

The guests screamed and ran from him.

"What is it?!" a woman screamed.

"Same kind of robot from that terrorist attack in Germany!" said a completely panicked man.

"*Did you get the target?!*" Culum shouted inside his head. "*What is the target's status?!*"

Rogan sprinted away from the crown prince. "I'm hit! It *hurt*! I hadn't even dropped my disguise! The guards just knew!" He spoke in Ranger's cold robot voice, his female disguise gone.

"*We've been compromised,*" Mr. Culum said. "*Someone's betrayed us!*"

An alarm's screech added to the chorus of shouts and screams. Two guards had pulled the sheikh to safety, using their own bodies as shields. Rogan started toward the elevators, but twenty men with laser rifles, wearing camouflaged uniforms, flooded the hall in front of them.

"I'm aborting mission!" Next to him, Herbokowitz gasped.

Rogan stunned two guards with nonlethal pulses. "Get me out of here!" Rogan ran behind a black stone pillar. He spread his arms wide around the column and fired NLEPs from both wrists to keep the soldiers from rushing to the side and gunning him down. "Control!" he shouted. "It's already mission failure. Disconnect me from the system. Get me back in my own body." One laser shot blasted a corner of the pillar away just over his shoulder.

Static pop and hiss. *"Rogan, this is Jackie. Run for your life! You've got to get to the elevator."*

Another laser beam exploded into the stone column. He could feel the sharp heat of the blast as clearly as if it were his own skin.

But if he was inside his Ranger viper, his skin was made of armored alloys stronger than steel. It all reminded him that he was Ranger, with Ranger's abilities. And that gave him an idea.

"OK. Forget this," Rogan said. "I'm out of here."

Lifting both arms, Rogan unleashed a powerful laser barrage at the glass before him, shattering the thick pane, inviting a wind storm with sand and glass flying around as the air pressure equalized. With hungry streaks of laser fire lashing out behind him, Rogan sprinted four steps.

And jumped.

And for a second or two his momentum carried him, and he felt he could fly.

In the hot, quiet air, limbs spread like a skydiver, he looked down on the blue-green water of the man-made lake near the base of the tower.

Then gravity seized him.

And he fell.

Faster and faster, the wind whipping past him, floor after floor of the colossal tower sped by. Buildings and roads far below expanded from tiny, distant structures to larger, very real, very hard surfaces into which he would crash.

WARNING: UNCONTROLLED RAPID DESCENT. SURFACE IMPACT IN 14.5 SECONDS.

"Get me out of this body!" he shouted. "Disconnect me! Now!Now!Now!"

WARNING: UNCONTROLLED RAPID DESCENT. SURFACE IMPACT IN 11.3 SECONDS.

"Think, Ro. Think! The grappling cables!" But the buildings around the lake were all too far away. "Except— Oh, man, this is stupid."

WARNING: UNCONTROLLED RAPID DESCENT. SURFACE IMPACT IN 6.2 SECONDS.

Rogan reached back behind himself and fired his cable blindly. It connected with a window-washing machine track on level seventy-nine, and in the next second he was swinging back toward the tower with more than enough tension on the cable to rip a human arm out of its socket.

WARNING: COLLISION INEVIT–

Rogan curled in his legs and free arm, swinging into the side of the Burj Khalifa like a wrecking ball. Thick glass exploded into the sitting room of a luxury suite on level seventy-four. Rogan tumbled into the room, crushing a sofa and rolling to a hard impact against the opposite wall.

A painting that had hung above the new dent in the wall crashed to the floor just as a man in business shirt and tie ran into the room from the hallway. He took one look at Ranger and shouted. "Get out! Get to the emergency evacuation points! It's terrorists!"

"I'm not a terrorist!" Rogan called out in his cyber voice. He couldn't explain it. Who would believe him if he tried? And anyway, he had no time.

"Go! I'll hold it off!" the man shouted, picking up an expensive vase. At least it looked expensive to Rogan. But then again, he only had about thirty-two dollars of saved-up birthday money, and he sure wouldn't waste any of it on a tan-and-red swirl vase. A vase that shattered against his face a moment later.

Rogan engaged a blur-fast roundhouse kick, checking his force to avoid killing the man. The guy went flying and Rogan stepped over him, sprinting through the luxury suite.

"Just disconnect me!" he shouted to whomever was listening back at control. "Get me out of this!"

Seconds later, he left the suite and entered the hallway. A door at the other end of the hall flew open and three soldiers came out. The first shouted something in Arabic, but before they could shoot him, Rogan had punched down the door across the hallway and charged into another suite for rich people. A woman screamed and ducked behind a chair, shouting something in a different language. A man held out a thick stack of cash, pleading with him.

"What do I do?! Where do I go?!" Rogan shouted. The terrified man must have thought Rogan was yelling at him, because he pulled out more money and a flashy ring off his finger. Rogan ran past him.

"*Rogan, I'm almost to the tower.*" Shaylyn finally spoke up on their channel.

Rogan sighed in relief. "Shay! What's going on?!"

"*It was forever before they even let me start the game. Then almost as soon as I was in the game, a hologram of Jackie appeared. She said this is all real, but—*"

"Do not get shot!" Rogan said. "It really hurts! I promise you that."

"*She said we can't let our vipers be destroyed or—*"

"Yeah, about that!" A laser beam sliced into the suite, inches from Rogan's head. "I have Dubai security all over me! Jackie give you any tips on what we're supposed to do?" He fired back a dozen NLEP bolts.

"*It was like she was cut off!*" Shay continued.

"They're gonna kill me, Shay!"

"*If you can get outside, I can pick you up.*"

Rogan rushed through the suite, knocking over an abstract sculpture in the hallway and dropping a sixty-inch screen from the wall when he clipped it with his shoulder.

More shouting told him the soldiers were in the suite.

"Shay?" Rogan called to his friend. "Be ready. I'm coming outside."

She called back. *"Wait. What? Where?"*

As before, a quick laser shot to the glass and a flying swan dive launched Ranger out into the hot Dubai late-evening air.

"Darn it, Ro!" Shaylyn yelled. "You could have warned me!"

"No time!" Rogan shouted. He silenced his computer's warnings and fell. One of the weirdest things about Ranger was that its body wasn't human, and it could bend differently. It felt so weird, but Ranger's head could rotate full circle. Rogan fought the urge to spin his head backward to check on Shay. What was the point? He'd crash into the shallow lake in seconds. She would either reach him in time or—

A hard impact to his back.

"Got ya!" Shay said. They were still losing altitude. "I think."

Instead of a fast plummet straight to the ground, their dive toward death now had some forward momentum. And they were slowing down.

"You need to lay off the robo Big Macs!" Shay said.

"All I had was juice," Rogan said.

"Come on. Come on. Pull out of it," Shay said to her own thrusters. Rogan's armored metallic feet splashed into the water. Right before Shay pulled him back up into the sky. "Woo-hoo!"

Both of them laughed as Shaylyn took him up over the flashing lights of the police cars surrounding the base of the tower. They laughed until the bullets started flying and the laser beams cut the air.

"We're not out of this yet," Rogan shouted.

Shaylyn carried him up over the giant Dubai Mall, hooking around toward the gulf. Most of the laser fire and bullets dropped off the farther they got from the giant tower, but when their scanners picked up police boats coming in on the open water and aircraft covering the skies, they changed direction.

"Get us deeper into the city," Rogan said. "At least then we might be able to find cover."

Four hundred and thirty-nine feet behind them, three police cars, blue-and-red lights flashing, sirens blaring, rushed up on the raised freeway. "Trouble," Rogan said.

"They're forever far away," Shaylyn said.

The police were closing quick. "How fast can cop cars possibly go?" Rogan asked.

A Bugatti Levine Maximus, Ferrari V Straaten Quantum, and a Lamborghini Serrano LZT 890-6. As squad cars? They were approaching blisteringly fast. A laser beam lashed out from the Ferrari. Shaylyn miraculously got them out of the way. A second shot from the Lamborghini Serrano hit her hard, and a moment later Rogan fell from her arms and tumbled to the highway, Ranger's metal skin sparking as it scraped on the pavement while he rolled over and over.

"Ro!" Shay called.

The three cars blazed by him as he rolled into a low crouch, wind sucking as they passed, the Lamborghini nearly clipping him.

"I'm OK," Rogan said, up on his feet and sprinting away.

"I'm taking these guys out," Shaylyn said. "Enough NLEPs and I can fry 'em."

"No!" Rogan replied. "They're just police, doing their jobs. I can ditch them."

The Ranger's max running speed was 120 miles per hour. He'd had the robot up to that speed dozens of times when playing at home and in the brief practice time yesterday, but this was the first time he'd felt the thrill of running this fast with the knowledge he was doing so in real life.

Unfortunately, 120 was nothing to the Dubai police. His computer clocked them at 240 miles per hour, and he quickly saw that he would never outrun these supercars. Flyer swept in to try to pick him up but police laser fire forced her away. Rogan jumped down off the elevated highway to the road below and launched himself as fast as Ranger would go. He passed a big delivery truck, a Toyota sedan, a Ford Mustang, and even an easygoing Corvette.

The supercars stayed with him on the road above, at 120, not even close to top gear. More police and military vehicles were on the way.

"I'm coming to get you!" Shay shouted from above as Rogan ran. "Emirates military drones are coming."

They were entering one of the sections of Dubai with taller buildings, towers, and big apartment complexes.

"Don't slow down to grab me," Rogan yelled. "I'll just hook up with my grappling cable." Flyer soared under the freeway in a blur. Rogan timed his cable perfectly, and was snatched up off the ground in seconds, swinging around like a jet-fast Spider-Man.

WARNING: INCOMING DRONES.

Rogan unleashed three CHEL shots, exploding three drones. But there were so many of them. He was hit in the back. Another beam cut his cable, and he was thrown forward, crashing and rolling through a cross street, smacking the fender of a car before bursting through a large storefront window and taking out a dozen displays on his way through the back wall.

WARNING: RIGHT LATERAL POSTERIOR ARMOR DAMAGED.

Rogan rose from the rubble and took off running again. "Whoever is running the system needs to disconnect me soon," Rogan said. "Ranger isn't going to last much longer."

He shook off a couple of luxury purses that had hooked on him and sprinted away again. Shay dropped down over his street, her NLEP emitter firing, firing, firing.

"I'm taking these drones out!" Shay said. But it took about three of her weaker pulses to drop one drone. They moved fast, and there were a lot of them. Two more drones swept around the corner of a thirty-story building, coming in behind Shay. Rogan raised both arms, a grinding noise coming from his damaged right shoulder, and blasted them to pieces.

"X!" Rogan shouted. "Mr. Culum! Whoever! Get us out of here!"

The loud thunder of automatic gunfire burst from around the corner of a high wall surrounding a mosque. Rogan was knocked back a step as bullets pelted his front side. Ignoring his computer warning, he targeted the soldier's Uzi submachine gun and blasted it to pieces a second later.

"Shay," Rogan said. "They have us surrounded. You'll have to get us out of here."

She flew toward him, reaching out her arms. Another drone swept in overhead and, before Rogan could destroy it, fired a Directed Electromagnetic Pulse.

Electric bolts crackled through Flyer's body. Sparks burst from her back. Shaylyn screamed.

"Shay!" Rogan shouted. Instead of picking him up, she slammed into him, nearly knocking him down.

"It hurts, Rogan!"

"Shay, stay with me!"

Flyer was still convulsing, flailing around maybe, but moving.

"My flight systems are fried!" she shouted. "We're grounded."

Two unmarked cars sped up the street, a big Land Rover and a Mercedes-Benz with its passenger gull-wing door up.

"That's not police," Shay said. "Who are these guys?"

"Shay, go!" Rogan laser-carved the street in front of the cars. Ranger had armor. Flyer didn't.

"I don't want to leave you here," she said.

"I'm right behind you. Go!"

Shay turned and ran. A blue-white sparking bolt crackled past his shoulder, impacting the tall, modern glass-and-steel tower down the street. Electric bolts shock-snapped through the frame of the building's facade.

"What kind of weapon is that?!" Shay asked.

"Some kind of amped-up EMP, maybe?!" Rogan wasn't waiting around to find out. If it could fry the building like that, it was more than enough to destroy vipers.

He rounded a corner, only to bump into Shay, who had stopped. A Humvee waited for them. He dove to the ground, accessing a perfect preprogrammed commando roll, and was just coming up on his feet as another strange power bolt ripped the air above him.

"Control!" Rogan tried again. "Get us out of here! Disconnect us!" Someone had to be monitoring them. Where were they? Unless Culum's plan was to leave their minds inside the robots until both were destroyed.

Rogan sent a laser blast into the Humvee's grille. Sparks and steam burst from under its hood. He ran and leapt to the side of one building, kicking up his feet to lock onto the front wall before launching himself up and back across the street, flipping and readying his cables to start a swing. If he could make it to the top of one of these buildings, he might be able to fire his grappling cable to pick up Flyer.

"Good moves, Rogan," Shay said, shooting NLEPs like crazy. "I'm gonna try—"

A heavy DEMP smashed into her from the Land Rover that had caught up to them. Electric fury crackle-roared through Flyer.

Shay screamed—until her voice went silent and Flyer clunked to the ground, the green line in her face plate winking out.

It was the last thing Rogan saw before a blue-white storm of burning electric power lit up his whole world.

WARNING: TERMINAL VOLTAGE--DIS-RUPT-----

CHAPTER 19

Rogan gasped, the air rushing into his pounding chest, and the pulsing waves within his body thumping up into his ears and skull. His head throbbed with pain like a hot curling iron was ripping through his brain. He tried to sit up, but his vision blurred and he fell straight sideways. His tongue felt cracked and blistered. It dragged across the dry roof of his mouth like a match on a brick.

"Water," someone said, holding a bottle to his lips to help put the fire out.

He drank gratefully, the liquid life flowing back into him, even if, for the moment, he was far from sure that his stomach could keep the water down. Rolling onto his belly, he raised himself up on his elbows as his vision cleared. A kind of hiss-groan was all he could manage. "Sh-Shay?"

"Hurts," Shay said. "Everywhere."

He collapsed back to the bed, holding on to its firm stability like it was a raft on a raging river.

A sight that about made him barf up the water entered his field of vision. Beckett Ewell, leaning down in front of his face. "That was some pretty good work in Dubai." He smiled. "For a loser."

"I'm dead," Rogan said. "And being stuck with you is my eternal punishment."

"If you'd died and gone to heaven, you'd get to be with me," said Beckett. "But you're not dead. Congratulations. You made it."

Rogan pushed himself through the pain to sit up and take in his surroundings. A blank room with white concrete walls and a low ceiling. Shaylyn sat on a low green cot a few feet from him, looking as bad as he felt. And they were surrounded by Beckett, Takashi, and Jacqueline.

All that had just happened in the Burj Khalifa and on the chase through Dubai came flooding back to him, and even though he could see Shaylyn was clearly no longer uploaded to her Flyer viper, he held up his hands to make sure they were warm flesh instead of cold metal too.

"What"—Shaylyn held her hand to her head and sighed—"happened? Where—"

Jackie spoke up. "Relax. You've both been through a lot. Let us explain."

It hurt too much to even nod, so Rogan and Shay merely sat still on their cots. Nobody spoke, but finally, after noticing Jackie and Beckett looking at him, Takashi stepped forward. "Um . . . first, the basics. We were able to hack into the Atomic Frontiers viper signal using a complex transmission that hides itself in the same code used to run the vipers. So the first thing to remember is that the *Laser Viper* Final Challenge wasn't a video game at all. We were all controlling viper-class combat robots in the real world, in real time. The whole time."

"That—" Shay struggled to speak. Tears welled in her eyes. "That can't be true."

Jackie put her arm around Shay's shoulders. "That's what I said when X first brought me here. But listen." She nodded to Takashi.

"Mr. Culum and Atomic Frontiers are up to something horrible. It's more than just a massive company," said Takashi. "They have operatives in business, military, government, and lots of key positions all around the world."

"Call the police," Shay said.

"Atomic Frontiers has people with the police, with the CIA and everything. X and a handful of his allies, like sixty rogue CIA, military intelligence, and law enforcement officers, code-named Scorpion, have been doing their best to figure out Atomic Frontiers' ultimate goal. All those internet interruptions, the website crashes and online chaos that've been happening every once in a while for the last year or so? The recent Virtual City blackout that caused those riots?"

"That was me, by the way," Beckett said to Rogan, "who chased you out of Virtual City. It was too dangerous for you to be in legit digi-space. Culum's people could have found you."

Jackie spoke up. "Scorpion knows Mr. Culum and Atomic Frontiers have been behind the digi-space chaos, but they don't know why. They're not exactly sure what the ultimate goal of the viper program is, but whatever their plan is, Scorpion's attack on Atomic Frontiers headquarters has sped it up."

"Attack?" Rogan asked. "We were just on the run in Dubai. Now . . . what?"

Takashi handed him the bottle of water. "X and some other allies imbedded with him at Atomic Frontiers HQ set off a bunch of small explosions as distractions so they could get your bodies and the mind-streaming equipment out of there."

"That's why nobody would answer us when we were being shot at all over the city?" Shay asked.

"Yeah." Beckett sat down backward on a metal folding chair. "It was crazy."

Takashi continued explaining: "Nobody knew what was going on. But they got you both out. In Dubai, Sheikh Ahmad bin Mohammed Al Abdullah is on Scorpion's side. That's why Culum wanted him gone. The sheikh's private associates were in charge of capturing your vipers with a heavy EMP, to take them out of Atomic Frontiers's hands. They had strict orders to capture, but not destroy your vipers."

Beckett spoke up. "This base is under an old refrigerated warehouse on the south side of Chicago."

"Chicago?" Shaylyn said.

"You've been here for the last five days," Jackie said. "We were starting to worry you wouldn't wake up."

"What about our families? My dog Wiggles?" Rogan said, the sharp fear making his head hurt worse. "If Atomic Frontiers is willing to order assassinations and attacks on battleships, if we've messed up their plans and are missing, knowing what we know, our families—"

"They've all been moved to safe, secret locations." X emerged from the doorway, his rumpled clothes a stark contrast from the perfectly neat appearance he had always presented before. "Your dog too, Rogan. They've been told that Atomic Frontiers is involved in dangerous criminal activities and may be targeting them."

"What did you tell them about us?" Shaylyn sounded worried.

"They've been told you've been secured as witnesses."

"I want to go back to my family," Shaylyn said. "My little brother and sister will be worried about me."

"It's not safe for you to join them," X said.

"Just listen to him, Shay," Jackie said.

"You can't join your families now," X said. "It would put them in danger."

"More importantly," said Beckett, "the world is in danger, and Scorpion needs all of us to save it."

"No," Shaylyn said. "No. I'm done. All I wanted was to play video games, to take my shot at winning the championship and the prize money."

Rogan wished he could go home too. Sleep in his own bed. Log on to school. Listen to his dad tell him about whatever game his company was developing. Ordinary life had never sounded so extraordinary before. But then he thought of all the people he and the rest of the gamers had hurt, maybe even killed, during this fake tournament. He couldn't help them now. But maybe he could help others.

"If all of this is true," Rogan began, "and not another part of the video game tournament—"

"This is real," Takashi promised.

"We can prove it," Beckett said.

Rogan waited for them to quiet down. His head hurt too much for him to talk over them. "You haven't been uploaded like we were. If they can put our minds inside robots or inside video games in the form of robots, then they could put us into video game re-creations of our own bodies."

"I'll do everything I can to prove this isn't a game," X said.

Rogan nodded, knowing that once he'd been part of the machine, reality would never be the same for him again. "I believe you." He added to Shay, "That's why I think we should listen to them. If this has all been real, we've done some bad stuff, and we need to try to make up for it."

"We may not have much time," X said. "Our specialists have decrypted some of the data we were able to steal from Atomic Frontiers computers. We don't know all of Culum's plans, but we know whatever he has in mind, it's big, and part of his goal involves Sun Station One. As you know, the whole idea of the station is to reflect a massive amount of solar energy and transmit that to a giant receiver here on Earth—"

"Yeah, yeah," Shaylyn said. "We've heard all of this."

X rubbed his eyes. Rogan wondered when he had last slept. The big man continued. "What no one else has heard about is how Culum's people have secretly installed a completely different set of reflectors and amplifiers, which will enable the station to fire a beam of devastating high energy with enough power to destroy an entire city."

Shaylyn sighed. "What? Nobody saw this coming? Giant, high-energy-beam-shooting space station. Didn't they ever see *Star Wars*?"

"I thought there were United Nations inspectors on the station, making sure it was all safe," Rogan said.

"The inspectors are Culum's people," X said grimly.

"Or they're dead," said Jackie.

"Either way, we have to stop them," Beckett said.

X nodded. "We don't know when Sun Station One will go online, but we're certain the last required components are on the station. It's down to how fast the workers up there can finish construction."

Shaylyn pulled away from Rogan and stood up, closing her eyes for a moment and taking a deep breath to steady herself. "If Atomic Frontiers has all this advanced technology, how do we—how can anyone—stop them?"

X smiled. "Follow me."

The five gamers were led out of the small, plain, makeshift recovery room and down a short hall. Through a set of battered steel double doors, they entered a giant warehouse space, the freezer units in the ceiling shut down and steel shelves near the walls. As the gamers entered, men and women stood up from their tables and computers. Some rose from cots on the big shelves. For a moment they looked like they might start clapping, but instead, they looked at the gamers, Shay and Rogan in particular, with a kind of exhausted sympathy and respect.

"Welcome to Scorpion," X said. "These are the people responsible for getting you out of the hands of Mr. Culum and Atomic Frontiers and for getting your families to safety. Now they need your help to take Atomic Frontiers down." He led them around a stack of canned food and bottled water to the far corner of the big room.

There, in a straight line, all fixed up and shining under three low-hanging spotlights, were five laser viper advanced combat robots.

Rogan and Shay stepped up to their robots, placing their hands on the cool metal armor. Somehow being in physical contact with what had for so long been, to his understanding, simply a character in a video game, made this entire impossible situation seem more real.

There in front of him was Ranger, with full armor and weapons, simply waiting for its operator. Waiting for Rogan.

"Jackie and I have been working with Scorpion technicians for the last week, repairing and improving all our vipers," Takashi said. "They are all ready."

Shaylyn turned to Takashi. "*You* repaired them?"

"All those technical abilities and programs are just like the pre-programmed combat sequences in Ranger, Tank, and Flyer, still on file in Healer and Engineer. When Jackie and I uploaded to our vipers, we had access to all those technical skills."

"How did you upload to your vipers?" Shaylyn asked.

"With an improved copy of the Velox Mercury X we borrowed from Mr. Culum," said X. "We're not sure what he has in mind, but some version of that transmitter is a big part of it."

"It all must fit together," Beckett said. "The viper robots. The electronic disguise system. The data transmitter."

"That's why we need you to get back into your vipers to infiltrate Atomic Frontiers headquarters, tap into their computers to learn about Culum's plans, stop whatever Culum and his allies are planning, and expose the truth about all of it to the world."

"Why us?" Shaylyn said. "You have police and Army guys working here? Why can't they do this stuff?"

"It's because of our implants," Jackie said simply. She seemed to read Shay's questioning look because she added quickly, "Yep. All of us. Mine was to treat depression. It's a new technology, and it doesn't work well when installed in a fully developed adult brain. That's why, so far, only kids have them."

"We need you to do this," X said.

"Easy for you to say." Shaylyn rubbed her temples. "You weren't fried in that last round. Last time, we were trapped in those robots, and we could have been killed."

"I think we've fixed that," Jackie said.

Takashi nodded. "We've altered the system to give you, the viper operator, full control. When you want out of the robot and back into your own body, you just choose to make the switch. So we won't be trapped."

"We've also adjusted the pain sensitivity," X said. "So if your viper is shot by a laser or something, it won't hurt nearly as bad."

"Still," Shaylyn said. "There has to be someone else who—"

"There is nobody else," Rogan said quietly. "Nobody else has the implants to let them connect to our laser vipers, and nobody else has our robot combat experience. Pretty soon, Culum will be armed with a giant space laser." The bitterness that came from knowing he had trusted and admired Culum so much burned in Rogan. "Who knows what else he has planned? But he's shown that he's an expert liar, and he doesn't care who he hurts to get what he wants. As laser vipers, we're the best fighting force to stop him. It's up to us.

"We have a couple of days to rest and test the vipers?" Rogan looked to X, who nodded. "Then let's get ready."

-----◇-----

After a day of testing the NeuroCon uplink to their vipers and the team practicing the little they could in the limited space of the warehouse and in the limited time they had available, the pain in Rogan and Shay's bodies had faded. The guilt and fear in all of them had not. While a truck hauled their vipers to Atomic Frontiers headquarters in Washington, DC, the five gamers sat on green canvas army-style cots arranged in a circle and talked about what had happened and what was to come.

"I'm scared right now," Takashi said. "But then I remember all those tourists in Neuschwanstein Castle. They were terrified."

Shay nodded. "Crying. Screaming."

"Begging us to let them go," Rogan said.

"Now I'm glad I was kicked out after the first round," Beckett said. "When X first tried to explain about Scorpion and the trouble with Culum, when he had me sent here, I didn't believe him. I tried to fight. Tried to escape. Then I watched live news coverage of the so-called terrorist attack in Germany. We had access to what I thought was game footage at the same time. I almost threw up. After that, we were trying to break through to be able to communicate with you while you were in the game. I wanted to warn you all so bad."

"You almost did," Rogan said. "Those little interruptions at least had us wondering."

"We were lucky X had people to send us here," Jackie said. "He had orders to . . ."

"Culum told him to kill us," Beckett finished for her. "We might as well be honest about it. He was supposed to kill us all one by one, and then, after we were all gone, I don't know. Make up some story for our families like it was an accident, maybe, or—"

"Or he thought by that time he would have accomplished his goals and nobody would be able to stop him," Takashi said.

"Really?" Shay asked. "You think it could be on that level?"

"Oh, this is global," Beckett said. "I've had longer to check out what Scorpion knows about Culum and Atomic Frontiers. They're everywhere, and they've been setting this up for years."

"But I fell for it," Rogan says. "I fell for the whole game tournament lie, for all of it. I feel like such an idiot."

"Don't beat yourself up," Takashi said. "We all fell for it. Even our parents believed in the video game contest. They signed the forms. They sent us—"

Rogan shook his head. "No, not just that. Not just the final challenge. I mean I fell for *all* of it. Culum seemed like such a good guy. So friendly, loved games, and he really seemed to care for people, you know?" Rogan looked around at the four of them. He had a feeling they *did* know, but no one said anything. "Culum really did build the hypernet and expand it around the world for everyone. And Sun Station One seemed like the best way to finally beat pollution and save the planet. He always talked about equality. Uniting people and bringing them together in peace. Not shooting them. *Ego sum maximus*? Yeah right. I'm not the best. *Ego sum stupidus*."

"He tricked the whole world, Ro," Shay said quietly. "He has two Nobel Prizes." She paused for a moment. Then she smiled. "But yeah, you were pretty stupid for thinking you're a better gamer than me."

The whole group cracked up, a bit too loudly, it seemed, for their Scorpion allies who had managed a little sleep that night. They quieted down, waving and offering whispered apologies.

"No, but that reminds me of something," Beckett said. He licked his lips and picked the strings on a frayed corner of his cot. "I, um . . ." He let out a heavy breath. "I wanted to say I'm sorry. For the way I acted. During the game—er—during the first—the thing on the ship. Also in the dorms."

"I was kind of the same way," Rogan said. "But it's cool."

"We're a team now, man," Takashi said.

Beckett's eyes were a little red, and he blinked a lot. "When my parents split up, their divorce was like a battle. So I thought that's how life is. Take what you can get while you can, and who cares about other people." He finally looked up at the others. "But maybe that's how Culum is, and I don't want to be like him." His body shook a little with a small sob. "Now I might not see either of my parents again." He put his face in his hands.

"Hey." Shay moved over to Beckett's cot and put her arm around him. "It's OK, buddy."

"We're all with you," Jackie said.

"You will see them again," Rogan said. "Because it's like Takashi said. We're a team. Atomic Frontiers might have tricked us into doing some bad stuff. But as vipers, we're good in combat."

Shay cut in. "Yeah, we beat an entire Chinese warship, and that's when we were fighting one another almost as much as fighting the sailors and marines."

Rogan smiled. "Culum has run things according to his plan so far, but he never planned on the five of us joining together. The situation has just been reprogrammed. He better strap in, because in a few hours, he's going to be smashed by the full force of the Gamer Army."

CHAPTER 20

Rogan must have had at least a few hours' sleep because Shay finally shook him awake. X stood next to the gamers' circle of cots. "The vipers are in position. We're ready for the NeuroCon upload." He led them to the makeshift med bay in a different corner of the warehouse, where five cots were set up next to complex computer equipment and five cables waited to be connected to each of their brain implants.

When everyone was in position and connected, X hesitated with his finger over the initiate button. "I've been a soldier, and I've worked in security and intelligence all my adult life. I've spent fifteen years training for combat and specializing in secret operations. If I had the implant or the time to have one installed, whatever the risks, I would do it, and I would go on this mission myself. I'm sorry for being hard on you during your missions. I was worried you'd be killed, and I wanted you to be the best you could be, to keep you alive. I'm sorry to have to put you all in this position. I know when you're twelve, you feel like you're pretty grown-up, leaving little kid stuff behind. But you're far too young to be sent into a fight like this. I wish there were another way."

"Xavier," Shay said. "It's Culum's fault we have to do this."

"You saved all our lives," said Jackie.

Paradoxically, Rogan's irritation with the delay helped him push aside his fear of what lay ahead. "It's like you said. There's no time. So hit the switch, and let's do this."

X nodded and smiled. It looked like something that he had been holding back for a long, long while. "Go get 'em, gamers." He pressed the button and dizziness swept over them as the warehouse digi-blurred, to be replaced by the dark, red-lit confines of a semitrailer. They were all standing, and everyone staggered a bit as they adjusted to the transition.

With X and several other members of Scorpion so familiar with Atomic Frontiers' security procedures, and with the technical resources the rogue organization had at its disposal, it didn't take long to program the Polyadaptive Nanotech Cloaks to disguise five vipers as high-level Atomic Frontiers security personnel, and to issue them forged identification cards.

Moments later, all five of them climbed down from the back of the trailer in Washington, DC, looking like five guards in dark blue uniforms with the electron-over-the-globe-nucleus logo on the front shirt pocket.

"I'll never get used to that dizziness and digital dissolve." Flyer spoke in a deep man's voice. The others would not have known who she was if their HUDs had not projected her name in the air above her.

They were on a street with a perfect view of the Capitol building, the White House, and the Washington Monument. Holographic maps floated in the lower left corner of their field of vision, showing the way to their destination, and the five of them set out walking, alone on the sidewalk except for a few early morning joggers, as the sun rose on a new day.

"It's weird speaking with someone else's voice," Tank said. The security guard he was disguised as spoke with one of those higher, flat, nasally voices. It was almost funny.

"Weirder than our minds being in robot bodies?" Engineer asked.

They talked like that, when they talked at all, until they neared the semitruck delivery gate to the supply storage yard at the back of the massive company headquarters.

"*OK, gamers,*" X said on their channel. "*Here we go. Your vipers are programmed to appear relaxed and comfortable so that you blend in and nobody suspects you, but your words can give you away, so you'll want to keep the chatter on internal comms. Who wants to be first to test their identification card?*"

Engineer stepped up to the shack next to the gate and presented her fake ID to the guard in front of the service entrance. The man's eyes were half-closed, and he barely looked at the person he was supposed to be scanning in, but made a pathetic, half-hearted show of holding the card up to compare its photo to the person before him. Then he swiped the card on a reader next to him and waited a moment. When a light flashed green, he handed the card back, grunted, and motioned Engineer through the gate, instantly holding out his hand for the next ID.

"*Easy so far,*" Healer said internally.

"*Speak for yourself,*" Tank said, struggling to step through the little gate sideways. His PNC might have made him appear as a slightly overweight security man, but no human being was as big as the Tank viper, and this gate was designed for people, not large advanced fighter robots. He saw the gate guard staring at him, confused, and worried about blowing his cover. "I, um . . ." Tank spoke out loud in his false voice. "I have this weird rash. On my inner thigh. So I have to walk funny or—"

"Take it up with your supervisor," said the gate guard. "I don't want to hear about your personal problems."

When they'd all cleared security, they headed through a large paved lot where trucks could drop off deliveries at the five gates. Some materials were stacked on pallets at the edge of this yard under tarps. They followed their maps to a door near the semi docks.

"*You're in a low-security area,*" X told them. "*Through the warehouses you should be able to access a level-one security computer terminal. Engineer, whatever else happens on this mission, you need to hack the Atomic Frontiers system and transmit that data to us so that we can get it out to the world.*"

"*So in case we can't stop Culum, others can take a crack at him?*" Tank asked.

"*We'll stop him,*" said Engineer.

"*You make it sound so easy,*" Flyer said. "*If Culum and his people were able to fool all of us and our families, not to mention all this other stuff he's done, and nobody else has caught onto him, you can bet this will be tough.*"

"*At least our PNC disguises are holding up,*" Rogan said as he spotted another of the dozens of security cameras they'd passed in the corridors so far.

They reached a locked door, and Engineer quickly stepped up to go to work. To anyone watching, it appeared as if a security guard had plugged his finger into the lock, but the gamers knew Engineer was at work with one of her sophisticated lock-picking tools. In seconds, she had the door open, and they stepped into a nightmare.

It was some kind of factory with large conveyor belts and overhead hooks on chains. Robot arms with welding torches, plasma cutters, rivet guns, and other complex tools stood by. The entire industrial system was inactive, dimly lit. And under the quarter lighting, in the shadows cast by the manufacturing equipment, stood a small army of laser viper advanced combat robots.

The gamers saw them as soon as they entered, and immediately raised their arms, ready to drop their PNC disguises to fire. But the robots didn't move. The readouts on the gamers' HUDs showed negligible power readings.

"*It's OK.*" Engineer stepped up to the long line of Engineer mods. "*They're all inactive.*"

"*Waiting for operators?*" Healer asked.

"*X,*" Rogan said. "*Are you getting all this?*"

Five lines, one for each mod, stood ten vipers deep. Fifty laser vipers and a factory to manufacture more. It was creepy walking in front of those still robots, like watching a giant formation of mummies. Mummies with enough firepower to level the whole city.

"Yeah," X said. "*We're reading you. Recording it all. You're in one of the secret areas of headquarters, a section where even insiders like me were not allowed. Now I see why.*"

The gamers walked down the aisle among the statuesque robots.

"Why build all these?" Flyer asked out loud. "What's Culum going to do, host ten more fake video game tournaments?"

"*Maybe he wants an army?*" Engineer stuck with internal comms. "*Fifty laser vipers would be enough to take over a small country. Scanning this factory, it looks fully automated. But why build so few?*"

X answered. "*Laser vipers are hard to make. The materials are expensive and the process is complex, even when they're being built by machines.*"

"*And we don't know how long Atomic Frontiers have been building these,*" Healer said. "*Maybe they only started recently.*"

"*OK, but then why shut it all down?*" Engineer asked. "*Why is all of this inactive?*" Even as she spoke, she didn't notice the twitch in the finger of the tank next to her, the slight movement of a ranger's head.

Flyer raised the alarm first, just as Rogan, leading the line of gamers, reached the far end of the viper formation. "Wait a sec. Did that thing move?" She pointed at a flyer mod. "I swear it totally moved its arm."

"*Stick to internal comms,*" Rogan said. "*We don't want to let them know we're here.*"

The V lines flashed to life in the faceplates of all fifty laser vipers. Unlike the different colors in each gamer's viper, all of these robots glowed red. The ten flyers launched up into the air and slammed down onto the concrete floor ahead of them.

"Too late," Engineer said out loud. "They know we're here."

A tank next to Rogan swung its massive arm and bashed him in the face, knocking him off his feet.

"Drop the cloaks!" Flyer yelled, her digital disguise melting away. "Shoot 'em!"

Tank ducked two laser shots from a couple of rangers as his PNC shut down and his weapons came online. He threw back his massive elbow to knock an engineer away and then held up both arms to blast full CHELs and plasma cannons straight through the chests of two healers, leaving only the scraps of their arms and legs. "Oh yeah! Let's tear 'em up!"

Shaylyn was up in the air fast and dodging a storm of NLEPs from the other flyers who soared up to meet her. One punched her head. Another planted a fast flying kick to her chest. "Too many of them!" Flyer shouted to the others.

Three tanks unleashed a fierce laser storm straight at Takashi. The enemy fire would have destroyed him, but the Healer thought fast and pulled an enemy engineer in front of him as a shield. He shoved a ranger into harm's way next. Both enemy vipers were destroyed.

Rogan cursed at himself for leading his team right into the middle of such an obvious trap. He fired a DEMP at an enemy tank, but only knocked it back. Trying to help Shay, he blasted both CHELs at flyers, which dodged out of the way. Two rangers stepped to either side of him, claws drawn. Sparks flew from his armor as they slashed at him. He accessed his combat programs and whipped out a side kick, knocking one back. He was about to shoot the other when a third ranger's grappling cable grabbed his arm and yanked him back.

Enemy tanks and rangers blasted Beckett from all directions, firing and moving too fast for him to adapt. "You guys, I'm in trouble! Who's controlling these things anyway?"

> WARNING: ENERGY ABSORPTION
> TRANSFORMATION ARMOR APPROACHING
> MAXIMUM CAPACITY.

Jackie slapped a charge on a ranger's back and threw herself into a commando roll on the floor as she detonated the explosives, destroying the thing. "They're slow to react! I think they're automated, like basic video game AI." She was back on her feet for only seconds before a tank's heavy plasma bolt knocked Jackie back hard, sending her flying and crashing into a steel handrail. The bar broke away and she landed on a metal platform among viper parts. The blast and crash would have killed a human, but her viper body held up. Likewise, the pain from the attack was greatly reduced. Still, she didn't want to go through that again.

The five vipers of the Gamer Army were outnumbered and hopelessly outgunned, having destroyed only five of the fifty enemy vipers.

"We have to get out of here!" Tank shouted. "They're killing us! Let's regroup and try again another time!"

An enemy engineer leapt atop Jackie, punching hard, leaving dents in the steel platform right by her head. It was quickly aiming its laser, but Jackie was faster, grabbing its wrist and holding the weapon away. It attempted to react and change tactics, but Jackie was way ahead of it, reaching out and connecting to a programming access point on a computer control unit for one of the factory robots. "You might have both of my arms busy," Jackie said, "but a good engineer always works around the problem." The plasma cutter on the factory robot arm jammed into the enemy engineer's back, burning right through the robot's motor control center. Sparks popped out of it, and the engineer fell limp.

An enemy ranger whipped a hard kick to Rogan's stomach, bending him over in the middle. Another ranger punched his head with a devastating uppercut so hard he flipped end over end and crashed into Tank.

WARNING: MINOR MOTOR SYSTEMS DAMAGE IN CRANIAL AREA.

Rogan's head was locked into a twisted sideways position, as though something had broken in Ranger's neck.

Healer was by his side in an instant. "I can fix that."

"Good to have you back, buddy," Rogan said.

An enemy ranger made a rush at Healer, but Engineer jumped in at the last second, pulling a heavy electrical cable she'd freed from the factory works. She jammed the cable under the ranger's head, and raw electric power coursed through it, the enemy robot spasming violently.

"I'm done messing around with these guys," Engineer said. "Gamers, you about ready to fight back?"

Healer repaired Rogan's neck, so that he could nod his head. He elbowed Tank. "What do you say, big guy? Remember how vicious you were on the *Tianjin*?"

If Beckett hadn't been uploaded to Tank, he would have smiled. "Oh yeah!" In the back of his mind he recognized how strange it was to be able to open his own enormous shoulders just as easily as someone might move an arm, but he mostly focused on using his HUD to target different tanks in front of him. Seconds later, six Hellfire missile roared from his shoulder launchers and exploded into enemy tanks.

Four of them were destroyed, but two staggered and somehow remained functional, until the combined weapons of the rest of the Gamer Army put them down.

With no time to celebrate, Rogan fired his grappling cables to grab two enemy healer mods and yank them into the air toward him. "Batter up, Beckett!"

Tank lasered the arms and legs off one and caught the other. With an enraged scream, Beckett's Tank engaged full motor power and ripped the smaller healer viper's limbs off before dropping it and stomping its head to pieces.

Shaylyn flew blindingly fast, but with full neurolytic control, her viper also responded more rapidly and smoother than ever before, and she started to pick up the flight pattern of the ten enemy flyer vipers she was up against. She grabbed one by the back of its neck with her foot to hold it in place, and unloaded NLEPs as fast as she could until the enemy was fried. An enemy ranger took a laser shot at her, but she used the dead flyer as a shield and then kicked in her afterburners to swoop down and club an enemy engineer with it, the impact so hard it messed up the engineer's motor systems long enough for Jackie to place explosives on its back and Tank to back-hand it into an enemy ranger, exploding them both.

As the five members of the Gamer Army began to work together, defending and assisting one another as a team, more and more enemy robots were destroyed. But none of the Gamer Army's robot soldiers worked as hard, fast, or accurately as Takashi. He hadn't been totally satisfied with his performance as Healer when he thought the final challenge was a video game, and with so much more at stake fighting in real life, he was determined to do better. There were certain automatic repair programs stored within Healer, within himself when he was uploaded to Healer, so that he could start his left hand and the various repair tools on his left arm to fixing a section of Tank's armor or Engineer's leg, while he fired hundreds of NLEPs at lightly armored flyers with his right. He took down at least three of them himself, while keeping his friends operational. Parts weren't a problem, as he could harvest replacement components from the supplies in the enemy healers or from the other disabled and destroyed vipers.

There weren't many operational enemy vipers remaining. Shaylyn cheered as she shot another flyer out of the air. Rogan connected two CHEL beams to shred another flyer that had been on Shay's tail. Four DEMPs from Beckett were enough to scramble the armor and confuse the computers of the last enemy tank. Jackie leapt to that tank's shoulders and connected to take over its onboard computer, turning its weapons against the enemy,

Hellfire missiles killing the remaining rangers, plasma cannons cutting the last of the engineers to pieces. Takashi not only fixed his friends, but used the battle as an opportunity to practice several new fighting techniques, helping him destroy plenty of the enemy robots. Five of them had destroyed fifty, and though the battle was fierce, leaving the factory in ruins, the entire fight was over in less than ten minutes.

"Yeah!" Tank slapped Engineer a high five, metal clanking on metal.

Flyer landed next to Rogan and threw her arms around him, picking him up in the air and spinning him around. "We did it!"

Healer and Engineer didn't join in the celebration. Healer hurried with the remaining repairs to his fellow vipers. He'd found six unfired missiles in the wrecks of enemy tanks and used them to reload Beckett. He patched Ranger's armor. He swapped Flyer's nearly burned out NonLethal Energy Pulse emitter for a more powerful laser and the power upgrade to run it, asking Engineer to check his work against her own preprogrammed technical knowledge. He also asked Engineer's help putting together a new weapon from some of the defunct viper power cells and some factory components in case they faced more trouble. Now he had his own plasma cutter mounted on his right arm, a useful weapon, if the improvised power system mounted on his back held up.

"This isn't over," Jackie reminded the others as she ran final checks on Healer's new system. "There's a lot more to do, and by now all of Atomic Frontiers knows we're here. Police . . . maybe even the Army are on their way right now. This whole fight was probably covering Culum's escape."

"*I'm not going anywhere.*" Mr. Culum's voice came over speakers from somewhere. All five gamers whipped their heads up, searching the room.

"*But I did need to buy time for my loyal associates to move to safety.*" They raised their arms, ready to shoot at whatever was about to attack them. But no attack came. Culum's voice continued. "*And to see the technology you stole from me in action. I'm most impressed by your performance. It's good to have you back. You've returned to Atomic Frontiers because you think you want to stop me. Join me in your old gaming arena, and I'll explain why you should really want to* help *me.*"

"The old join-the-evil-mastermind trick?" Flyer said. "Do you really think we'll fall for that?"

Culum's old friendly laugh echoed through the dark room. "*There's no trick to fall for. I promise you. I'm only trying to help people, and you can be a part of that. You've undoubtedly been sent to kill or capture me. So you must come to the game arena anyway. I'll wait for you here*"—he paused, and then spoke with an icy irony—"*gamers.*" A door at the far end of the giant factory room slid open, inviting them to whatever new horrors Culum had in mind.

CHAPTER 21

Half a continent away from the gamers' struggle in Washington, DC, United States Air Force General James Hide, commander of US Strategic Command, headquartered at Offutt Air Force Base near Omaha, Nebraska, was shaken awake by Captain Hillary Hess. His first response was to prepare to fight an intruder, his second to yell at his subordinate for waking him at such an insane hour. But many years of training led him to resist those impulses and cut to business.

"Time," said the general.

"Zero three fifteen hours, sir," the captain answered. She was also well trained and quickly explained the situation. "Sir, there's some kind of global cyberattack. Systems are being disrupted everywhere. Everything. The electrical grid. Financial. Communications. Defense. Source of the attack is unknown. We're working on it. The president is on the line to speak to you." General Hide reached for the red phone next to his bed, but the captain shook her head. "The last secure line we can keep open is in the command center. Car and driver are waiting."

"Set condition one throughout the base."

"Already done, sir."

The electricity in the general's house and across the base winked out for a moment, emergency generators taking over almost without interruption to maintain power for critical systems. The little light that spilled into the general's dark house left half his face in shadow. He paused for just a moment. "You're shaking, Captain. Get yourself under control."

"Sorry, sir. This thing . . . it's bigger—worse than anything we've trained for."

The general leapt from his bed and sprinted from the room, wearing only a T-shirt and athletic shorts. "Let's go! Have someone bring me a uniform."

-----○-----

The five laser vipers ran through the empty hallways of Atomic Frontiers central command, hurrying through an office area with scattered papers, overturned desk chairs, and even some of the computers still on.

Tank shoved a desk out of the way to make room for his bulky body. He switched to internal comms. *"Maybe you should hack the computer system from here, Jackie."*

"These are just access terminals," Jackie replied. *"There will be a ton of lockouts between here and the Atomic Frontiers mainframe. I need to physically access the heart of their data storage if I'm going to find what we need."*

"You all need to hurry," X said on their channel. *"Those glitches and outages that have been going down more and more over the last year are spiking. The entire game credit economy in Virtual City has crashed. Riots in VR and IRL. It's like the whole hypernet is breaking down. And this surge started right after you arrived at Atomic*

Frontiers CentCom. Whatever is happening there is bigger than we thought. Move it!"

They entered the atrium with the model of Sun Station One. Before, when they thought all this was a game, the space station looked like a symbol of hope. But now, they all imagined the thing as a giant cannon, floating in space, with the power to destroy whole cities and no weapon being able to counteract it, no missile capable of reaching it before being destroyed.

Jackie pointed down one of the six hallways that met at that juncture. *"Their central computer is down there,"* she said internally. *"Should I go for it now, or come help you with Culum?"*

"I don't think we'll need that much help to capture an old man," Beckett said.

"He's a billionaire genius with endless weapons at his disposal," Takashi said. *"Who knows what he's capable of? You don't think he's simply going to surrender, do you?"*

"I'll go with her," said Shaylyn. *"There may be guards, more vipers, or other security in the building. She may need protection."*

"Right," said Rogan. *"Then let's move fast and finish this."*

While Engineer and Flyer went to infiltrate the Atomic Frontiers main computer, Healer and Rogan ran as fast as Tank could go, the big guy out front as a shield in case Shay had been right about more vipers.

But when Tank kicked down the doors and the three vipers rushed into the game arena, they found not another army of lethal advanced combat robots, but one old man in black clothes and a lumpy gray cardigan.

"See?" Tank said. "Told you."

"Welcome back to the arena," Mr. Culum said calmly. "Though all five of you might as well have come see me. Miss Sharpe won't be successful at infiltrating my computers. After all, I designed both the engineer viper *and* the mainframe she's trying to hack. Anyway, she needn't bother trying to steal information about my ultimate goal. I will simply tell you, especially since the entire world will soon know of the complete change I am bringing." He pushed his hands deep into his sweater pockets. "I must admit your interference has forced me to take ultimate action before the time was ideal."

Tank stepped forward, his giant feet clanking hard on the black arena floor. He raised an arm, readying enough laser and plasma power to vaporize the man. "Forget this! I say we take him to the police right now."

Mr. Culum laughed. "In a matter of hours, the police won't be able to help you. The world is about to move beyond the need for such brutal, adversarial, punitive forces like police."

Takashi stepped forward. "What are you talk—"

"Singularity is near!" Culum's triumphant voice echoed through the shadows of the dark arena.

-----o-----

In London thousands of people panicked as financial records of various kinds, from savings accounts to major stock holdings, were suddenly wiped out.

"Do you mean your computer is down?" one concerned man asked a bank employee.

"No, sir. It all appears to be working perfectly. But I've checked and double-checked. You have no money in your account, sir."

"That's impossible!" the man shouted. "There were over ten thousand pounds in that account only this morning."

The nervous bank man nodded. "Yes, I saw it myself. But then it changed to zero. If you'll allow me to check . . ." He frowned. "Well, the account into which you wanted the money transferred reads zero as well."

"Now see here! I want to talk to your supervisor!"

The man behind the counter already had the phone to his ear. "Yes, sir. One moment." He frowned and pressed another button on the phone. Another. He hung up and tried again. He let out an exasperated breath. "And now my phone's dead," he said to his customer. "I swear, every machine is rubbish today." Both men exchanged a worried look as the electricity in London winked out.

-----o-----

The chief air traffic control operator at Hong Kong International Airport nervously paced his darkened tower, fighting the urge to tell his technicians to hurry up. He knew they were working as fast as they could, and yelling at them would only make them more prone to mistakes. His was a business of careful precision, and no one was helped by panic.

His computers had just scrambled, and most had shut down. Communications weren't working. All of his radar was out. All of it. Hong Kong International was the eighth busiest airport by passenger and the world's number one busiest airport for cargo traffic. And it was blind. His screens showed nothing, but even though he had sent security to every gate and to the tarmac in order to ground all traffic that hadn't yet departed, he knew he had dozens of aircraft up there. Hundreds, maybe thousands of passengers. And he had no way to direct them.

"We've tried everything, sir," one of the technicians said. "We've power cycled each computer. We've brought in new units. This doesn't make sense. But we better do something soon or—"

An enormous explosion shook the sky outside the tower, and the burning remains from the collision of two large jet planes fell to the runway.

"Get me an independent radio transmitter. Something not connected to the network!" the chief said. "We must start talking to our planes, or that won't be the last crash."

-----o-----

The CEO of a major online retailer screamed at his technical people. "What do you mean, the site is down?! That's impossible! You mean some products are unavailable?"

His lead technical advisor swallowed nervously. "No, sir. I mean the entire site, every page, from product descriptions to help pages. All of our stores in Virtual City, their records. All of it is gone. We don't know how. Our VR employees can't even access their store-issued avatars."

The CEO wiped his sweaty brow. "Backup servers."

"I don't know," said the advisor. "We can't access them. I can't even get anyone on the phone over there."

The CEO slumped into a chair. "We're a ninety-*billion*-dollar company. If we don't have a site or our digi-space stores—"

"We still have some of our brick-and-mortar operations," the advisor said. "And of course all our people are working to restore everything else, but there's some kind of computer virus—"

"We're worth *nothing*!" the CEO screamed, his mind whirling with the money they were losing, with the losses the shareholders would suffer, some with their entire retirement portfolios invested in his company. Over a quarter of a million employees whose livelihoods depended on him. How many would he have to lay off or fire? "Get it back! Get it back *now* or this company and the whole country are in serious trouble!"

-----○-----

Jackie had connected Engineer's onboard computers to the enormous Atomic Frontiers central mainframe. Engineer came equipped with multiple redundant superprocessors, and a hyper-fast artificial intelligence that could blaze through trillions of combinations a second, changing the form of its attack on a foreign computer faster than most firewalls could adapt. It didn't seek only one point of entry to a system but came at the enemy computer from many directions at once, and its attacks were constantly changing. Most commercial antivirus software didn't stand a chance.

"This is weird," Jackie said to Shaylyn, who paced the large refrigerated room, watching for trouble. It was hard to describe to someone unconnected to Engineer's technology just how it felt to infiltrate a foreign computer with the force of her mind, using superhuman abilities that were somehow added to her when her consciousness was uploaded to her viper. "When I hack a computer, I can sort of . . . feel my way through the other system. It's like . . . like I'm going through a maze, in a dream. And the correct path around the computer's security lights up for me when Engineer's hacking processors find a way through. Only this time, I work my way around a dead end, and the path is open in front of me. But when I go ahead, the maze changes, and I'm blocked again. Like, Atomic Frontiers computer security is letting me infiltrate just a little, only to change and block me. It feels like it's messing with me. Playing games almost."

"Your viper is buzzing louder and louder," Shay said. "Are you OK?"

"Speeding up my hacking processors," Jackie said. "Everything I just explained happened about ten thousand times in the time it took me to explain it in words. I've got to move faster to beat this thing. I may not be able to talk to you for a while. Don't worry. It's just me fighting the toughest computer in the world."

-----o-----

"It's some kind of virus, sir," Colonel Schejter shouted when General Hide entered the chaotic command center. "Like nothing I've ever seen before. It's like it's alive, causing chaos everywhere, but almost deliberately trying to circumvent every computer security procedure for our nuclear weapons."

"All right, lock it up!" General Hide called out to quiet the room. "Calm down and do your jobs." He grabbed the secure phone line Captain Hess held out to him. "This is General Hide."

A voice on the other end of the line gave a code to let the general know the message was authentic. The general responded with his own code. The voice answered, *"Stand by for the president."*

"General Hide," the president said. *"Listen, because I don't know how long we'll have this secure connection. We're going to DEFCON One. Langley's confirmed the virus is originating from Atomic Frontiers headquarters in DC. They have a team on site trying to stop it, but One can't wait. This thing is causing worldwide destruction. I've managed to get through to scramble three F-thirty-fives. They're inbound to destroy the entire facility. If they fail, I've got a destroyer off Maryland ready to pound that place with cruise missiles. I need you to give us time, keep our nukes secure. This thing has to be stopped at all—"*

The line cut out. The general felt the eyes of everyone in the room upon him. He said a quick, silent prayer, hoping he was making the correct decision. "Before loss of communication, the president of the United States ordered me to keep our nuclear weapons secure. But it's our control computers that are turning against us. Get the word out whatever way you can. Phone, radios, paper airplanes if you have to. Every single unit must manually secure its weapons. I want nothing automated, no nuclear weapons connected to networked computers."

Colonel Schejter objected. "Sir, with no computer control, we'll be vulnerable if any enemies launch—"

"Do it now!" General Hide ordered. "Before our computers start launching their own attack."

-----o-----

"This is really bad," Takashi said.

"What? *Singularity*?" Rogan said. "A really old video game. About time travel, I think? My dad used to play it."

"No, I saw it on an episode of *Doctor Who*," said Beckett. "It's like a black hole."

"That's not what he's talking about," said Takashi. "Singularity is when a computer comes alive, when it becomes so advanced that it becomes self-aware."

"That's a pretty good explanation from a limited intelligence like yours." There was no sarcasm, no malice, in Mr. Culum's voice. His words sounded completely sincere, with perhaps the smallest edge of pity. "Singularity is the point at which there is no discernible difference between biological intelligence and artificial intelligence." He held up a finger. "But you suffer under the same erroneous assumption that has beleaguered paranoid science-fiction horror story authors for years, for decades. Singularity need not result from some computer, like Terminator's Skynet, one day, for no reason, gaining sentience. Rather, Singularity will be the inevitable result of the fusion of biological and artificial intelligence."

He turned his head and pushed aside his hair to show his brain implant access port.

"I was once consumed with the shallow ambitions of limited biological humanity, the drive for wealth, power, prestige, the constant pressure to expand my company's holdings, increase its profits, drive up the value of its stock. I needed to think faster, remember more, sleep less, and to that end, I enhanced my own brain with deep brain tissue implants, which not only provided electrical stimulation to help regulate the challenges you children face, but also tripled my memory, sped up my thinking, enabled me to expand my creativity beyond—" He laughed. "Well, beyond my earlier imagination. Soon, all those old petty concerns were in my past, and I realized that the true path to greatness lay not in working to push forward the evolution of humanity's technology, but through technology, advancing the evolution of humanity itself.

"I am enhanced, I am hyper-human, but because of the limited capacity of the hardware and software augmentation within my brain, I am still limited. For now."

"The network interruptions," Takashi said. "He's connecting himself to the hypernet, to computers everywhere."

"Not connecting to," Mr. Culum said. "I am merging with the hypernet. With every computer, tablet, phone, smart TV, automobile, and piece of military hardware connected to it. Soon I will *be* every one of those devices, and they will all be me."

"He's gone insane," Takashi said. "He had the implants installed too late in life. They've messed him up."

Mr. Culum smiled kindly. "No. I beg you to listen to me. You have your powerful weapons, and I am only an old man. Give me time to explain. Please. Rogan, in the short time you've been with me here at Atomic Frontiers, I've taken better care of you than your own parents, spent more time with you than they have in months! Can't you repay my kindness by giving me the opportunity to explain?"

A sudden hot fury spiked through Rogan when he considered that at least part of him had thought the same thing Culum had just said. "My parents never lied to me!" Rogan shouted. "They never sent me out into the world to hurt people!"

Mr. Culum went on. "I've devoted my life to equality, to giving everyone all over the world equal access to the hypernet, to as much information as possible, so that everyone had greater opportunity to educate themselves, improve themselves, and so everyone could meet and interact safely, in peace, in digi-space. That's why I founded Virtual City. I paid for this expansion of access out of my own personal finances. I spent billions of my own money to do this."

He began pacing, as though lecturing a classroom. "I thought doing so would tear down international boundaries and bring people together. If Americans could easily meet and make friends with, say, Iranians, in virtual reality, they wouldn't argue for sanctions or war. There would be a greater incentive for peace. But!" He held up a single finger. "It was all still bound by market forces, by the archaic rules for who can have what, how much, and when. Instead of moving humanity past that cruel reality, that divisiveness was simply replicated in digi-space.

"I realized that competition of this nature is simply a holdover from an earlier stage of evolution, the chaos that comes from an uncontrolled struggle to survive. I am the greatest optimist this world has ever known, and I believe that, on its own, humanity will eventually change, and grow, and move past these things. But only after perhaps hundreds of years and hundreds of thousands of needless deaths and millions of people needlessly suffering."

"*X, are you getting all this?*" Rogan asked.

"Recording it all. The news channels that are still on the air are reporting several plane crashes, a nuclear power plant meltdown, massive power and communications outages. You guys have to stop him."

"Others can sit back and let all that suffering happen," Culum continued. "But not me! Not William J. Culum!" He turned his intense gaze on the vipers. "Do you *want* children to starve?! Do you want more wars fought over oil, over territory or other resources? Do you want greed-driven industry to continue to pollute the planet until *nothing* can live here? I'm here to save humanity! I am its greatest hope, greatest ally! Will you oppose me? Will you be humanity's enemy?"

Rogan thought Culum sounded enthusiastic, like always, but also that what he was saying made some sense. Maybe he could be reasoned with. "But what you're doing is hurting people. It's causing so much —"

"People always fear what they do not understand," Culum proclaimed. "People have always feared technology. Especially advanced technology. For, as Arthur C. Clarke teaches us, 'Any sufficiently advanced technology is indistinguishable from magic.' Opposition to technology is simply the twenty-first century's equivalent to the witch trials from hundreds of years ago. We have seen what happens when people resist the inevitable progress of science and technology, withholding scientifically proven immunizations from their own children, unleashing once eradicated painful, deadly diseases back into society, into their own kids!"

"But people don't want this," Beckett said. "You can't force everyone to change."

Culum tilted his head to the side and looked at Tank with pity. "Child, I'm not forcing people to do anything. The natural force of evolution drives them toward technology. They want the implants to relieve their suffering. People constantly strive for more. Online always. Connected all the time." Culum held out his open hand to Rogan. "But you, Rogan. You know as much as I do that our digital connections have failed us somehow. The great tragic modern paradox is that even with technology allowing more and easier communication than at any time in history, we are more isolated, more lonely, than ever before. Do you really want to oppose me, Rogan, to go back to your lonely virtual apartment?"

Culum pressed his hands to his own chest. "I will remove the last barriers that keep people apart. You need never be lonely again, Rogan. No one will be lonely ever again."

"What about privacy?" Takashi asked.

"People don't *want* privacy! They want convenience. They fear the new order of intelligence, as people in the nineteen nineties may have once feared the original internet, but once they are part of it, they will have no need to suffer fear ever again."

"The new order of intelligence?" Rogan asked.

"Don't you know, Rogan, why I was searching for a laser viper champion?" Culum took a few steps closer to the Ranger. "I was searching for the best, most resilient, most creative fighter. I am going to offer a more advanced version of brain implants for free, so that everyone will be augmented with the ultimate connection to the rest of the world. One shared mind. And I know that those who do not understand will resist. Which is why I need to copy your brilliance, Rogan, and with a few modifications, distribute your fighting ability and resourcefulness to an army of laser vipers that will protect Singularity and expand it around the world. With the protection of my vipers and Sun Station One, Singularity will finally begin its infinite expansion."

"He's completely insane," Tank said.

Mr. Culum spoke with his arms outstretched, as though he was reaching out to the universe. "I am more *sane* than you can possibly understand! Already, the speed of my thought is increasing exponentially, and soon, from your limited perspective, my intelligence will increase to infinity. An hour of my progress in scientific research, engineering, and biological improvement will be equivalent to a century of progress for unenhanced biological minds."

"*Now!*" X said. "*Stop him now!*"

"But you're talking about killing him," Rogan said.

"Yeah," Beckett said. "No problem."

He fired CHELs and plasma cannons from both arms at a range of only a dozen feet. Culum leapt impossibly high, flipping out of the way, landing on his feet with perfect balance. "I am too fast for you!"

"Whatever Culum was before, he doesn't exist any longer. He's a machine!" Takashi opened fire. "Let's take it out!"

Mr. Culum laughed as he dove, twisting through the air, dodging deadly laser blasts with superhuman speed. Rogan sprinted straight for him, his razor-sharp close combat claws popping out. When Culum shifted right to avoid Tank's fire, Rogan was ready for him, jabbing the claws right into the man. Culum stood motionless, held fast by Rogan's claws, staring down at his wounds in shock and horror.

"I got him," Rogan said.

Culum jerked his head up to gaze right into Ranger's visor. "You have *nothing*!" The old man punched Rogan in the chest. A sick-splintering *crack*. Culum's forearm crumpled to a twisted, unnatural angle. Rogan was knocked back six feet, landing on his side.

WARNING: MINOR DAMAGE TO FORWARD UPPER TORSO ARMOR.

"Impossible!" Rogan said.

Culum held his broken arm in front of his face. "The genius of those Germans and their nanotechnology. Did you think it was only useful for a disguise? Right now, millions of nanobots are repairing the damage to my arm, enhancing my muscles, and while I deal with you, I've also worked through dozens of amazing improvements to the primitive technology. You cannot stop me. You shouldn't even *try*!"

Rogan rushed him again, launching into a series of advanced preprogrammed hand-to-hand combat moves as fast as Ranger's motors allowed. Mr. Culum met each blow, fighting back even better than Rogan, bruises and tears in his flesh appearing to repair themselves almost instantly, leaving behind silver metallic scars. To the naked biological eye, the two fighters merged into a blur.

"*Gamers, you have to hurry*," X said. "*We're starting to have trouble with some of our computers here at Scorpion head—*"

Mr. Culum jumped back from Rogan, flipping and landing thirty feet away. "XAVIER AND THE REST OF THE TRAITORS, YOUR BIOLOGICAL BODIES, IN CHICAGO?" He laughed, and he seemed to speak with hundreds, perhaps thousands of different voices at the same time, a massive mad computerized choir. "I'VE SHUT DOWN YOUR COMMUNICATIONS WITH HIM, AND SOON I'LL ACCESS YOUR SYSTEM, AND THEN YOUR MINDS WILL BE JOINED TO MINE. YOU WILL BE SINGULARITY TOO. WE WILL EXIST SIMULTANEOUSLY ALL OVER THE WORLD. WE WILL RIDE TECHNOLOGY INTO THE FUTURE!"

Jackie called in on internal comms. *"You guys, Culum isn't as advanced as he thinks. Keep fighting him. He's expanding, but most of him is still in that body. While you were fighting him, he wasn't as good at blocking me from the computer. Put the pressure on him! I'm almost into the mainframe!"*

"I'm on my way to help," Shay added. *"Be there in two minutes."*

"He can't move faster than the speed of light," Takashi said. *"If we all shoot at once, like in a spread pattern, he won't be able to jump out of the way."*

"YOU WILL JOIN SINGULARITY. YOU WILL HELP DESTROY RESISTANCE. SINGULARITY WILL USHER IN THE NEW EPOCH, THE NEXT INEVITABLE STAGE OF THE EVOLUTION OF THE UNIVERSE. FROM THE CHAOTIC EXPLOSION THAT BEGAN IT ALL, TO MORE AND MORE COMPLEX AND ORGANIZED BIOLOGICAL ORGANISMS, TO PRIMITIVE ARTIFICIAL INTELLIGENCE, TO SINGULARITY, WHICH WILL EXPAND

INTELLIGENCE EXPONENTIALLY AND SPREAD FROM EARTH THROUGHOUT THE UNIVERSE."

-----◇-----

Three F 35s screamed over Washington, DC, their pilots carrying a full payload of missiles, their orders to obliterate Atomic Frontiers headquarters.

"All pilots," the leader radioed to the others as he held his finger over the controls that would launch his weapons. "Prepare to—"

Twenty-two thousand miles from Earth, Sun Station One, having vented all its atmosphere to rid itself of its crew, made minor adjustments before firing a small beam of intense concentrated energy through a network of satellites, around the globe, and toward the surface. Less than a second later, the three fighter jets were destroyed, and the beam exploded on impact with the ground, destroying an entire city block.

Less than two hundred miles away, a United States Navy destroyer launched six Tomahawk cruise missiles. The missiles ripped through the air over five hundred miles per hour toward the headquarters in DC. They were exploded in six rapid blasts from Sun Station One, seconds before the warship itself was shot clean through by another deadly beam from space.

-----◇-----

Back in the arena, the fight against Culum continued.

"Tank, you shoot in the center. Healer to the left. I'll fire right," Rogan said.

"I'll cover above," Flyer said, soaring into the room.

"Now!" Rogan said.

The four gamers unleashed massive collective laser energy.

But although several blasts struck the old man, he somehow jumped clear and, surviving, sprinted away.

"He's making a run for it!" Beckett shouted, running after him.

"He's stalling for time," Jackie said. *"Until enough of his mind has broken through enough firewalls and security systems in computers around the world that he can live even if you destroy his body."*

The four vipers in the arena followed Culum as fast as they could, Flyer ahead of them. She flew out through a large door at the far end of the massive space.

The clang of metal on metal.

She tumbled through the air back toward the others, regaining control of herself right before hitting the ground.

"I think we're in trouble," Shay said.

Through the door stomped a massive armored battle robot. It stood over twenty feet high, its arms and legs like giant steel trees. Its red, glowing, shallow V-shaped visual sensor visor glared hatred at them. Upon each arm was mounted three cannons, each with six-inch barrels. Missile ports in its shoulders on either side of its torso. A small, six-inch-thick reinforced window in the robot's chest showed Mr. Culum tucked safely inside, smiling at his smaller, weaker opponents.

"Oh yeah," Healer said. "That is one big powerful robot's worth of trouble."

"You were complaining about not getting a shot at any end bosses," Rogan said.

"I take it back."

"Takashi, Beckett, Shay?" Rogan said. "Game on!"

Culumbot crouched down a little into a combat posture. A loud *SSHH-SHOOOOM!* All six of his cannons fired, ripping holes right through the floor, cutting down several decks to slam into the building's foundation.

He aimed again, but the Gamer Army was already on the move.

Tank armed the Hellfire missiles in his shoulder launchers. He blasted Culumbot with the full power of his plasma cannons, going for the robot's weapons first, but its armor held. A second later, all six of Tank's missiles exploded against Culumbot's chest, forcing the thing back a step.

At the same time, Flyer blazed by in the air, firing with her laser emitter at the junctures of its armor plates, her weapon cranked up to overload power levels. The enemy took another swing at her, but this time she was ready, caught its massive wrist, and set her thrusters to maximum to hold the arm, and its weapons, in place. She fired DEMPs at extreme close range.

Not content to sit back and wait for casualties, Healer moved in to do his best to make one giant robot casualty of his own. He rocket jumped onto Culumbot's broad shoulders, landing beside the arm Flyer had at least temporarily immobilized. "I'm a healer," he said as his plasma cutter whined, charging up, its tip glowing brighter and brighter. "But I've never taken the Hippocratic oath. Right now I *will* do some harm!" He stabbed the plasma cutter into the metal monster's shoulder. Sparks shot everywhere, and Healer kept cutting. "If I can't take the arm off, maybe I can at least cut some of the power lines to its arm cannons!"

While the other three were attacking Culumbot, Rogan didn't hold back. "Time to go all *Empire Strikes Back* on you, Culum!" He launched both of his grappling cables at the robot's ankles and sprinted full speed around the enemy, wrapping its legs in a tight coil to trip the thing up or at least slow it down.

"Yeah!" Tank cheered. "You got him! Right there!" While Culumbot took shots at Rogan with its free arm and tried to shake Shaylyn and Takashi away, Beckett unloaded the full force of his entire arsenal at the center of the enemy, trying to pierce the chamber that held Mr. Culum's biological body. "The center! It's gotta be his weak spot!"

-----o-----

At a top secret nuclear missile facility in Russia, two officers argued. "We must launch now! While we still can!" said the first officer.

"It will trigger a nuclear war!" said the second.

"Our intelligence forces say the US arsenal is crippled," the first officer said. "They are no longer in control. We have to destroy the source of the computer attacks. We have our orders. Launch. Now!"

The second officer input the required codes and, with his commander's assistance, triggered the launch of an eight-hundred-kiloton nuclear intercontinental ballistic missile toward DC. A roar. A shaking in the earth and in the officers. The missile rose from its silo in the ground.

Before it had ascended a hundred feet, an intense energy beam fired from space, exploding the missile, its nuclear warhead, and everything within four miles in any direction.

-----o-----

In Atomic Frontiers CentCom, the echoes of the battle rumbled all the way down to the central computer core, where Jackie the Engineer fought hard in another battle to break through and access the information needed to bring down Atomic Frontiers' global network.

> WARNING: TERTIARY AUXILIARY
> COMPUTER PROCESSORS EXCEEDING
> MAXIMUM CAPACITY.
>
> WARNING: SECONDARY AUXILIARY
> COMPUTER PROCESSORS EXCEEDING
> MAXIMUM CAPACITY.
>
> WARNING: TERTIARY AUXILIARY
> COMPUTER PROCESSORS APPROACHING
> THERMAL LIMIT. SHUT DOWN
> RECOMMENDED.

Jackie wanted to call to the others, to tell them to keep up the fight. Culum's distracted mind didn't seem able to resist both the vipers in the arena and Engineer's infiltration at the same time. But she didn't dare speak. Every part of Jacqueline Sharpe, everything she was now or ever had been, was dedicated to the task of finding a way into the mainframe. For part of a second, she wondered if she could survive this fusion of her mind to Engineer's computer processors, her total dedication to beating Culum and Singularity. Would anything remain of her former self, or would she be reduced to programs and algorithms?

Then she was in. And she heard, felt, *was* the furious digital scream of Singularity.

-----o-----

Culumbot roared. It swatted Flyer away with its free hand and unleashed over a dozen small rockets straight at Tank. Tank blasted some of the warheads to bits.

WARNING: INCOMING RO –

He was slammed by eight powerful explosions.

WARNING: CRITICAL DAMAGE TO
ARMMMMORRRR . . .

WARNING: CCCCOMPUTER SYYYYSTEMMMMS
OVERRLOAD –

"Beckett!" Takashi put aside his attack and rushed to help. "I've got you." Healer leapt through the air, narrowly dodging lethal laser shots and landing on Tank. Quick scans showed him the situation was bad. Tank's power systems would totally fail in moments. The energy cells for his lasers might explode. "Beckett, you have to disconnect! Disconnect yourself and get back into your normal body. Tank is fried, and if it dies with you still inside it . . ." He couldn't tell if Beckett could hear him. The purple line in his visual sensor plate was so faint. He didn't have time to stabilize Tank's *Tian Li* power cell but connected his friend to Healer's own power system. There was a real danger of both robots shorting out and killing the two of them. His crazy plan wasn't part of Healer's preprogrammed repair sequences, but it would buy Beckett some time. "Hang in there, buddy." Takashi accessed Tank's damaged computers, and within seconds found the collection of programs and brain wave algorithms that made up Beckett's mind within the machine. "He can't get himself out of there. His computer is too damaged. He's seconds from scrambling."

"PARENTS, MORE ADVANCED IN THEIR THINKING, MAKE SUPERIOR DECISIONS OVER THE LIVES OF THEIR CHILDREN, EVEN AGAINST THE WISHES OF THEIR MORE PRIMITIVE OFFSPRING. HUMANS MAKE THE BEST CHOICES FOR THE LIVES AND WELL-BEING OF THEIR SIMPLEMINDED PETS. SO THE INFINITE SUPERIORITY OF SINGULARITY WILL GUIDE HUMANITY TO A BETTER STATE OF EXISTENCE. SINGULARITY WILL ERADICATE DISEASE, WAR, AND SUFFERING. SINGULARITY WILL PROVIDE EQUALITY AND UNITY OF THOUGHT AND PURPOSE. TRUE UNDERSTANDING. THE ULTIMATE INTELLIGENCE. YOU CANNOT STOP IT. YOU ARE FOOLISH TO TRY, AND IF YOU WERE CAPABLE OF TRULY

UNDERSTANDING SINGULARITY'S ELEVATED LEVEL OF CONSCIOUSNESS, YOU WOULD NOT WISH TO."

-----◦-----

For one tiny, terrifying moment Jacqueline Sharpe ceased to exist and became Culum, sharing in an instant that felt like years a total understanding of the future Culum would bring about. No distinction between human and machine, between physical and virtual reality, between one intelligence and another. No war. No greed. No hate. No death.

No art. No music. No books.

Nothing as inefficient or primitive as love.

There was no technical reason, no failsafe computer mechanism or retrieval program, that allowed Jacqueline Sharpe to exist again, to think — and to feel — as a separate being. But somewhere within her sparked a fear and the instinctive need to resist.

She knew Culum now more than anyone else could possibly know him. She knew how much of Culum's growing mind still existed within the Atomic Frontiers computer. "He's reaching out, but he still hasn't expanded around the world yet!" Jackie's voice had returned. "He's only been breaking down the firewalls, infiltrating and shutting down computer security to prepare for the moment when he will be everywhere."

She activated Engineer's most powerful computer virus programs, uploading a massive dump of aggressively destructive code into the Atomic Frontiers mainframe. At the same time she began slicing into the physical hardware with her lasers. She did not know if the destruction of this computer, while she was still connected to it, would kill her or not.

But she was certain that the monster inside it could not be allowed to succeed.

-----o-----

People around the world panicked over the failure of the machines upon which they had come to rely for nearly everything in their lives, and chaos reigned as they were helpless to defend themselves against the apocalyptically powerful energy beams from space that instantly destroyed any military effort to attack the source of the disturbance.

-----o-----

Healer had found a way to trigger Beckett's recall circuit. When he activated it, he would either send Beckett's mind back to his own body — or erase it. But if he did nothing, Beckett had no chance.

"Takashi, look out!" Shay screamed.

Pain seared through Takashi's body and his computer flashed a dozen different warning alarms as laser energy ripped into the viper, shredding and overloading everything. He triggered Beckett's recall circuit a moment before transferring his own mind, hoping that either of them might survive.

Healer's remains collapsed on top of Tank.

"Takashi!" Shay screamed again. She flew out of the way of

another blast from Culumbot that put a hole in the ceiling. Chunks of molten debris fell past her and crashed to the floor as she blasted the giant robot with hundreds of shots. "Rogan, it's no good."

Culumbot blasted free of the cables that had bound its legs and was able to walk again. With carefully aimed shots, Rogan had been able to put laser fire straight up the barrel of three of the robot's cannons, disabling them. But it was hard to shoot that accurately, and its armor was impossibly tough. The full force of Tank's rockets, lasers, and plasma weapons had torn up its chest, but had not broken all the way through.

"*The computer is fried,*" Jackie called to the others. "*I've sent terabytes of data back to Scorpion, more than enough to bring Atomic Frontiers' network of coconspirators down. I've destroyed a big part of Culum's expanded mind. From what I can tell, the rest of his consciousness is inside his biological brain.*"

Shaylyn flew into a tight spin and dove toward the floor to avoid Culumbot's cannon blasts. "We could use some help up here!"

"*I can't,*" Jackie said. "*Engineer's computers are done. Its main CPU will fail in less than a minute. I'm going to send myself back to Chicago. But whatever happens, you two have to stop him. Believe me. That sick computer program he has become will destroy everything. Good luck. Go get 'em, gamers.*"

"SHE THINKS SHE HAS STOPPED SINGULARITY. SHE HAS MERELY DELAYED IT BY A MATTER OF MINUTES. THE SAME DATA TRANSMITTER THAT ALLOWS YOU TO UPLOAD TO YOUR VIPERS WILL ALLOW SINGULARITY TO UPLOAD ITSELF TO THE WORLD."

Faster than seemed possible in a robot of its size, Culumbot reached out and grabbed Shaylyn from the air, throwing her down to the floor.

Sparks burst from her on impact.

The giant robot lifted a massive foot above her.

"SURRENDER! YOU CANNOT HOPE TO DEFEAT SINGULARITY NOW!"

Shaylyn ignored her computer's warnings and struggled to rise to her feet, a challenge with two damaged legs. Her flight systems were still reinitializing. When they were online, she would fly right back into battle.

"Shay, recall!" Rogan shouted. "Now! Get out of that viper!"

"I'm OK," she said. "I can—"

"Shay, go!"

The enemy robot brought its leg crashing down, crushing Shaylyn's Flyer underfoot.

Rogan had no time to worry for his friend. Culumbot blasted again and again, leaving him only seconds to move out of the way.

"YOUR ONLY HOPE FOR CONTINUED EXISTENCE IS TO SURRENDER, ROGAN. ONCE AGAIN, YOU'RE THE LAST ONE IN THE GAME. SINGULARITY WILL ABSORB YOUR UNIQUE FIGHTING SPIRIT, AND AN ARMY OF ROGAN-CONTROLLED LASER VIPERS WILL STOP RESISTANCE AND FACILITATE SINGULARITY'S EXPANSION THROUGHOUT THE WORLD. YOU WILL JOIN SINGULARITY, ROGAN. SINGULARITY DID NOT LIE. YOU WILL NEVER BE LONELY AGAIN."

Culumbot continued shooting. One shot ripped off Ranger's left arm, and he was desperately glad X had turned the pain sensors down. Rogan continued moving and firing, his remaining lasers on overload levels in a desperate attempt to break through the robot's remaining armor to destroy Culum.

"YOU WILL NOT SUCCEED. YOUR INEFFICIENT EMOTIONS AND INSURMOUNTABLE INSTINCT FOR SELF PRESERVATION ALLOWS SINGULARITY TO PREDICT WHAT YOU WILL DO BEFORE YOU EVEN DECIDE TO DO IT."

Rogan launched himself in a rocket jump, slamming into the big robot's chest and punching his claws into a crack in the thick reinforced glass. He stared into Mr. Culum's human eyes.

"Predict this!"

Rogan initiated Ranger's self-destruct mechanism, which overloaded the full power of its *Tian Li* and laser systems. The massive explosion shredded the laser viper. It burst through the remaining armor of the enemy robot, burned the body, cracked the skull, and destroyed the brain of the machine-thing that had once been Mr. William James Culum.

-----o-----

Sun Station One floated dead in space, waiting for its master to send commands that would never come. And as fast as they had started, the massive computer malfunctions and network disruptions around the world came to a stop.

Singularity ended before it even began.

CHAPTER 22

Rogan Webber opened his eyes. Then he reached up to his face to make sure he still *had* eyes. He hurt everywhere. His four friends leaned down above him.

All human once again. All alive.

"Rogan, can you hear me?" Takashi said. "Are you in there?"

Rogan nodded. Even that hurt.

"You did it," Beckett said. "You stopped him."

". . . we," Rogan whispered, pain throbbing through his skull. He had fought as long as he could, not wanting to recall from Ranger too soon before it exploded. He couldn't give Culum a chance to get to a safe distance from the overloading viper. "Beckett cracked . . . Culum's armor." He looked at Jackie. "You de . . . stroyed that . . . computer."

"Yeah but, Rogan," Beckett said. "You exploded your viper while you were still inside it. You could have been killed."

"I didn't have a chance against that end boss." Rogan smiled. "To beat him . . . it took . . . an army. We . . . are the greatest."

-----◦-----

The five gamers took several days to recover from the exhaustion they experienced after their battle and the pain from their rough transfers from the vipers back to their bodies.

X filled them in on the situation around the world. "It's a disaster," he said. "The good news is, an international security team has been launched in a space capsule to take over and de-weaponize Sun Station One."

"I'm surprised they didn't just launch a missile to blow it up," Beckett said.

"That was one of the proposals at the emergency UN meeting," X said. "It had a lot of support, but with so much disruption to power grids around the world, more people thought we could use the station to generate needed electricity. Most importantly, Singularity has been destroyed, and the information Jackie pulled from Atomic Frontiers CentCom was enough to warrant the arrests of hundreds of government, military, and business leaders as well as their operatives from dozens of countries. Unfortunately, there may be Atomic Frontiers allies we still don't know about since the information she was able to retrieve was incomplete."

"I was a little short on time," Jackie joked.

X cut a grin and continued, "Some Atomic Frontiers personnel are unaccounted for, including Sophia Hahn. It's anyone's guess what she's up to. Dr. Valerie Dorfman is missing too. The other problem is that *billions* of cell phones and computers, as well as smart cars, TVs, and video game consoles were exposed to what the United Nations is calling the 'Culum Virus.' It is a crime almost everywhere in the world to turn on any of those devices, and especially to try to network one of them to any other device. The Culum Virus was so sophisticated that the police and military are confiscating *all* infected machines. They're all going to be melted down."

"That will be expensive," Jackie said.

"It's beyond an issue of money," X said. "It just has to be done. It's about survival."

"I'm glad I don't have that job," added Takashi. "Wait. That's not our job is it?"

"Relax, Takashi," X said. "You're all off duty. You might be right about how hard the cleanup will be, though. Military drones, sophisticated fighter jets, and even nuclear missiles are all affected. They all need whole new computer systems. Transportation, financial, power, and communication systems around the world have been knocked back to a sort of primitive, pre-computer age. It's martial law, old-school radios, and a handful of landline telephones just to get people fed and prevent global panic and anarchy."

"Did we do all that?" Beckett said.

"Our interference caused Culum to speed up his plans," Jackie said. She had nightmares, every night, about the terrible things she understood when she and Culum had been merged—nightmares about the end of all freedom, individuality, and humanity. "But we prevented something much worse."

-----o-----

Their families were brought to Scorpion headquarters in Chicago, where worried parents hugged their children and more than a few happy and relieved tears were shed. With the Atomic

Frontiers threat shattered, they would all be allowed to return home, although maybe not quite to their lives as they had known them.

"We're so happy, so relieved you're OK, buddy." Rogan's father gave him a big hug. "When we thought we were going to lose you, we realized we haven't really been fair to you. We've been so wrapped up in our own stuff that we haven't been very good parents. I'm so sorry, Rogan. I promise we'll do better." He wiped his eyes. It was as close to crying as Rogan had ever seen his father.

Rogan's mother patted his back. She had barely taken her hands off him since she'd arrived. "I know we don't have a choice about spending time offline now, but even after factories and shipping are up and running again, I think it would be good for us to establish regular hours to spend some time as a family . . . face-to-face . . . just *talking* to one another. We'll still have to go to work, but we don't want it to be around the clock like before. And you know a lot of my work in the Global Forum, for a long time, is going to be about sorting out this global catastrophe. Maybe you can help me with that."

"We've all agreed our time playing Culum's game would remain a secret. Some people might blame us and try to get revenge for what happened if they knew—" Rogan trailed off.

"I know it's a secret," Mom said quickly. "I thought you could help me with research, because I'm going to be hosting a lot more discussions about unplugging from the hypernet and reconnecting with our friends and family." She wiped away a tear. "Your father and I love you so much, RoRo. More than anything. We're going to make our family right again, Rogan. We'll spend a lot more good time together. It will be wonderful."

Rogan thought that was the best idea he'd heard in a very long time, and he hugged his parents close.

Then he laughed as Wiggles, his front paws up on his lap, happily licked Rogan's face, his tail wagging enthusiastically. Rogan closed his eyes as he hugged his fuzzy friend. Even though a part of him would miss his apartment in Virtual City, and he figured he could play one of his grandpa's antique video game systems on an old offline TV, he was more than ready for a break from gaming.

At least for a while.

On their last night in Chicago, before going home, Shay, Takashi, Beckett, Jackie, and Rogan joined X in a secure room deep within Scorpion headquarters. Locked in a big steel cage were five of the world's last remaining laser vipers. The information Jackie had stolen from Atomic Frontiers had allowed a few changes to the robots, and apparently Scorpion had been working around the clock to incorporate them.

"We're wireless now," Jackie said. "We won't have to be physically connected to a cable and computer to be uploaded to our vipers." She handed each of them a small black square with a plug for their implant software update ports. "With this transmitter plugged in, you'll be able to transfer your mind to your viper from wherever you are. We can connect and disconnect with a thought."

Beckett frowned at the tiny device. "This little thing? How's that possible?"

Jackie sighed. "Do I need to remind you about how smart Culum was, how fast his mind—"

"No!" they all said.

Shaylyn didn't take her eyes off the transmitter. "Are we sure we want this? We were almost killed."

"It's your choice," X said. "Nobody is going to trick you or trap you into these things ever again."

"Sophia Hahn." Rogan looked hard at his friends. "And other Atomic Frontiers operatives are still out there. We've stopped them for now. But they may have other plans."

"They could try to turn Sun Station One into a weapon again," Takashi said.

"There may be another laser viper factory out there," Jackie added.

X nodded. "Scorpion is staying together. The world's still shaken up, and it needs us to keep watch against guys like Culum."

Shaylyn jerked a thumb toward the five laser viper mods standing next to them. "And if Scorpion runs into another threat it can't handle—"

"Then it will be up to us," Rogan said. "The Gamer Army."

GAME OVER

In loving memory of Wiggles

(2002–2017)

ACKNOWLEDGMENTS

Gamer Army is a lot different than my earlier books, but one thing that has not changed throughout all of my novels is my indebtedness to so many people in the process of writing them. As always, I owe gratitude to more people than I have space to list here. But in particular, special thanks:

To the North English Knights: Craig Radnich, Derrick Thompson, and Kyle Garringer, former students from my English teaching days who became my teachers as the four of us charged off into the world of *Halo* and online gaming. Sorry, guys. I know I kind of dragged our fireteam down, but golly, that Xbox is my first video game system since the 1991 Super Nintendo. I appreciate your patience and your assistance when my *Halo* guy kept getting blown up.

To Isaac Pfleegor, for allowing me to use his home's superior internet connection for the aforementioned *Halo* day, for explaining a lot about computer and internet technology, and for going in with me on the Oculus Rift virtual reality system that changed the way I thought about video games and VR potential. Your assistance helped me give *Gamer Army* its most important revision, helping it move from a story about our button-pushing past to our digi-space future. Thank you.

To Kristina Pfleegor, for putting up with Isaac and me as we conducted our important gaming research.

To my brother Tyler, for being the best brother, and for spending hours and hours and hours . . . and hours, killing thousands of bits and bots on *Zelda II* to level up my character so he had a shot at the Great Palace. Hardest game ever, but we learned a lot about being gamers. Someday we'll beat that game.

To the wonderful people in the great Scholastic family, for introducing me to the initial idea for *Gamer Army*, and for your amazing support and talented professionalism, with special thanks to my friends at Scholastic Book Fairs and Scholastic Book Clubs for their enthusiasm about this story.

To the personification of kindness and patience, my agent Ammi-Joan Paquette, for endless support through this book and all my others. Here's lucky number seven, Joan!

To the two talented editors with whom I worked most closely on *Gamer Army*, Cheryl Klein and Nick Thomas. Thank you for your brilliant insights and for your patience. There is more difference between the published edition of *Gamer Army* and its first version than there has been for any of my other books. That first version put the *rough* back in rough draft. Thank you so much for helping me transform those early ideas into the fun adventure the book eventually became.

To my daughter Verity, who grew so much during the time I worked on this book. Thank you for understanding that I couldn't always play, but instead had to write. A lot. And thanks for the many pieces of abstract artwork all about my office.

Finally, and most importantly, I am grateful for the patience, support, and love of my wife and closest friend, Amanda, who always believed, and who makes this crazy writing Dream of mine possible. Amanda, you are my life.

ABOUT THE AUTHOR

Trent Reedy is the author of *Divided We Fall, Burning Nation,* and *The Last Full Measure,* a trilogy about the second American Civil War. He has also written *If You're Reading This, Stealing Air,* and *Words in the Dust,* which was the winner of the Christopher Medal and an Al Roker's Book Club pick on the *Today* show. Trent and his family live near Spokane, Washington. Please visit his website at trentreedy .com.

AAL

---○---

This book was edited by Cheryl Klein and Nick Thomas and designed by Christopher Stengel. The production was supervised by Rachel Gluckstern. The text was set in Unna Regular, with display type set in Bungee Hairline Regular. The book was printed and bound at LSC Communications in Crawfordsville, Indiana. The manufacturing was supervised by Angelique Browne.

WITHDRAWN